DATE DUE

SAVAGE GUNS

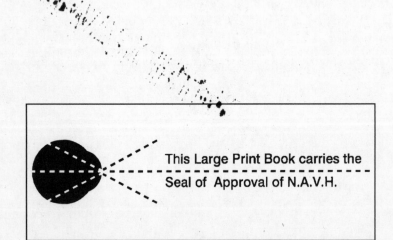

This Large Print Book carries the
Seal of Approval of N.A.V.H.

SAVAGE GUNS

WILLIAM W. JOHNSTONE
WITH J. A. JOHNSTONE

THORNDIKE PRESS
A part of Gale, Cengage Learning

GALE
CENGAGE Learning™

Detroit • New York • San Francisco • New Haven, Conn • Waterville, Maine • London

GALE
CENGAGE Learning™

Following the death of William W. Johnstone, the Johnstone family is working with a carefully selected writer to organize and complete Mr. Johnstone's outlines and many unfinished manuscripts to create additional novels in all of his series like The Last Gunfighter, Mountain Man, and Eagles, among others. This novel was inspired by Mr. Johnstone's superb storytelling.

Thorndike Press® Large Print Western.
The text of this Large Print edition is unabridged.
Other aspects of the book may vary from the original edition.
Set in 16 pt. Plantin.

LIBRARY OF CONGRESS CATALOGING-IN-PUBLICATION DATA

Johnstone, William W.
   Savage guns / by William W. Johnstone with J. A. Johnstone.
     p. cm. — (Thorndike Press large print Western)
   ISBN-13: 978-1-4104-3548-4 (hardcover)
   ISBN-10: 1-4104-3548-2 (hardcover)
   1. Large type books. I. Johnstone, J. A. II. Title.
PS3560.O415S33 2011
813'.54—dc22   2010049042

Published in 2011 by arrangement with Pinnacle Books, an imprint of Kensington Publishing Corp.

Printed in the United States of America
1 2 3 4 5 6 7 15 14 13 12 11

SAVAGE GUNS

ONE

I was mindin' my daily business in the two-holer when I got rudely interrupted. Now I like a little privacy, but this morning I got me a bullet instead. There I was, peacefully studying the female undies in the Montgomery Ward catalog, when this here slug slams through the door and exits through the rear, above my head.

"Hey!" I yelled, but no one said nothing.

"You out there. Don't you try nothing. This here's the law talking. I'm coming after you."

But I sure didn't know who or what was in the yard behind Belle's roomin' house. I thought maybe a horse was snorting or pawing clay, but I couldn't be sure of it. I wanted to see what was what, but the half-moon that let in fresh air was high up above me, and I had my business to look after just then. You can't do nothing in the middle of business.

I don't know about you, but I wear my hat when I'm in the two-holer, just on general principles. A man should wear a hat in the crapper. That's my motto. It was a peaceful enough morning in the town of Doubtful, in Puma County, Wyoming, where I was sheriff, more or less. So that riled me some, that bullet that slapped through there knocking my good five-X gray felt beaver Stetson topper, which teetered on the other hole but did not drop. If it had dropped down there, I'd a been plumb peeved.

I thought for a moment I oughta follow that hat through the hole and get my bare bottom down there in the perfumed vault, but that was plum sickening, and besides, how could I slide a hundred fifty pounds of rank male through that little round hole? I don't need no more smell than I've already got. When I pull my boots off, people head for the doors holding their noses. It just wouldn't work. If someone was gonna kill me, they held all the aces.

The truth of it was that I wasn't finished with my business, and all I could do was sit there and finish up my private duties, and rip a page out of the Monkey Ward catalog, and get it over with. Like the rest of us who used the two-holer behind Belle's boardinghouse, I was inclined to study ladies' corsets and bloomers and garters for entertainment, saving the wipe-off for the pages brimming with one-bottom plows, buggy whips, and bedpans. Them others in Belle's boardinghouse, they felt like I did, and no female undie pages ever got torn out of the catalog. That sure beat corncobs, I'll tell you.

"Sheriff, you come outa there with your hands up and your pants down," someone yelled. I thought maybe I knew the feller doin' all that yelling, but it was hard to tell, sitting there with pages of chemises and petticoats on my lap.

"Hold your horses," I said. "I ain't done, and the longer it takes, the better for you, because I'm likely to bust out of here with lead flying in all directions."

That fetched me a nasty laugh, and I knew that laugh, and I thought maybe I was in more of a jam than I'd imagined.

But no more bullets came sailing through, and I finished up, and ripped out a page of men's union suits, and another page of hay rakes and spades, and got it over with. I wasn't gonna bust out of there with my pants down, no matter what, so I stood, got myself arranged and buttoned up, drew out my service revolver, and with a violent shove, threw myself out the door and dodged to the left just to avoid any incoming lead.

It sure didn't do me no good. As my mama used to tell me, don't do nothing foolish.

Sure enough, there before me were eight, nine ratty-assed cowboys on horses, all of the lot waving black revolvers in my direction, just in case I got notions. And also a dude with a buckboard, holding some reins.

"I shoulda known," I said to the boss, who was the man I figgered it was.

"I told you to come out with your pants down, and you didn't. That's a hanging offense," the man said. "You do what I say, and when I say it."

"My pants is staying put, dammit," I replied.

I knew the joker, all right. I'd put his renegade boy in my jail a few months earlier, and now the punk was peering at the blue skies through iron bars. This feller on a shiny red horse waving nickel-plated Smith and Wesson at me was none other than Admiral Bragg. And the boy I was boardin' in my lockup, he was King Bragg, and his sister, she was Queen Bragg. Mighty strange names bloomed in that family, but who was I to howl? I sure didn't ask to have

10

Cotton hung on me, and Pickens neither, but that's how I got stuck, and there wasn't nothing I could do about it except maybe move to Argentina or Bulgaria.

Them names weren't titles neither. Bragg's ma and pa, they stuck him with the name of Admiral. If he'd of been in the navy, he might have ended up Admiral Admiral Bragg. But the family stuck to its notions, and old Bragg, he named one child King and the other child Queen. It was King Bragg that got himself into big trouble, perforating a few fellers with his six-gun, so I caught him and he would soon pay for his killin' spree. I think the family was all cheaters. Name a boy Admiral, and the boy's got a head start, even if he ain't even close to being an admiral. Name a girl Queen, and she's got the world bowin' and scrapin' even if she ain't one.

I was a little nervous, standing there in front of his pa with seven or eight Bragg cowboys pointing their artillery at my chest. Makes a man cautious, I'd say.

"Drop the peashooter, Sheriff," Admiral Bragg ordered.

I thought maybe to lift it up and blow him away, which would have been my last earthy deed. It sure was temptin' and my old pa, he might've approved even as he lowered

11

the coffin. Nothing like goin' out in style.

But there was about a thousand grains of lead pointing straight at me, and I chickened out, and set her down real slow, itching to pull a trick or two on these rannies. I sure was mad at myself for not spitting a few lead pills before I got turned into Swiss cheese. It just put me out of sorts, but I figured at least I was alive to get my revenge another day. So I set her down slow.

"Now you get into the buckboard, Sheriff," said Admiral Bragg. "We're taking you for a little ride."

I got in, sat next to the old fart who held the reins. I knew the feller, old and daft, with a left-crick in his neck that some said was from a botched hanging. He spat, which I took for a welcome, so I settled in beside him. There was still about a thousand grains of lead aimed at me, so I sat there and smiled at these gents.

The old feller slapped rein over the croup of the dray, and we clopped away from there, heading down the two-rut road out of Doubtful in the general direction of the Bragg ranch. I sort of had a hunch what this was about, and it wasn't too comfortable thinkin' about it.

Bragg was one of the biggest stockmen around Doubtful, and had a spread up in

12

the hills north of town that just didn't quit, and took a week with a couple of spare Sundays to ride across. He called it the Anchor Ranch, and it sure did anchor a lot of turf. He controlled as much public land as anyone in the West, and had an army of gunslicks to pin it all down, given that it wasn't his turf but belonged to Uncle Sam.

I guess that wasn't so bad; he raised a lot of beef and his men kept the saloons going in Doubtful. Admiral was a tough bird, all right, but I didn't have no occasion to throw him into the iron-barred cage in the sheriff office, so I pretty much ignored him and he ignored me until now.

I sort of didn't like the way this buckboard was surrounded by his gunslicks and we was headin' out of town, me a little bit against my will. But the bores of all them pieces aimed my way kept me from doing much complainin' about all that.

Old Admiral, perched on that shiny red horse, he ignored me, so I didn't have a notion what this was all about or how it would end. Or maybe I did. All this here stuff had to do with that scummy son of his, King Bragg, who grew up twisted and bad, and got himself into big trouble. From the moment King was big enough to wave a Colt six-gun around, he was doing it, shooting songbirds and bumblebees and gophers and snakes. It must have been a trial for old Admiral to keep that boy in cartridges, because that's about all that King did. He got mighty fine at it too, and could shoot better and faster than anyone, myself included. He could put a bullet through the edge of the ace of spades and cut that card in two.

Well, that kid, soon as he was big enough to ride into town on his own, without his ma or pa, was bent on showing the good citizens of Doubtful who was who. It wasn't lost on that boy that his pa was the biggest rancher in those parts, and maybe the biggest cattleman in the Territory, if not the whole bloomin' West.

He also was fast. Throw a bottle or a can or a silver dollar into the skies, and King would perforate it, or pretty near sign his name with bullet holes in a tomato can. I had to chase the kid out of a few saloons because he was only fifteen or so, and he didn't take kindly to it, but that was all the trouble I had, until the day he turned eighteen.

He come into Doubtful that day, few months ago, on his shiny black stallion, wearing a brace of double-action Colts, a birthday gift from his old man. I didn't pay no attention, but maybe I should have. I was busy with all that paperwork the Territory wants all the time, full of words I never heard tell of. I don't lay any claim to being more than fifth-grade schooled, so sometimes I got to get someone who's got more smarts to tell me what's what. But I make up for it by being friendly and enforcing the law pretty good.

Anyway, King Bragg tied his horse up on Saloon Row and wandered into the Last Chance wearing his new artillery. I wasn't aware of it, or I'd of kicked his ass out. He's too young to hoist a few shots of red-eye, and I'd of turned the brat over my knee and paddled his butt for pretendin' to be all growed up.

Well, next I knew, there was a ruckus, a bunch of shots to be exact, and I pop out of my office and hustle over to Saloon Row. There's a mess of shouting from the Last Chance, so I hurry over there and it was plain awful. There were three dead cowboys sprawled on the sawdust, leakin' blood. A few fellers were trying to stanch the flow some, but it was hopeless, and that threesome finished up their dying while I watched, and then people were just staring at one another. King Bragg was sitting in the sawdust, his emptied revolver in his hand. The barkeep, he was starin' over the bar, and them cowboys in there, they were staring at the dead ones, and there's me, law and order, staring at the whole lot, wondering who did what to who and why. It wasn't a very fine moment.

Well, I asked them cowboys a few questions and then pinched the kid, brought him in and locked him up, and got him tried by Judge Nippers, who told the jury the kid was guilty as hell, and sentenced him to hang by the neck until dead. And Doubtful, Wyoming, was going to see a hanging in just two weeks. In fact, I'd just hired Lemuel Clegg and his boys to build me a gallows and charge it to Puma County. Meanwhile, the Bragg family lawyer was screechin' and hollerin', but it didn't do no good. That punk killer, King Bragg, was going to swing in a few days. Me, I'm all for justice, and with all them dead cowboys lying around, I'm thinkin' it ought to be sooner, but all that was up to Judge Nippers.

I sorta thought maybe this was connected to that, but I don't take no credit for smart thinking. Whatever the case, I was being transported by a rattling old buckboard out of town by some pretty mean-lookin' fellers with a lot of .45-caliber barrels poking straight at me, so I didn't feel none to comfortable.

"What's this here all about, Admiral?" I asked.

But that wax-haired, comb-bearded blue-eyed snake wasn't talking. He was just leading this here procession out of Doubtful, with me in the middle. I sure was getting curious. But I didn't have to wait too long. About two miles out of Doubtful, right where a bunch of cottonwoods crowded the creek, they were steering toward a big old tree, with a mighty thick limb pokin' straight out, and hanging from that limb was a noose.

Two

I sure didn't like the looks of that noose. That thing was just danglin' there, swaying in the breeze. That rope, it was thick as a hawser, and coiled around the way them hangmen do it. Like someone done it that had done it a few times and knew what to do.

Them cowboys and gunslicks was uncommon quiet as we rode toward that big cottonwood, which was in spring leaf and real pretty for May. But I wasn't paying attention to that. All I was seein' was that damned noose waiting there for some neck. I was starting to have a notion of whose neck it was waiting for, and that didn't sit well with my belly.

It got worse. That old goat driving the buckboard headed straight to that noose, and when it was plain dangling in my face, he whoaed the nag and there it was, that big hemp noose right there in front of me.

None of them slicks was saying a word, and none of them had put away their artillery neither. I knew a few of them. There was Big Nose George, and Alvin Ream, and Smiley Thistlethwaite, and Spitting Sam. They didn't think twice about putting a little lead into anything alive. You had to wonder why Bragg kept those gunmen around. Times were peaceful enough, at least until now.

"Admiral, this ain't a good idea," I said.

He laughed softly. You ever hear a man laugh like that, like he was enjoying my fate? Well, it's not something a person forgets.

"I'm the law, Admiral, and you'd better think twice."

I was thinkin' maybe I'd go down fighting, but before I could think longer, that old boy beside me wrapped his knobby old arm around me, and one of them slicks grabbed my hands, yanked them behind me, and wrapped them in thong until my arms were trussed up tighter than a fat lady's corset. Me, I'm not even thirty and had a lot of juice in me still, and I wrestled with them fellers, but it was like kicking a cast-iron stove. They knew what they was up to, and had me cold.

I began thinking that them spring leaves coming out on the cottonwood would be about the last pretty thing I'd ever see. I don't rightly know why I kept that sheriff job, but I had. I sorta liked the fun of it, and I was never one to dodge a little trouble. I kinda thought one of my deputies might be hunting for me now, but I was just being foolish. Them fellers slept late and played cribbage or euchre half the night in the jailhouse.

I didn't need any explanations. Admiral Bragg, he was getting even with me. Hang that boy, hang me. There wasn't no point in asking a bunch of questions, and no point in trying to talk him out of it. The hard, belly-grabbing truth was that this thing was gonna happen and there wasn't no way I could jabber and slobber my way out of it.

But I wasn't dwelling on it. I was eying the bright blue sky, and hearing some red-winged blackbirds making a racket down on the creek, and feeling good mountain air filling my lungs, and thinkin' of my ma and pa, and how they brought me into the world and raised me up.

I writhed some, but there was a passel of them around me in the buckboard, and strong hands pinning me while one of them slicks pulled off my five-X gray beaver hat and dropped that big, scratchy noose right over my neck. It was the first time I ever

20

felt a noose and it wasn't a very good feeling. It was just a big, cold, scratchy twisted rope, and now it rested on my shoulders, and one of them slicks tugged it pretty tight, and tipped it off to the side a little so as to break my neck.

So I was standin' there in that buckboard with a noose drawn tight on my young neck, and all trussed up, and they all backed off and left me standing there, my knees knockin' and waiting for the final, entire, no-return end. I wondered if Admiral Bragg was gonna preach at me some, tell me this was his brand of justice, or whatnot, but he didn't. He just nodded.

That old knobby-armed geezer, he settled down in the wooden seat of the buckboard, me standing in the bed, and then he let loose with his whip, smacked the dray right across the croup, and away it went, jerking me plumb off my pins as the wagon got yanked out from under me. Then I tumbled past the wagon and started down, feelin' that hemp yank hard at my neck and jerk my head back, and then I felt myself topple to the ground, and couldn't figure what happened. I wasn't dead yet. Maybe this was just the last gasp. I bunged myself up some, hitting that dirt so hard, and landing on a cottonwood root too, so that I was really hurtin' and that noose was as tight as a necktie at a funeral, and pretty quick I was starin' up at the sky and seein' lots of blue, and the pale green of them cottonwood leaves.

"Now you know what a hanging is," Admiral said.

That was the dumbest thing ever got said to me.

They rolled me over and cut that thong that had me tied up like some beef basting on a spit. I felt some blood return to my wrists and hands, and I flexed my fingers, discovering they was alive, all ten or eleven, or whatever I got. And they loosened that scratchy hemp and pulled that thing loose and tossed it aside. One of them slicks even slapped my gray beaver Stetson down on my head. And then they let me stand up, even if my legs was trembling like a virgin in a cathouse.

I couldn't think of nothing to do, so I slugged Admiral, one gut-punch and a roundhouse to his jaw, and he staggered back as my boot landed on his shin.

That might not have been too smart, but it sure was satisfying. He let out a yelp and in about two seconds half of them slicks was pulling me off and holding me down. I figured they'd just string me up for certain, and make no mistakes this time, but Admiral, he got up, dusted off his hat, wiped some blood off his lip, and smiled.

This sure was getting strange.

All them slicks let go of me, and I was of a mind to arrest the bunch for manhandling a lawman, but the odds weren't good. I never got a handle on arithmetic, and took long division over a few times, but I know bad odds when I see them.

Admiral Bragg, he spat a little more blood and nodded.

That old knobby-armed geezer, he fetched that hemp rope and brought her over to me, but he wasn't showing me the noose end. I was more familiar with that end than I even wanted to be. No, he showed me the other end, which had been razored across, clean as can be, save for one little strand that sort of wobbled in the morning breeze. I hated that strand; it pretty near did me.

They'd cut that rope for this event, and I sure wondered why. This whole deal was to scare the bejabbers out of me, and it sure as hell did.

"King won't be so lucky," Admiral Bragg said.

"No, but neither was them three he killed."

"He didn't kill them."

"I saw them three lying in the sawdust. Every last one a cowboy with the T-Bar Ranch."

"And you jumped to conclusions."

"There was the barkeep and two others saying King Bragg done it, and they testified in court to it."

"You've got two weeks to prove that he didn't do it. Next time, the rope won't be cut."

"You tellin' me to undo justice?"

"I'm telling you, my boy didn't do it, and you're going to spring him."

"That boy's guilty as hell, and he's gonna pay for it."

Admiral Bragg, he sort of scowled. "I'm not going to argue with you. If you're too dumb to see it, then you'll hang."

Me, I just stared at the man. There was no talkin' to him.

"Get in the wagon or walk," Bragg said. "I'm done talking."

I favored the ride. I still was a little weak on my pins. So I got aboard, next to the geezer, and the buckboard rattled back to town, surrounded by Bragg and his gunslicks and cowboys. They took me straight to Belle's rooming house and I got out, and they rode off.

The morning was still young, and I'd

24

already been hanged and told I'd be hanged again.

It sure was a tough start on a nice spring day.

I looked at them cottonwoods around town and saw that they were budding out. The town of Doubtful was about as quiet as little towns get. I didn't feel like doing nothing except go lie down, but instead, I made myself hike to the courthouse square, where the sheriff office was, along with the local lockup.

Bragg made me mad, tellin' me I was too dumb to see what was what.

It sure was a peaceful spring morning. Doubtful was doing its usual trade. There was a few ranch wagons parked at George Waller's emporium, and a few saddle horses tied to hitch rails. A playful little spring breeze, with an edge of cold on it, seemed to coil through town. It sure was nicer than the hot summers that sometimes roasted northern Wyoming. I was uncommonly glad to be alive, even if my knees wobbled a little. I smiled at folks and they smiled at me.

I got over to the courthouse, which baked in the sun, and made my way into the sheriff office. Sure enough, my undersheriff, Rusty, was parked there, his boots up on a desk.

"Where you been?" he asked.

"Getting myself hanged," I said.

Rusty, he smiled crookedly. "That's rich," he said.

I didn't argue. Rusty wouldn't believe it even if I swore to it on a stack of King James Bibles.

"You fed the prisoner?"

"Yeah, I picked up some flapjacks at Ma Ginger's. He complained some, but I suppose someone with two weeks on his string got a right to."

"What did he complain about?"

"The flapjacks wasn't cooked through, all dough."

"He's probably right," I said. "Ma Ginger gets it wrong most of the time."

"Serves him right," Rusty said.

"You empty his bucket?"

"You sure stick it to me, don't ya?"

"Somebody's got to do it. I'll do it."

Rusty smiled. "Knew you would if you got pushed into it."

I grabbed the big iron key off the peg and hung my gun belt on the same peg. It wasn't bright to go back there armed. King Bragg was the only prisoner we had at the moment, but I wasn't one to take chances. I opened up on the gloomy jail, lit only by a small barred window at the end of the front corridor. Three cells opened onto the cor-

26

ridor. King was kept in the farthest one.

He was lyin' on his bunk, which was a metal shelf with a blanket on it. The Puma County lockup wasn't no comfort palace. King's bucket stank.

"You want to push that through the food gate there?" I asked.

"Maybe I should just throw it in your face."

"I imagine you could do that."

He sprang off the metal bunk, grabbed the bucket, and eased it through the porthole, no trouble.

"I'll be back. I want to talk," I said.

"Sure, ease your conscience, hanging an innocent man."

I ignored him. He'd been saying that from the moment I nabbed him out at Anchor Ranch. I took his stinking bucket out to the crapper behind the jail, emptied it, pumped some well water into it and tossed that, and brought it back. It still stank; even the metal stinks after a while, and that's how it is in a jailhouse.

I opened the food gate and passed it through.

"Tell me again what happened," I said.

"Why bother?"

"Because your old man hanged me this morning. And it set me to wondering."

King Bragg wheezed, and then cackled. I sure didn't like him. He was a muscular punk, young and full of beans, deep-set eyes that seemed to mock. He was born to privilege, and he wore it in his manners, his face, his attitude, and his smirk.

"You don't look hanged," he said, getting smirky.

I sort of wanted to pulverize his smart-ass lips, but I didn't.

"Guess I'm lying to you about being hanged," I said. "So, go ahead and lie back. Start at the beginning."

The beginning was the middle of February, when King Bragg rode into Doubtful for some serious boozing, and alighted at Saloon Row, five drinkin' parlors side by side on the east end of town, catering to the cowboys, ranchers, and wanderers coming in on the pike heading toward Laramie.

"You parked that black horse in front of the Last Chance and wandered in," I said, trying to get him started.

"No, I went to the Stockman and then the Sampling Room, and then the Last Chance. Only I don't remember any of that. Last I knew, I took a sip of red-eye at the Last Chance, Sammy the barkeep handed it to me, and I don't remember anything else.

I couldn't even remember my own name
when I came to."

THREE

There's some folks you just don't like. It don't matter how they treat you. It don't matter if they tip their hat to you. If you don't like 'em, that's it. There's no sense gnawing on it. There was no sense dodging my dislike for King Bragg. I don't know where it come from. Maybe it was the way he kept himself groomed. Most fellers, they got two weeks to live, they don't care how they look. But King Bragg, he trimmed up his beard each morning, washed himself right smart, and even washed his duds and hung them to dry. That sure was a puzzle. The young man was keeping up appearances and it didn't make no sense. Not with the hourglass dribbling sand.

Now he stood quietly on the other side of them iron bars, telling me the same story I'd heard twenty times, and it didn't make any more sense now than the first time he spun it. It was just another yarn, maybe concocted with a little help from that lawyer, and it was his official alibi. Actually, it was more a crock than an alibi.

What King Bragg kept sayin' was that he had dozed through the killings, and when he woke up, he was holding his revolver and every shell had been fired. So he'd gotten awake after his siesta and got told he'd killed three men. And that was all he knew.

Well, that was a crock if ever I heard one.

"Maybe you got yourself liquored up real good, got crazy, picked a fight with them T-Bar cowboys, spilled a lot of blood, and got yourself charged with some killings."

That was the official version, the one that had convicted King Bragg of a triple murder. The one that was gonna pop his neck in a few days.

He stared. "I have nothing more to say about it," he said.

"Well I got nothing more to ask you," I said.

"Why are you asking? I've been sentenced, I'm going to hang. Why do you care?"

"Your pa, he asked me to look into it."

"Admiral Bragg doesn't ask anyone for anything. He orders."

"Well, now that's the truth. He sort of ordered me to."

"What did he say?"

"He didn't. He just hauled me out of Belle's crapper and hanged me."

"Now let me get this straight. My father — hanged you?"

"Noose and drop and all."

"I don't suppose you want to explain."

"It sure wasn't the way to make friends with the sheriff, boy."

"You calling me boy? You're hardly older than I am."

"I got the badge. I get to call old men boy if I feel like it."

"So my father, he hanged you?"

"Complete and total. And when I'm done here, I'm gonna haul his ass to this here jail and throw away the key."

King Bragg laughed. "Good luck, pal."

He headed over to his sheet metal bunk, flopped down on it, and drew up that raggedy blanket. Me, I was satisfied. That feller wasn't gonna weasel out of a hanging with that cock-and-bull story. As for me, I was ready to hang him whether I liked him or not, because that was justice. A man shoots three fellers for no good reason, and he pays the price. I'd just have to deal with Admiral Bragg one way or the other. Now I'd talked with the boy to check his story and nothing had changed.

I didn't much like the thought of pulling

the lever, but it would be my job to do it. They made me sheriff, and now I was stuck with it. I could quit and let someone else pull the lever that would drop King Bragg from this life. But I figure if a man's gonna be a man, he's got to do the hard things and not run away. So when the time comes, I'll pull the lever and watch King drop. Still, it sure made me wonder whether I wanted to be a lawman. It was more fun being young and getting into trouble. I was still young, but this wasn't the kind of trouble I was itching for. My ma used to warn me I had the trouble itch. If there was trouble somewhere, I'd be in the middle of it. Pa, he just said, keep your head down. Heads is what get shot.

I thought I'd ask a few more questions, just to satisfy myself that King Bragg done it and his ole man was being pigheaded, more than usual. Admiral Bragg was born pigheaded, and sometime it would do him in.

This sheriff business wasn't really up my alley. It would take someone with more upstairs than I ever had to ask the right questions. I could shoot fast and true, but that didn't mean my thinkin' was all that fast. There was a feller I wanted to jabber with about all this, the barkeep over to the

Last Chance Saloon, Sammy Upward. That was his sworn-out legal monicker. Upward. It sure beat Downward.

The Last Chance was actually the first bar you hit coming into town, or the last one if you were ridin' out. That made it a little wilder than them other watering places. The rannies riding in, they headed for the first oasis they could find. It didn't matter none that it charged a nickel more for red-eye, fifteen cents instead of a dime, and two cents more, twelve in all, for a glass of Kessler's ale. It didn't matter none that some of them other joints had serving girls, some of them almost not bad lookin', if you didn't look too close. And it didn't matter none that the other joints were safer, because the managers made customers hang up their gun belts before they could get themselves served. No, the Last Chance was famous for rowdy, for rough, and for mean, and that's why young studs like King Bragg headed there itching for some kind of trouble to find him.

It wasn't yet noon, but maybe Upward would be polishin' the spittoons or something, so I rattled the double door, found it unlocked, and found Upward sleeping on the bar. He lay there like a dead fish, but finally come around.

"We ain't open yet, Sheriff," he said.

"I ain't ordering a drink; I'm here for a visit."

"Visits cost same as a drink. Fifteen cents."

He hadn't yet stirred, and was peerin' up at me from atop the bar. That bar was sorta narrow, and he could fall off onto the brass rail in front, or off the back, where he usually worked, and where he had easy access to his sawed-off Greener.

"We're gonna visit, and maybe some day I'll buy one," I said.

"Someone get shot?"

"Not recently."

"I could arrange it if you get bored. If I say the word, someone usually gets shot in this here drinkin' parlor."

He peered up at me. He needed to trim the stubble on his chin, and maybe put on a new shirt, and maybe trade in that grimy bartender's apron for something that looked halfway washed.

"Tell me again what you told the court," I said.

"How many times we been through that, Sheriff? I'm tired of talking about it to people got wax in their ears."

"All right, pour me one."

"I knew you'd see it my way, Cotton."

The keep slid off the bar, examined a glass in the dim light, decided it wasn't no dirtier than the rest, and poured some red-eye in. The cheapskate poured about half a shot. I dug around in my britches for a dime and handed it to him.

"I owe you a nickel," I said. "Start with King Bragg coming in that night."

He didn't mind, or pretended he didn't.

"Oh, he come in here, and he was already loaded up. I could see by how he weaved when he walked."

"Why'd you serve him?"

"I make my living by quarters and dimes and nickels, damn you, and I'd serve a stumbling drunk if he had the right change. Hell, I'd even serve you, Cotton, even if it made my belly crawl. Just lay the change down, and I'll take it, and that's the whole story."

"You sure are touchy. How come?"

"I'll be just as touchy as I feel like, and I'm tired of telling you the story over and over. I ain't gonna tell it to you no more. You heard it, you've tried to pick it apart, and you can't. Now finish up and get out. I don't want you in this place. It's bad for business."

Upward was polishin' the bar so hard it was pulling the varnish off.

But I wasn't quitting. "What did King Bragg say to them T-Bar cowboys?"

"He said — oh, go to hell."

"That what he said?"

"No, that's what I'm telling you. I'm done yakking."

"How many T-Bar cowboys was in here?"

"I don't know. Just a few."

"Was Crayfish with the boys?"

"I don't remember. You want another drink? Fifteen cents on the barrelhead."

The man I was talkin' about owned the T-Bar, a few other ranches, and wanted Admiral Bragg's outfit too, just so he could piss on any tree in the county and call it his. His name was Crayfish Ruble. I don't know about that Crayfish part, but since I got Cotton hung on me, I don't ask no one about their first names. Not Crayfish, not Admiral. Crayfish Ruble had a Southern name, but I'd heard he was from Wisconsin, and who knows how he got a name like that. He come West with some coin in his jeans and bought a little spread, and then began muscling out the small-time settlers and farmers, paying about ten cents on the dollar, and pretty soon he was the biggest outfit in Puma County, and the T-Bar kept Doubtful going. Without the T-Bar, Doubtful would be a ghost town, and no one would know Puma County from New York City.

I sorta liked Crayfish. He was honest in his crookedness. Ask Crayfish what he wanted from life, and he'd not mince any words. He wanted all of Puma County, as well as Sage County next door, and Bighorn County up above, and half the legislature of Wyoming, along with the judges and the tax assessor. I asked him, and that's what he told me. I also asked him what else he wanted, and he said he wanted half a dozen wives, or a good cathouse would do in a pinch, and his own railroad car and a mountain lion for a house pet. He got no children, so there ain't nothing he wants but land and cows and judges and women. You sorta had to like Catfish. He was a plain speaker, and he sure beat Admiral Bragg for entertainment. Catfish tried to buy out Admiral, but Admiral, he filed a claim on every water hole and creek in all the country, and that led to bad blood and they've been threatening to shoot the balls off each other ever since. There's no tellin' what gets into people, but I take it personal. I gotta keep order in this here Puma County, and I know from experience that when a few males got strange handles, like Admiral and Crayfish, or Cotton, there's trouble a percolatin' and no way of escaping it. The feller with the worst handle usually wins, and I've always figured Admiral is a worse name than Crayfish, and even worse than Cotton, though I'm not very happy with what got hung on me.

Well, I was gonna go talk to Crayfish again, for sure.

"Sammy, I think I asked you a question. Was Crayfish Ruble in here when the shooting started?"

Upward just polished the bar, like he didn't hear me.

"Who pays your wages, Sammy?"

I knew who. It was Crayfish. He owned the Last Chance, but didn't want no one to know it, so the name on the papers was Rosie, but she didn't have a dime more than she could make on her back, and someone put up a wad to buy this place, and it was Crayfish.

"I get my pay from Rosie," Sammy said.

I leaned across the bar and grabbed a handful of apron and pulled him tight. I seen his hands clawing for that Greener under the bar, so I just tugged him tighter.

"Don't," I said. "Who owns this joint?"

"Never did figure that out," he replied.

"You're a card, Upward. I think I'm going to look a lot closer at this here triple murder. Somebody shot three of Ruble's hands, and maybe it was King Bragg, just like the court says it was, but maybe it was someone else, you know who, and ain't saying. And I'm poking around a little more until I got a better handle on it. This ain't makin' me happy."

Upward, he didn't like that none.

FOUR

Sammy Upward, he polished that bar so hard he was scrapin' varnish. I sure liked him even if I didn't trust him none. He's got a full deck in his head, more than I got, and he's always trying to deal aces to himself. So I just stood there and waited for him to outsmart himself.

"Pickens, I never give anything away. You want something from me, you pay for it."

I'd heard that before, so I just waited.

"Maybe trade. I'll trade for things."

I nodded.

"Like, you tell me something and I tell you something. You want news, you tell me news."

I nodded. "Don't call me Pickens," I said. "It's bad enough alone, but when you put Cotton in front, it's good for a punch in the nose."

"Well, do you think I like Upward? What am I, a choirboy?"

41

"What do you want to know, Sammy?"

He quit polishing. "This is a cold case. How come you're opening it up?"

"I ain't very happy with it, is all."

"You ain't squaring with me, Sheriff. What got into your bonnet?"

It's true, I wasn't squaring with him.

"I got just about hanged myself. So I thought I'd have another look at things."

"Just about hanged? Just about hanged? Get outa here, Sheriff, or make sense."

"I got shot in the outhouse."

"Shot in the outhouse! Now I've heard everything. Pickens, you're either drunk or you belong in the funny farm."

"It was in Belle's crapper, and they surrounded me and put a bullet in. Now you tell me something."

"Me tell you something! You got shot in the crapper and hanged, and now you want something from me!"

This was getting impossible. "I quit," I said, and clamped the Stetson down on my lumpy head. I'd had enough of Sammy Upward.

"Who hanged you? Who shot you? It had to be Admiral Bragg. Right?"

"I've done enough confessing, dammit."

"How come you're alive if you got hanged and shot?"

"The bullet went over my head and the rope didn't hold."

"Sheriff, I ain't getting the whole monte."

"That's because I don't feel like telling it. Now I'm outa here."

"Wait! Don't go out that door. I'll tell you something. This here place, it's owned by Crayfish Ruble, not Rosie."

"So?" I yawned and headed for clean air. That saloon stank like the vault of an outhouse, especially when the air was moving from Sammy in my direction.

I hadn't got anything from Upward that I didn't know, and me getting shot in the crapper would be all over Doubtful anyway.

"Up yours, Upward," I said.

Maybe that wasn't very smart, but I never can think of anything catchy to say. Some men, they've got just the right word for every occasion, but not me. Upward had got a confession out of me, and I got nothing in return. So all I could think of was Up Yours.

I sure hated the way it was going to play around town. There'd be whispering and laughing behind my back. Admiral Bragg, he dang near hanged the sheriff! Strung him right up and kicked the wagon out! Put a slug through Belle's crapper, too, caught the sheriff with his pants down! Every time

I walked into one of the town's five saloons, they'd be smilin' and snickering and I'd be as ornery as a two-hump camel.

I'd be hearing about it for a month. Hell, I'd be hearing about it until I quit and got out of Doubtful. Which I was of a mind to do. This thing was wounding my pride.

I wondered how Rusty was doing over to the jail, so I plowed back there, still pissed at Upward. I'd get even somehow.

My inquiry wasn't going nowhere, for sure.

Rusty was a typical redhead who'd get into a fight before he knew why, and then forget to quit before he got hurt. But he made a good deputy, mostly because people liked him, which is more than I can say about me. Red-haired people got no brakes.

He was sitting in my chair, reading *Captain Billy's Whizbangs,* which had more death and dismemberment and arsenic in its pulp pages than ten cents could possibly buy. The thing was published in Chicago, or Natchez, or some cesspool like that.

"Hey, Cotton, I was reading about a jailbreak in here," he said. "Forty people dead in Poughkeepsie, New York, including the warden and six guards. You think Admiral Bragg's going to try to spring King before the hanging?"

"It passed through my head a few times," I said.

"But it didn't stick?"

"The day they convicted King Bragg, I told his old man that King would get the first bullet if they tried to bust him out."

"They got the manpower, Cotton."

"Admiral's got maybe twenty cowboys handy with a six-gun."

"And what do we have? You and me and DeGraff and Burtell."

"It's a worry," I said, trying to dismiss him, but Rusty wouldn't be dismissed.

"What if they try something slick? Like a hostage? Like they capture you, and want to trade you for King? Or me? Am I worth King Bragg to you?"

"Rusty, if they grabbed you off the streets, I'd just laugh."

He wasn't very happy with that. "Well, same goes for you," he said. "They snatch you and want to trade you for King, I'll just laugh."

That riled me some. Why was I so riled this day? Maybe it was because I'd already got shot and hanged this morning. It was fixing to be a lousy day.

"Rusty, if they highjack me and want King for me, tell 'em to go to hell."

Rusty, he stared at me. "You really mean that?"

"And tell them if they come for King, they'll collect the body, but not the boy."

"What if they grab me?" Rusty wanted to know.

"Same thing. I'll tell them they'll collect King's body but not King."

"You mean you'd not trade me for King Bragg?"

"Nope."

Rusty, he sort of took a moment to swallow that. 'Cause I was saying if he got took hostage, he wasn't gonna get any help from me.

"Maybe I'll get me another job," Rusty said.

"Maybe you should," I said.

Rusty, he sort of stared at me respectful. It was the first time in living memory my deputy ever treated me respectful. It was like his red hair didn't count.

"They might try a trick, like coming in here to talk, and then holding us at gunpoint, snatching the keys, and freeing King. So I worry some. I told the mayor, if Admiral Bragg shows up with a lot of gunmen, get under cover because there's going to be a lot of lead pills flyin' around. This jail is gonna get itself shot up."

46

Half the time, there's no one on duty at night, but since King Bragg was our guest, I'd kept a deputy on at all hours with instructions to keep the front door locked. This place ain't no fortress, but it would take some work to bust in, and I figured anyone knocks down the door, they get a load of double-ought from the Greener aimed that way. So far, anyway, no one had showed up to spring King Bragg, and I doubted anyone would. But you never knew. I'd not put it past his old man to toss a stick of DuPont Hercules through the barred window up high just to put a little respect in us.

"Rusty, you hold the fort around here, and don't let no one in, not even some drunk saddle tramp. You just keep the scattergun handy. I'm going for a ride."

"Where you headed?"

"Time to have a little talk with Crayfish Ruble."

"What for?"

"I don't rightly know except this whole thing don't sit good with me. Them three hands of his got kilt; I hardly know a thing about them. Maybe I'll find out. One was Foxy Jonas, and his kid brother Weasel Jonas, neither of which was a sterling citizen of this republic. They'd steal their mother's

47

false teeth and let her starve. And the other, Rocco, that's the only name he ever had, this Rocco, he kidnaped girls and sold them. So King Bragg done the world a favor, except it was murder and he's going to swing for it. But I'm just curious why Crayfish Ruble had three jacks like that in his deck, so him and me are gonna talk."

"King Bragg, he done us a favor," Rusty said. "Them three buried out in the potter's field."

"Don't start thinkin' that way. Murder is murder."

I stomped out, headed for Jasper Turk's Livery Barn, where I was keeping Critter these days. Critter didn't like it at all. He liked being out on a pasture, with the sun and wind and rain and snow on him, and a chance to bite anyone come close.

He wasn't exactly the friendliest nag, and sometimes I thought to shoot him, bam, right between the eyes, and send him to the cat food canner. Critter and I, we were growing ornery side by side.

I didn't much care for this place, but in a town the size of Doubtful, I didn't have much choice. Turk, he treated horses worse than he treated people, and that always ticked me off. Only, he was careful no one ever saw him at it. But I could tell. I'd lead

Critter toward Turk, and Critter would lay back his ears and start clacking his molars and I got the picture real good.

I found Critter gnawing pine off the planks of his pen.

"Wreck your teeth," I told him.

He snorted. I stepped in and he bit me on the forearm. I always allow him one bite, but if he bites again, we get serious.

"You ain't got teeth hard enough to draw blood, you old coot," I told him.

He bit me again, this time gnawing on my shoulder.

"Cut it out!"

He snorted, so I raised a knee to his ribs, and he whoofed up some air, and tried to lay a hoof into me. I dodged just as he kicked with his right rear and whirled around to nip my ear.

"You sure are ornery this afternoon," I said, but he paid me no heed and was calculatin' how to kick me in the crotch. He's a smart horse, all right.

"You been in here too long," I said. "We'll take some air."

He lowered his ugly head and shoved it into my chest.

"Yeah, I like you too," I said.

Critter could get sentimental at times. We'd been partnering for nine years, and he knew me better than I knew myself. He was a good horse, not fastest at all, but with bottom. That bottom, that no-quit running, saved my life a time or two. So I sort of got along with him, at least most of the time.

I put a bridle on him and watched him lip it, working it with his tongue. He always did that. He hated a bit with a big curb in it, and had a conniption if I got too bossy. But now he settled down, so I brushed him good and led him into the aisle, where I blanketed and saddled him, after kneeing the air out of him so I could pull the girth up tight.

Turk was nowhere in sight, which was good. I didn't want to see anyone, not after getting hanged and shot that very morning. It sure seemed like a long time ago, between sitting in Belle's crapper and saddling up Critter.

I let myself out of the livery barn, leading Critter, and then I got on board. He was stiff-legged while he was deciding whether or not to pitch, but finally he sighed and I knew him and me were going to get along on this day.

But it was already deep into the afternoon, and Crayfish Ruble's spread was miles up the valley. Maybe I should go in the morning. But I decided against it. The last thing Crayfish would expect to see would be the sheriff of Puma County riding in seven, eight o'clock in the evening.

I steered Critter toward the jailhouse, which stood solid and tan, built of sandstone and intended to last a while. I wrapped Critter's rein around the hitch rail, just in case, and wandered in there.

Rusty was playin' euchre through the bars with King Bragg.

"I'm heading up the valley to talk to Crayfish. You'll be on duty here," I told him.

"You sure you want to go at this hour?" Rusty asked. "Can't it wait?"

"No, it can't. A man gets hanged in the morning, he wants answers by sundown."

"Pay me overtime then," Rusty said.

King Bragg stared at me. "Ask Crayfish why he shot his own men," he said.

FIVE

It sure was a fine day. Critter thought so too, and farted his way up the valley, scaring lizards and offending horseflies. The two-rut road ran beside Chippy Creek, where the red-winged blackbirds were festooning the red willow brush and making a racket.

I was packing a slicker and a bedroll, just in case, because May is as fickle as a bored wife. I let Critter pick his own pace, which was a jog. I didn't know when I'd get out to Crayfish's big ranch, or whether anyone would be awake. But it didn't matter. It was May, and the whole world was happy to be alive.

You have to wonder where Crayfish got that name. Or how I got to be stuck with Cotton. There's no telling about parents. My pa, he told me up in New England, everyone gets named for a virtue. The women are Faith, or Charity, or Temperance. There's men named Serene or Parsimony. One feller from Vermont named Diligence Brown showed up in Doubtful, and he was a bookkeeper. But down South, pa said, people scratch where they itch. Now someone named Crayfish simply has the itch for crayfish, and someone named Toad, that's what he's like. I've knowed a couple fellas named Toad, and it fits. Or sometimes a Southern boy gets named for something that scared his ma. I knew a Funeral Jones once, right out of Macon, Georgia. And my uncle was named Digger. That's what he did. I had an auntie named Sweet and I once knew a Candy Cane too. I prefer the Southern method of namin' babies. It's more honest. I don't care much for Cotton, but it's better than Boll Weevil. So I already knew a piece about Crayfish just from his name. Tell me the name of a Southerner, and I've already got a handle on him. I knew two Turkeys and three Chickens and one Buzzard, two Possums, and a Packrat, and all of them born south of the Mason Dixon Line. One feller from Alabama was called Possum Pilgrim, and it was a puzzle. I knew a Pecker Smith once, but didn't want nothing to do with him. I met a Carolina gal named Sassy once. The fellers called her Peach Fuzz, but that's because her skin was fuzzy. Only girl I ever met with a mustache and a hairy chest.

Crayfish, he mostly had Southerners on his spread. And they had Southern names, too. Like those that got kilt by King Bragg, namely Foxy and Weasel Jonas, and Rocco. That's what I was riding twenty miles each way on a May day to find out about. Foxy and Weasel were from South Texas, and there ain't nothing worse, especially down around Waco. Seems like ever time I had trouble bite me, it was someone from Waco. I don't have kindly thoughts about anyone from Waco or a hundred miles in any direction from Waco. I don't think anyone in Waco ever growed up straight or true. I wish someone would build a fence around Waco and not let anyone out. There was a rumor that Crayfish came from outside Waco, but I wasn't gonna hold it against him until it got proved. There's always a bad rumor or two floating around Doubtful, Wyoming.

It was a long ride, but I didn't mind. I quit a couple of times, and let Critter chomp on anything he could get his buck teeth around, while I looked for snapping turtles along the creek, without no luck. I've been meaning to catch a couple of snappers and give them to my deputies. I know Rusty, he'd like one, but them other two, DeGraff and Burtell, they might not know what to do with a snapper. Give 'em to a lady, of course. You never know. Maybe some gal in Doubtful is pinin' away for a snapping turtle, seeing as how lots of women have the same nature as them turtles.

Critter got into a commotion while I was wetting a stump at the creek, and next I knew, he had a prairie rattler between his teeth and was shakin' it every which way. That fat rattler was not taking it kindly, but it was pretty cold for rattlers to be out, so all it did was wiggle some until Critter bit it in two and left the two parts dancing in the grass.

"Critter, don't you never do that to my arm," I said. "I got all my fingers and I'm keepin' 'em."

Critter yawned.

Pretty soon I began seeing bunches of T-Bar cattle. They was all ornery little things; Crayfish wasn't much on breeding. Admiral Bragg, he was buying good short-horn bulls and crossing his range cattle on them, and getting more weight, but Crayfish didn't give it a thought. Them cows was chopping that tender May grass right off, and there was sure a lot of them skinny beeves chewing down the range, but I didn't much care. A man's got a right to ruin his ranch if he chooses, and Crayfish was the sort who'd chomp her down to dirt and then move on.

I didn't see no one around, but that was usual enough. The T-Bar was spread over so much land it'd take every person in the state of Missouri to staff it right. So there was simply bunches of cattle gnawing away as Critter jogged himself up the road.

Most horses, a jog is real comfortable, but not Critter. His jog bent my tailbones and sent aches up my back. But it was a mile-eater pace, so I just stood in the stirrups now and then and let Critter ruin his own bones instead of mine. I figure if he wanted to wreck himself, that was his business. Let him; why should I care?

Twilight came, and then night, and the crickets started up, and the air chilled real quick. But I rode into the T-Bar just when the last light was fading. Log buildings made it solid. There was a main house, well lit with lamps, a bunkhouse, a barn, a couple of sheds, and pens. The log house had a comfortable porch stretching across it, facing the mountains, and it looked like a fine place for a man to sip a toddy and eye his empire. The place wasn't fancy, just solid, but that was not Crayfish's doing. That's how he bought it from Thaddeus

56

Throckmorton.

It looked like I was too late to chow down. Lamps were shining from the bunkhouse, and I could see cowboys, mostly in their long underwear, playin' cards in there. I figured it wasn't too late to come callin', so I wrapped Critter's rein around the hitch rail and banged on the door. I was curious about Crayfish's domestic arrangements, and when the man himself opened up, I wasn't surprised. I couldn't imagine no woman staying with Crayfish for more than an hour or two. A day would be stretching it. A day and night would be beyond imagining.

There he was, wearing his eye patch. This time it was gold. He had a dozen of them, all sorts of colors, and I hardly ever saw him wear a black patch. This here one, gold colored, had a turquoise stone set in the middle.

"You're looking at the wrong eye, Sheriff," he said.

"Never saw that one," I said.

"I got more patches than women got hats. You want to come in, or are you gonna stand there all night?"

He waved me into his lamplit parlor. He was medium short, with black hair slicked straight back. There never was a hair out of place, and the word was that he glued his hair down, using the juice of boiled-up pigs feet. His hair lay so shiny and flat you could pretty near ice skate on it.

"You want something to wet your whistle?" he asked.

I nodded.

"This here's for guests," he said, holding up a decanter. "That one's for me."

He poured some red stuff into a cut-glass beaker and added a splash. When he handed it to me, I noticed he had a ring on every finger. Then he poured another from the other decanter for himself.

"Always like to treat guests to what's tasty," he said.

I sipped. That stuff, it cut a channel down my tongue and scraped the hide off the rest of my mouth. I coughed, swallered, and downed it, expecting to start quaking.

"Mighty nice," I said.

He leered at me, and sipped cheerfully at his own beaker.

"Strange hour to come calling," he said.

"Well, that gets me straight to it," I said. "Say, this is mighty fine stuff, mighty fine." I sipped again, felt savaged, and swallowed that varnish, feeling it scrape paint off my innards all the way down. "You treat company better than you treat yourself," I added.

"Well, when I sell this spread, I'm going into the hospitality business," he said. "This is just a way of fattening my wallet. Give it another year, and I'll be in some metropolis. I'm thinking Kansas City."

"What'll you do there, Crayfish?"

"Run the best whorehouse in the United States," he said.

"That your dream, is it?"

"You don't know the half of it," he said. "Gambling parlor downstairs, fiddlers and pretty bar maids, poker tables, no one walks in except he's all dressed up, top hat and tails, boots shined, and a fat purse on him too. And upstairs I got the prettiest girls in the world, all refined, bedsheets washed, the girls bathing at least once a week, and perfumed just fine. Ten dollars a pop, and most of it for me."

"That's a dream, all right, Crayfish."

"Beats ranching in Wyoming," he said. "And I get to graze wherever I want."

He sipped. I sipped and coughed.

"This ain't a social visit," he said, not quite making a question out of it.

I wasn't in no hurry. I just wanted to see if he'd sweat a bit if I didn't come direct to my business.

"Mighty fine stuff here," I said, swirling the glass. "Just right for company."

"Brought it up from Utah," he said. "Them Saints make mighty fine Valley Tan."

I figured it was something like that. "I imagine you can afford any hooch from anywhere," I said.

"I could afford a lot more if I had more land," he said. "These foothills, they're not half the pasture that Admiral's got. Now if I had his spread, I'd been sending you a barrel of whiskey once a month."

I listened real hard to that.

"I guess you would, if I wanted it," I said. "But I don't. I'm not a drinkin' man, and not a dry man neither. Once in a while, I take a little sauce for the kidneys. My ma, she said do whatever you want, but don't do it often."

"Smart woman, I'd say." He downed the rest of his stuff, and built hisself another, with a generous splash of springwater in it. "This a social call?" he asked.

"Oh, I've got me a few questions, loose ends, things that didn't get tidied up," I said.

"Well, I'll be glad to help any way I can, Sheriff."

The social moment had vanished, that's for sure. He wasn't one to sit and yarn with a law officer if he could help it.

"Them three got kilt, the ones working here. You know, I need to git ahold of next of kin. I never let their ma and pa and brothers and all know what happened. That's a part of being a sheriff. A peace officer, he's got to send along the bad news. I thought maybe you could tell me something about each of them, and I'll send along a wire or a letter to their folks."

He seemed almost to deflate. For a while there he was all ballooned up, trying to look six inches taller than he was, but now the gas was leakin' from his bag, and he just smiled some.

"Oh, that. Well, I don't know much. The pair of Jonas brothers never did tell me much about themselves."

"Where'd you meet 'em, Crayfish?"

"Beats me. I think they were from down deep in Texas but I wouldn't swear to it."

"Texas, eh? Well, you Texas fellers can spot each other easier than I can."

"Why do you think I'm from Texas, Sheriff?"

I shrugged. "Just a hunch. If I got her wrong, you can put me straight."

"I'm from all over the place," Crayfish said.

"Well, these Jonas boys. Them that got kilt. The county put them in a potter's field out of town, seeing as how you didn't feel like buryin' your own men. Foxy and Weasel was their handles, but I need to know what names they got christened by."

"Blamed if I know, Sheriff."

"They had a ma and pa, and probably got named something like Elmer and Harry, and got the Foxy and Weasel names later. If I'm gonna write their kinfolk, I kinda need the names."

"Funny, Sheriff, but I never asked. Here, it ain't polite to ask a gent."

"Well, at least you know where they came from."

"Waco, maybe. Someone once told me Waco."

"They was pretty slick with six-guns."

"That's what I want, Sheriff. I got crooks and rustlers and land grabbers to deal with. I need men who know cows and guns real good."

"You reckon if I just shot a wire off to any Jonas in Waco, it'd get to their folks?"

The rancher shrugged, and downed his whiskey.

"Well, tell me why you hired them. They must of got some sort of reputation, carrying names like that. Now why'd the one call himself Weasel?"

"Weasels is mean, Sheriff. You know that.

You can figure it as well as I can. Foxy, too, you get the man's character without any more than the handle."

"I guess I sort of do," I said. "Now how about that other, the third that got kilt by King Bragg. What was he doin' here?"

"Oh, Rocco, poor devil. Just a drifter. I hired him straight off. I need all the hands I can get, and he seemed fit enough."

"How do I get ahold of his folks, Cray-fish?"

"Blamed if I know, Sheriff."

"Any reason that King Bragg would pump lead into those three?"

"Yes. He was drunk. He and his pa don't much care for me. And those three were all of my hands that were in the saloon when he wandered in, looking to cause trouble." He shrugged. "I guess you know the rest."

I wasn't so sure I did.

Six

Crayfish Ruble stared at me from his good eye, a liquid brown one, with an eyebrow showing a few gray hairs. It was that gold eye patch with the turquoise sewed on that done me in.

"You don't like my eye patch," he said. "An eye patch should be dignified."

"Well, it gets attention, Crayfish."

"Now then. You ride clear out here late in the day looking for something that could be gotten any time I'm in town. And you come out here weeks after my men got shot. That's mighty interesting, Sheriff. I think you'd better tell me what's going on."

"Oh, I was just looking at things that ain't finished up yet, like getting word to those poor relatives."

Crayfish sort of grinned at me. "And maybe a little pressure on you from Admiral Bragg to see if his boy can get sprung."

"Well, he ain't getting sprung unless

there's something didn't get said in the trial."

"And of course you're looking for it."

"Things don't add up, is all," I said.

"Word I got is that you had yourself a rough morning," Crayfish said. "How does it feel, having a noose around your scrawny neck and dropping off a wagon?"

Word got around, all right. I shoulda knowed I couldn't keep anything a secret for long. "Well, I didn't much care to be hung, Crayfish."

"It's hanged, Sheriff. The correct word is hanged. That's when you've got a noose around you. Hung is something else. If you're hung, you get to please the ladies."

I blushed clear through. My ma, she never told me the difference, and five grades of schoolin' didn't help me none. He was standin' there sort of smirky, and I was thinking maybe I ought to do something else with my life. I never was any good with all them highfalutin words anyway. I got a few basic ones, and that's all I ever needed. Here he was, maybe the richest rancher in Wyoming, making a fool of me. I am a good shot, and fast with a handgun, but there ain't much else going for me.

"How about a refill, Sheriff?" he asked.

I debated it, but not for long, and pushed

my tumbler his way.

"You know of any reason King Bragg woulda shot Weasel and Foxy and Rocco?"

"I think King Bragg would have shot his own grandmother if he felt like it," the rancher replied.

"I'm lookin' for reasons," I said. I wasn't gonna let him give me windies instead of facts.

"He was drunk, by just about everyone's account. What a man does with that much booze in him is beyond knowing, Sheriff."

He handed me the Valley Tan, which was awful stuff that bit and snarled its way down my throat. He sure didn't drink it himself. My ma used to tell me you could get a handle on anyone just by seein' what he served up for company.

"Well, you tell me what you heard again," I said. I wasn't gonna quit on this.

"I don't have the details."

"You're the boss, and you don't have the story?"

He sighed. "By the time I got there, my men were laid flat, cold, and gray. They'd all been shot in the chest, just once. And Upward was holding a shotgun on King Bragg, who was sitting stupidly on the floor, too drunk to stand. Upward had looked at the kid's six-gun. King Bragg fired six shots, killed three of my men."

"I'm still lookin' for reasons," I said.

That Valley Tan was awful, but it was doin' its work in my belly.

Crayfish eyed me a moment, I mean with the brown eye, not with the turquoise stone on gold. "To get a look at King, just have a close look at Admiral," he said. "King's a good son, taking his pa's side always. The Braggs, they ain't glad to have Ruble around. It's almost, but not quite, range war, with big ranchers collecting gunmen and having it out. Only it's not. I'm too busy trying to turn this place into a bonanza and get out of here. This is the loneliest and most godforsaken land a man could get mired in. I want city lights, Sheriff. Ruble's no enemy of the Braggs. Crayfish Ruble would like to clean up. In fact, I was hoping to sell everything I possess to the Braggs, and even do it on generous terms. But there's a little fly-in-the-ointment, Sheriff. The Braggs don't see me like I see me. You know? They're not my enemy, but I seem to be their enemy. And they've worked themselves up about the T-Bar Ranch, my brand, and now they kilt three of my men."

It made sense. I got to thinking about trouble in Doubtful, and it wasn't the T-Bar drovers that was causing trouble. They were

67

mostly quiet fellers, downing a few ales in Upward's watering hole. It was the Bragg men raising hell, when there was hell-raising in town. But I wasn't feelin' very good about all this.

"Crayfish, how come you're out here if this country don't appeal to you?"

That question caught him off guard, for sure. For a moment he just flapped his lips, trying to come up with something.

He smiled and shrugged. "How'd you end up sheriff?" he asked.

"It got laid on me," I replied.

"Well, this got laid on me, Sheriff."

"You coulda stayed in the city."

He yawned. It was clear he wasn't eager to continue this little talk. "That's what separates you and me from Admiral Bragg and his strange-named brood, Sheriff. Bragg likes it here. He likes cows and cowboys and land. He likes this cold weather. He likes no one being around. He likes having his own trees and grass. He likes being alone and being lord of his whole universe. Me?" He shrugged again. "Accident. I won the original T-Bar in a poker game. I bet a night with my lady friend, Maybelline, against Arnold Austria's ranch, and a full house won. So there it was. I got turned from a gambler into a rancher. Everything in my life's a turn of the card, Sheriff. I have no ambition. If Admiral Bragg beat me out of my place tomorrow, I'd pack up and walk away. What does it matter?"

"You coming in to watch King Bragg hang?"

"I wouldn't miss it, Sheriff."

"Then maybe you care more than you're saying."

That sure surprised him. He frowned some. "You know," he said, "it's the justice of it I care about. Yes, three of my men got kilt, and that's something to care about. I'll be in Doubtful watching real close when you spring the trap," he said.

Something wasn't right with Crayfish. "You didn't care enough to contact their next of kin," I said.

He stared at me. "What are you up to?"

"I'm up to making sure justice is going to be done."

"You're a card, Pickens." He began crowding me toward the door, and then he opened it. "Long ride for nothing," he said.

"I got two weeks," I said. "And I'll use them."

I handed him the tumbler and stepped onto his porch. Behind me the door closed quietly.

The bunkhouse was dark. Them cowboys

sure didn't burn any oil. But they were up before dawn, and out with the cattle while there still were stars showing. Chill air was rolling down from the mountains. It sure as hell would be a long ride back, but me and Critter, we'd manage it if I let him rest.

I collected my nag. Critter snarled at me. He was lookin' for some hay and a good roll after the saddle was off, but here I was getting on him and steering him away from the pens and hay ricks.

We rode out quiet, in starlight, and I let Critter pick the way. Horses can see better than people, and he had no trouble takin' me down that road. It sure was peaceful. Night is when it's a joy to be out in the country, with no one nowhere, just walking along and owning the whole universe.

My stomach was tellin' me it was owed some chow, but I had none, so there was nothing to do but ride them long miles back to Doubtful, so that's what I set out to do. Wasn't anyone gonna drop a rib roast and mashed potatoes and gravy into my mitts.

I like my sleep, but this was such a fine spring night I didn't mind. It'd be maybe one or so when I raised Doubtful, more if I let Critter graze and fart along the way. I always use a single loop rein, so I just let her ride behind the horn, and stretched my arms and cracked my fingers some.

I was dozin' along, letting Critter find his way back to Doubtful, when I got woke up sudden. I didn't even know where I was. But a soft voice ripped out of the night.

"Stop," said this female voice. I don't rightly know why I thought it was female.

I woke up fast, and debated kicking Critter into a gallop, but instead I reined him in.

"I've got you skylined, Sheriff. I can see you but you can't see me. You're where the stars are blotted out. There's a Greener loaded with buckshot aimed at you, and if you mess with me, you'll be hamburger. That clear?"

"Mighty clear," I said.

"Then I'll put this shotgun away. I just want to talk to you, and not get shot at by an itchy lawman."

"Well, you coulda chose a better way."

"I'm sorry. It's dark, and I thought if I called, you'd pump a bullet at me."

"What do you take me for? I want to know what I'm shootin' at, especially if it sounds like a woman."

"You mind if I ride with you a way, and just palaver a bit?"

"I ain't used to riding with strangers in the night, ma'am."

There was a long pause, and I wondered whether she would beat a retreat.

"I'm Queen Bragg. Call me Queenie."

Well, that wasn't no surprise. "All right, what?" I asked.

"I'm getting my mare and we'll ride together," she said.

I wasn't too pleased with that. This here day started out with a Bragg, and was ending with a Bragg.

I sensed her steer her nag close in. I kept my six-gun in my hand, just in case this was another abduction. I wasn't gonna let any more Braggs haul me to any more hanging trees.

But she settled in beside, and I could sort of make her out in the dark. Everything I knew about her was gossip, because she'd never given me the time of day. The story was, she was another high-handed Bragg, like her old man, only worse.

I didn't say nothing, and let her ride beside for a while. We were sort of taking the measure of each other. I knew what would come next. Another demand. Braggs never asked anyone for anything. She'd demand that I stop the hanging.

"I'm sorry my father did that to you," she said.

I pretty near fell off Critter. I'd never

72

heard a Bragg apologize for anything, not even a fart.

"I don't ask you to forgive him, or me," she said. "It's his way, and it's what got King into trouble, and why I don't have friends."

I just grunted something. I don't come up with words very good.

"He shouldn't have shot at you in the outhouse. That was reckless. And it wasn't necessary."

I could hardly believe my ears. Here I was, listening to a Bragg actin' halfway civilized.

"It sure was reckless. What if I'd been standing up and getting my pants up? I'd be dead."

"I know," she said. "They laughed about it. They know you usually sit for twenty minutes reading the Montgomery Ward catalog."

I sure didn't have any handle about how this was going to play out. Critter, he kept eying the mare like he was going to bite it, which he probably would pretty soon. But I just reined his head away a little, and let the two nags pick their way through the black night.

"You sure you're Queen Bragg?" I asked, not really believing.

"I'm Queen. And I'm apologizing."

I didn't know what to say to that.

She laughed. "It doesn't figure, does it?"

I shook my head, and then realized she couldn't see it. "Always a first time," I said.

"And I'm sorry he tried to scare you half to death with that noose and the whole hanging. And I'm sorry he's pushing you the way he is. You must be angry."

"All in a day's work," I said.

"I don't think the way my father does. We all want to enlist your help, but he thinks you've got to be pushed."

"I don't get enlisted," I said. "I do my job and try to do it right."

"That's what I told Admiral. But he just smiled, like I was some simpleton girl, and said, 'Well, look at him now. He's got the case wide open and talking to everyone that was caught in it. Scare a man enough to wet his pants, and he'll do his best for you.' I don't agree."

"Well, in fact he got me running, all right."

"Yes, you've talked to the barman, Upward, and to King in jail, and to Crayfish Ruble this evening. Did you find out anything?"

"Enough to make me itchy is all."

"You've got two weeks to be itchy, and then King dies," she said.

"How come you're here? Scaring me in

74

the night?"

"To ask you to keep looking. To thank you for doing what you can do."

That sure wasn't the usual Bragg talk. Braggs never asked anything of anyone. And no living person ever heard a Bragg say thanks.

"And to tell you I apologize for all of us."

I didn't much like it. I'd like it if all the Braggs were the same type, and I could count on 'em to be ornery.

"All right, you run along now, and don't point loaded Greeners at lawmen. It ain't right, and you're lucky I'm not hauling you in and tossing you in with your brother."

"Why are you itchy?" she asked, gently ignoring me.

"Some things don't match up with the trial. Like King saying he don't remember none of it. Like Crayfish in an uproar at the trial about the death of three of his best men, and demanding fast justice — at the same time he let the county put them dead bodies in a potter's field, and he never did try to find their next of kin. It's all nothing, just Ruble being his usual self. But it makes me scratchy."

We reached the turnoff to the Anchor Ranch, her place, which she recognized a lot better than me, and she drew up her mare there.

"I guess this is where we part," she said.

I was sure uncomfortable, and itching to get back to Doubtful.

Then she leaned over, until she was half out of her saddle, and I grabbed for my six-gun not knowing what came next. But it was a quick kiss on the cheek. One quick peck on my stubble, and then she turned her nag into her lane, and I found myself rubbing my cheek, like I had been branded.

SEVEN

I cussed Queen Bragg clear back to Doubtful. I thought I had all them Braggs figured out. But she was running against form. I imagine I was the first person on earth to hear a Bragg ask for something, or hear an apology from a Bragg. It made me feel cranky. Just when I thought I knew something, it turned out I didn't. I tried to think what my ma or pa would say about that, but I came up with nothing. They likely never heard of someone goin' against the grain.

It was bad enough that she apologized, but worse, she kissed me. Maybe it was just a swift peck, but it was a kiss, all right. Last time she got that close to a male, she beat him with a riding crop. I guessed she'd beat me with one soon enough. She'd do anything to get the sheriff to reopen the case. That's all there was to it. Absolutely nothing more. Just another Jezebel stirring a man up.

I put Critter in the livery barn. It sure was dark in there in the small hours of the night. I didn't know what time, only that Doubtful was quiet and peaceful. Critter was out of sorts himself, having got ridden too long, and cussed out. Between cussing at Queen, I was cussing at Critter and tellin' him he was about ready to get hisself sold at the next auction. He bit me as I was hauling the saddle off his back, so I got kissed and bit in the same day I got shot at and hanged. Or hung. I called it hung, no matter what Crayfish Ruble thought. I didn't give a hang.

I found the door locked, which was good. I banged on it until Rusty slid open the peep.

"Lemme in," I said.

"You could say please," he said from the other side of that massive door. He swung it open, and first thing I saw was the big old Dragoon Colt in his hand. He seemed to favor that antique. That was good too.

He had a lamp lit at the rolltop desk, but the rest of my office was pitch dark.

"All right, you can go home," I barked.

"You mad at something?"

"No, it was a good ride, and now I'm here. Go home."

He shoved that cannon back into its holster. "Quiet here too," he said.

"Prisoner quiet?"

"Sleeping, last I knew." He stared at me. "What's wrong?"

"Don't ever trust a woman. You think you know a woman and she's the exact opposite."

"You run into a woman?"

"She run into me."

"What's the deal, Cotton?"

"Never mind. It ain't nothing. Now git."

"You could thank a man for staying late and putting in extra."

"I never thank anyone. You done your duty, so you're dismissed."

Rusty smiled. "It's a woman," he said. He collected his gray felt Stetson and headed into the night. I slammed the door behind him and latched it tight as it would go.

There was not much night left, but I could snatch an hour or two in the other cell. And I'd be ornery all day. I checked for messages, but it had been a quiet night. And nothing on the log either. No drunks spent the night sleeping it off; no cat burglars snatched any woman's brooch. No one busted into the hardware and stole all the shotguns.

It was chill in there, but it wouldn't matter. I'd pull a jail blanket over me and settle down. I put the cell key in my britches, so I wouldn't lock myself in. Them bunks was nothing but a sheet of metal, but I'd slept on worse. So I peered into the other cell, which was murky black, and then lowered myself. Cold iron ain't exactly a comfort, but I was so tired it didn't matter none.

"You were talking about my sister."

That was King Bragg. I peered into the murk. He was standing in the cell across the aisle, his hands on the bars.

"Yeah, Queen. She pulled a Greener on me."

"For what?"

"So she could talk. I can't figure you Braggs out."

"Neither can I," King said. "But she's breaking the mold. Maybe she's the lucky one. I got stamped in my father's cookie cutter. I've never asked anyone for anything, and I never will."

I was tired and out of sorts but he stood there waiting, and I needed someone to talk to, so it might as well be him. "She said she was sorry about what your pa did, shooting and hanging me, and she asked me to help you if I would. Now ain't that something?"

"It runs contrary," King said. "Pa always told us never to apologize."

"It was like an earthquake. A Bragg apologizin' to me. Asking for help. In all my years, I never heard of it."

"You're not old. Just a few years older than I was."

He was calling himself *was*. It fit.

"I'm getting some rest now. I rode out for a little talk with Ruble. It didn't come to much."

"In a few days you'll walk me out to the courtyard and up some steps. There won't be a thing I can do about it. If I don't walk, you'll carry me. If I don't want to go, I'll be taken. And my hands will be tied behind me, so I'll be helpless. Then you'll put the hemp noose over me and tighten it some and turn it off a little so it breaks my neck clean. Then I'll feel the floor go out from under me, and I'll fall fast and then there'll be a crack, and then nothing. A flash of pain and then nothing. No heaven, no hell, no hearing birds sing in the morning. I just turned eighteen. And that's as far as it went."

I felt bad, and wanted to tell him to shut up, but I just lay there. I didn't feel much better about it than he did.

"Are you satisfied I did it?"

"I ain't heard nothing to the contrary."

I sure wasn't enjoying this.

81

"Maybe I did it. I don't know. I have no memory of it."

"The court heard you were fallin'-down drunk."

"I'd had one or two. I wasn't falling down. But next I knew, I was on the floor looking up. People standing over me. Gunsmoke in the air. They were checking my six-gun, and said all six rounds got fired. And there were three dead."

I didn't say nothing. He was working up to pleading that he didn't do it. I'd heard that song a few times.

"You know them three? Rocco and Foxy and Weasel?"

"No. But they were T-Bar riders. Everyone in there's T-Bar."

"Tough customers. Some wanted dodgers on them. I looked through all them dodgers come into this office, and they weren't upright citizens."

"Why did I shoot them?"

"You asking me, boy? Answer it yourself."

"The Jonas boys were horse thieves and rustlers. Rocco was a con man, crook, ravisher of women, and things like that. They tell me that's why I shot them. If I did. Somehow I supposedly knew all that, and went in there and killed them, just like that. And never popped a shot at the regular

82

T-Bar cowboys."

"That's how the testimony went, King."

"I guess I knew more than I thought I did, killing off three crooks."

"Guess you did. Your pa, he must've given you the scoop on them three."

"No."

"Then someone else did."

He sighed. "It doesn't make any difference. When you've got a few days left, it doesn't matter. I don't know what happened, and that's how I'll die."

"Who else was in the Last Chance?"

"I don't know, Sheriff. I walked in, asked for a drink from Upward, he hands one to me, and I don't remember the rest."

"I guess there's fellers who blank out, get just enough sauce in them."

"Maybe I deserve hanging," he said.

"Not for me to say, King."

He didn't reply. I could see he wasn't standing at the bars any more.

I didn't like lying there in the same jail room with him, so I took the jail blanket with me and settled into my swivel chair and tried for some shut-eye. It wasn't far from dawn anyway, and I might as well look a little like I was on duty.

But I didn't like sitting there in the office with him back in the cell. What he did, he did, but maybe he wasn't even aware of it. Didn't give them kilt men a life back, but maybe he didn't know what he was doing. Maybe they should have shipped him to the asylum instead of hanging him. I couldn't say. I was as helpless as he was. In a few days I'd have to do stuff I didn't want to do. I wouldn't want to tie his hands behind him, lead him out to the courtyard, and up them steps. But I had to do it, just as he had to submit to it.

I quit thinkin' like that. His pa, Admiral Bragg, he'd tried to scare the bejesus out of me just one morning ago. Pretty near did me in. Let the boy hang. Hang all the Braggs, Queen too, and the world would be a better place.

I got under that blanket in the chair, but pretty quick, there was hammering, and I let DeGraff in. He pitched his hat onto a peg — a trick I never could master.

"How come you're here, Cotton?"

"How many times do I tell you, don't Cotton me. Just call me Sheriff. I never liked the name that got hung on me, and hold it against my parents. They were okay in the rest, except Pa never earned nothing, but they hung that name on me and I'd just as soon trade it."

He grinned. "How come you're here, Cotton?"

He was bein' inflammatory, and he knew it.

"I been riding," I said.

"Story is, you get held up by Queen," he said.

"Word sure gets around," I said. "A man can't take a leak in Doubtful but everyone knows about it."

DeGraff poured some ancient java from the speckled blue pot, which hadn't had a fire under it for days, and began sipping. He saw the cell block door was closed, and then settled close.

"I wandered into the Last Chance last night, just to give it the eyeball, and Upward nodded to me sort of strange. It was full of T-Bar men, and they were all sucking beers, one or two sipping red-eye, and mighty quiet. None of them had hung up their artillery either. It was all just dangling from their waists, not on the pegs Upward put in the wall. It was peaceful enough, except that it was all-fired quiet. I just smiled a bit and went out, and hung around under a porch in shadow, and pretty soon they came out of there, got on their nags, and rode out. There was maybe ten of them."

I waited for more, and sure enough, it was

coming.

"I let 'em go. They wasn't causing trouble, and they was heading out. But I was a little curious, so I slipped back in there later. Just a couple of old soaks in there then, trying to blot out what's left of themselves. Well, Cotton, I leaned into the bar and asked Upward what it was about, and he just smiled.

"But then he fessed up. Them T-Bar men, they were doing a little practice run. One of these moments they're going to hit the jail, drag King Bragg out, and lynch him at the nearest cottonwood tree."

"Upward told you this?"

"He did, while polishing the bar top like he always does when he's talking. And one more thing. He said word is out that Bragg's putting some heat on you to free the boy. If you keep poking around, trying to open a closed case, then the T-Bar will settle the case its own way. With its own rope. Just a little warning, was how Upward put it. You quit poking around, and they won't break down the jail door."

"That makes two bunches wanting to bust in," I said. "Bragg wants to spring the boy and get him out of Wyoming. And this Ruble bunch wants to speed up justice a few days. I imagine we got our hands full.

You up to it?"

"I always knew I'd get myself kilt," he said.

EIGHT

I got a little shut-eye, not half enough, and headed back to the office. They was all there when I knocked and got let in. Three ornery deputies. Rusty, who come over from the wild side a year or so earlier and joined up with me. He was the only one in the lot who was cheerful now and then. And them pals of his, DeGraff and Burtell, both a good piece older than me, tough as barbwire, and the sort never to waste a bullet because they always hit their target the first time. Them three made a bunch, all right, and the county was halfway safe because I had good men standing with me. None was married, and none wanted to be. They all had been drifting cowboys once, selling their skills to ranchers for forty and found.

I was glad to see them together, because we had a little talkin' to do. Rusty, he poured himself some week-old java from the blue speckled pot, took a sip, and managed to get it down his gullet. The others, they were kinda waiting for me, like they had expected a little talkin' this afternoon. They were right.

"King Bragg is enjoyin' his visit?" I asked.

"Last I looked," said Rusty. "He ain't taking doom easily, and has gotten to pacing. Not any direction you can go in a ten-foot cage."

"He should of thought about that before he kilt them T-Bar men," I said.

I got myself some of that coffee, and it was so bad I spit it out. "Make some fresh one of these weeks," I snapped.

But them deputies, they just lounged around, staring at me.

"All right. We gotta do some thinking. It's hard enough for me to do any, so maybe you can do better. There may be trouble coming at us any time. Admiral Bragg's itching to bust his boy outa here, and we can count on it if I don't come up with something to spare the boy. He'd like to get aholt of his boy and ship him to California or some ugly place like that, outa my grasp. He's got his own way of putting some heat on me, and it just riles me up some. Now, he ain't the only one rubbin' me sore. Crayfish Ruble's rannies are getting ready to bust in here and hang King Bragg before the execution. They've got word that Admiral Bragg's putting some heat on me to spring his boy, and they've warned me to quit looking; it's over and the boy's gonna get his neck in the noose. And the word is, if I don't quit lookin', they're gonna bust in here and have their own necktie party."

"Both sides?" DeGraff said.

"Both sides. Maybe twenty, thirty men on each ranch."

"And we're forted up." Burtell said. He was sort of smilin', knowing how bad it really was.

"It ain't easy for them to bust in," I said. "This here place is made from quarried sandstone. It's got a slate roof. There's big wooden shutters for the windows, and they got a few firing ports in them. We got a few scatterguns in here, just in case they bust the door in and try to rush us. I'd hate to try to break through four ten-gauge loaded with double-aught buckshot."

"Chimney," Rusty said.

"That's a bad one. If we got a fire in the stove, they can plug the chimney and smoke us out. That means, no fires in our stove. We drink cold coffee from now on."

They didn't mind it much.

"They're likely to try to draw us out," I said. "Trouble out there somewhere. But

90

trouble, lawmen needed, so we rush outa here. I ain't got much of an answer to that. If there's trouble, one or more of us gotta go. I'm thinkin' maybe I'll stay out of here, and you three guard the prisoner. I'll do better roaming around."

Rusty grinned. "You're jailing us and keeping the best job for your lonesome self."

I ignored him. "Now we got another possibility. They might try to starve you out. A siege where they got the jail surrounded and hope we run outa food and water. DeGraff, it'll be your job to keep plenty of water in there, and keep them chamber pots and thunder mugs emptied, and keep some hardtack or crackers or jerky or something in there. Stock up and put it on the county bill."

DeGraff, he nodded. They had twenty years on me, and I felt some ridiculous, giving 'em orders like that. Still, the sheriff job got dumped on me during a set-to a year or so earlier, and the town was happy with me — so far. No telling how they'd feel if I drove off their best customers.

"There's more," I said. "If Admiral Bragg and his bunch rush this place, you let him know he's putting his boy's life on the line. I hate that, but if it's war, they can expect us to do what we gotta do. That won't work

91

with them Ruble boys, who'd just tell us to hand the boy over."

"Cotton, that's not good. Our job's to protect King Bragg any way we can," De-Graff said. "That's the law and that's justice."

"You sure are right," I said, seeing the merit in it. "I'll back off. We'll protect that boy as best we can, any way we can. Thanks, DeGraff."

The man barely nodded. He was as lean as a hungry crow, and had the look of a hawk in his skinny face.

"That do it?" I asked.

"I think we got it covered," Rusty said. "Ain't nobody gonna bust in here without paying a price."

"And I hope they know it," DeGraff said. "I'll see how we're fixed for powder."

"Good idea," I said. I was pretty sure we had plenty of cartridges and shotgun shells, but it never hurt to check it all out.

We worked out a schedule that would keep two deputies in there at all times. DeGraff headed out to the pump and jacked some water into a pail, and then filled up the spare. After that he would head for George Waller's store and get some food that would last and keep a man's belly at bay. I didn't want no hungry, thirsty, desperate men in here if the place was under fire.

Three or four men defending a jail against maybe twenty-five. I didn't like them odds, even if we had got ourselves into good shape. But the thing was, it probably wouldn't happen. Neither Crayfish Ruble or Admiral Bragg would be as dumb as that. Busting a jail and shooting at sworn peace officers would put them on the wrong side of the law for the rest of their days.

There was still a worry or two, when I got to chewing on it. In a few days a crew would start to put up the gallows in the courtyard square. What if them Bragg men tried to stop it? Tore everything out? Well, I'd deal with it. Maybe a town posse could make sure them timbers rose they way they should. I'd talk to the town merchants about it.

Still, the whole thing made me itchy. This was war, and a good way to win a war was to hit where no one expected to be hit. What had I missed? Where was my weak spot? I sure didn't know. I wish I had a few more aces in my deck, but I don't know how to be anyone else, and as far as I could see, I'd got us set up for trouble pretty well. There was a few odds and ends, though. I wanted to make sure that someone in town slipped away to get help from the next county if it came to that. I'd need to talk to some of them merchants, and work up a plan. Puma County was a long way from anywhere at all, at the ass-end of Wyoming, and it'd take three, four days to get a force together to break the siege. It wasn't no fun to think about. But my pa, he always said not to worry about what you don't know and can't fix. So that was that.

I made sure my boys was getting the place ready for whatever might come, and then I left the deputies and headed toward Saloon Row. I wasn't done lookin' into this business, not by any means.

The town looked quiet. There was a few ranchers and their women loading up at the mercantiles. The Wyoming flag barely flapped at the courthouse. The square in front of the courthouse was quiet. I wanted the gallows builders to put it in the middle of the square, well away from the streets. I'd asked Will Wiggins at the lumber yard about getting the gallows built, and he said he would bid on it.

"I'll see about a proper design, and get to sawing the timbers," he'd said. "I think some good solid pine eight-by-eights should do it. Regular two-by-fours and plank for the deck. I got some hinges here for the drop, which I'll throw in, since I get 'em back anyways. That deck's gotta be about eight feet up, so there's a good neck-cracker fall. Seems to me we don't want to be hard on the boy, and a good fall's important."

He had seemed uncommon eager. I guess it'd give him something to talk about at the potluck suppers over at the Rock of Gibraltar Chapel where he and his woman went at nine o'clock every Sunday morning. The services at that outfit lasted three hours, with a lot of hallelujahs, and I was awful glad I wasn't of that persuasion.

But after that Sunday, he'd backed off and said he didn't want the business, so I got Lem Clegg to do it. There was something else I didn't know nothing about, which was makin' a noose. A hanging rope is no lariat. It's entire different, and I was still looking around for someone who could make me one. I'd asked around some, but so far I hadn't come across anyone to make one for me. That was a noose for sure that Admiral Bragg's rannies dropped over me, but I sure wasn't going to get anyone from that outfit to make one for me.

I hitched my holster around. I hated carrying heavy metal all the time, but nowadays I had to. I drifted along Wyoming Street, and finally hit Saloon Row, where the smell of stale beer drifted out of every batwing door. It wasn't much different from the rest of town, mostly board-and-bat buildings thrown up fast, but it had a different smell.

I went into the Last Chance, looking for Upward. The place was dark and quiet, and I couldn't see him nowhere, but he wouldn't be far away. I finally discovered he was out back, liming the outhouse. The outhouses behind Saloon Row stank so bad they sometimes made the whole town stink. Upward and Mrs. Gladstone at the Sampling Room was the only ones that did anything about it, dumping a few loads of lime down the holes once in a while. Doubtful sure didn't smell like lilacs most of the time, especially on Sundays, after Saloon Row had seen a Saturday night.

He come in, carrying an empty dipper.

"Keeps it down a little," he said. "You want a shot?"

"No, just want to talk some."

"What have you got for me, eh?"

There it was again. To get anything out of Upward, you had to whisper something to him.

"I had a little meeting with Queen Bragg in the middle of the night," I said.

Upward's eyebrow arched.

"It didn't come to nothing."

Upward sighed. "That's because you don't

have what it takes, Sheriff. Now, if she met with me in the middle of the night, it'd be different."

"Okay, where are them two witnesses, the ones that testified that King Bragg plugged three T-Bar men?"

"Oh, you mean Plug Parsons and Carter Bell."

"Yeah, them two. They're the ones saw it happen. And you were there too."

"I heard they left the country, Cotton. Right after the trial. They drew wages from Crayfish. The word was, they were scared that Admiral Bragg would string them up, and I can't say as I blame them for pulling outa here. That's what I heard, but I don't know the truth of it."

"They say where they was heading?"

"Nope, and they didn't want no one to know. Crayfish told me they'd drawn wages."

"That leaves you as the sole witness, Sammy."

"Me, I didn't see nothing. I was in the storeroom."

I remembered at the trial, Upward had testified he'd served up some red-eye to King Bragg, and then gone to the storeroom to find a bung starter. The shooting had come in a burst when he was back there, and he was afraid to come out until things quieted, and then it was just a quick peek. King Bragg was standing there with an empty six-gun and there were three T-Bar men down, leaking blood and life.

"King, he says he didn't know anything, and first thing he knew, he was lying on the floor looking up at you and some others," I said.

Upward smiled. "He never was down."

"The jury thought so too."

"I heard all the shots, and a lot of breaking glass, and stayed low until it quieted. He was standing there holding an empty gun when I come out of the storeroom."

"Anything else happening?"

"Sure, half the bottles on the backbar, they were busted and my best booze was draining into the sawdust."

"How come bullets was coming into the bar? I thought King Bragg was at the bar when he shot them T-Bar men."

"How should I know? Bullets fly all over the place." Upward was getting annoyed. "All this because Queen batted her big eyes at you in the night?"

I got to feeling sort of dumb, and started to make excuses, and thought better of it.

"Think what you want," I said.

Upward, he was enjoying himself.

"Did King Bragg start to reload?" I asked. "Get out of here? A man with an empty gun, he's pretty quick to shuck the empties."

"I'm tired of the palaver, Cotton. You find something else to tell me, and I'll find something else to tell you."

I tipped my hat and left, with Sammy Upward staring at my back. The sunlight felt good. The two witnesses were gone, and Upward said he didn't see the shooting. King Bragg said he was knocked out and lying on the floor; but Upward said King was standing with an empty gun in his hand. Upward said a bunch of his bottles got busted; the court testimony was that King Bragg was shooting from the bar into the rest of the saloon. It sure was a puzzle.

NINE

Critter was nipping at me, and I didn't blame him. I'd been neglecting him. He hated being in Turk's livery barn, and usually took it out on me with his big buck teeth. If I had big teeth like his, I'd nip him back.

I tried to get over to see him every day, but sometimes I got waylaid. He kept track, and let me know when I was lettin' him down. If I really messed up, he kicked the hell out of me.

I found some oats and poured some into the manger, but he wasn't done with me. He backed around until he was shoving me into the side of the stall, just to let me know who came first.

"All right, we'll get out this afternoon," I said. "So cut it out."

He decided his oats were more interesting than me, and got to licking them out of the manger.

"That horse'll likely kill you some day," Admiral Bragg said.

He had ridden into the livery barn on his handsome blood bay, and Queen was beside him on a palomino. She was riding sidesaddle this time, though she was sitting astride the other night when she stopped me. I guess maybe she did what her daddy wanted when he was around, and what she wanted when he wasn't. But in town, she was always riding sidesaddle, very ladylike. I never quite knew why no woman was supposed to ride astride, but it had to do with their anatomy, and I never did figure it out. I thought maybe it was something preachers invented, but mostly it was a way of riding for rich women. It sure was nothing I was gonna worry about.

I thought she might favor me with a little smile, but all I got from her was a haughty stare. I should've known. Queen was just being Queen, and Cotton Pickens was nothing but a worm. Oh, well. My ma used to tell me, look twice at a woman because she'll change in a flash. I hardly have had a chance to test that one out, but I sure been meanin' to.

I greeted the pair and helped her down, as he dropped off the bay. Her hand was colder than a glacier. Lazarus, the hostler, took them horses off, and began brushing them down.

"I'm glad I found you here, Sheriff. We're going to visit my boy."

Admiral Bragg wasn't asking, but I don't suppose he had to.

"All right. I don't keep family from him."

We stepped onto Wyoming Street, and first thing I noticed was a mess of horses, most of them with the Anchor brand on their left hip, tied to the hitch rail in front of Mrs. Gladstone's. That was the name of the saloon, a few doors up from the Last Chance. Mrs. Gladstone's Sampling Room was where the Anchor cowboys collected. I knew a few of them nags. Jesse Tilton was in town, and so was Wiley Wool. Both of them were handy all-around cowboys, tough as they come. Wool was quick with fists, and knew some Oriental moves that meant he could usually flatten someone he was brawling with. And there were other Anchor rannies over there, most of them plenty familiar with sidearms. Sure as could be, there was Big Nose George's dun horse, and Spitting Sam's and Smiley Thistlethwaite's plugs right next door. Most of the Anchor Ranch outfit had pulled into Doubtful, and I knew they was all wetting their parched throats in there.

This was starting to get interesting.

"All right," I said to Admiral and Queen, "come along."

We hiked to the courthouse square and the county sheriff office and jailhouse, and I knocked.

"Who?" yelled Rusty.

"Me, with Mr. Bragg and Miss Bragg, come to visit."

"Is that all right?" he asked.

That meant, was everything okay?

"Yeah, open up."

The door swung, and Rusty was in there with a drawn six-gun. He let us in and then locked the door behind him.

"Rusty, put on the log that the Braggs are here," I said.

Then I remembered he couldn't write none. "Never mind, I'll do it," I said. I can spell pretty good, and didn't have no trouble with Queen. It was Q-W-E-E-N.

Rusty, he's lookin' at me and then at Admiral, who was all swelled up in a gray swallowtail coat that seemed to bulge here and there. I nodded to Rusty.

"Looks like we got to do a little checking here," I said. "I mean, we got to frisk you, sir."

He was annoyed. "No, you don't."

"Well, I can't let you in there to palaver

with King unless we do. And come to think of it, I can't let Miss Bragg in there. She ain't friskable."

That got me two icy stares.

"Take me to the boy, and be quick about it," Bragg said.

I sighed. There was no way I could back down. Not against a man like that, who probably had a few derringers, toad-stabbers, stilettos, and loose cannons under that lumpy coat. Plus a couple of jail keys, a hacksaw, a file, and lock-pickin' stuff. And there was no tellin' what Queen Bragg had under there, and I got red in the cheeks just thinkin' about all them hiding places. But there wasn't any way outa this except a frisking.

"You can take off that gray coat, and slide out of the boots, and Rusty here will give them pants a quick pat."

I could feel the fires blazing in that rancher, and I thought he was about ready to explode like one of them steam boilers. Either that or he'd pull out one of them hidden cannons and start givin' us what-for. But I guess he remembered he had a daughter beside him, so he curbed the volcano building up in him.

"Bring the boy here," he said.

"No, he stays locked safe and tight."

"Tell the boy he will live a lot longer than you."

"I might tell him you said it."

"Tell the boy if they harm a hair on his head, there's going to be not one stone standing of this jail and the courthouse; that Doubtful will disappear; that Puma County, Wyoming, will vanish from memory. And every official with it."

"I guess that's a threat. Sure sounds like a dilly. We'll write it up."

"If you can write," he said.

That made me mad. I did five grades and part of the next.

I turned to Queen. "You want to add anything, miss?"

She closed her eyes, and for a moment I could see pain radiating from her face. Then she stared at me.

"That goes double for me."

Rusty, his hand was never far from his six-gun. He saw them lumps under the gray swallowtail. I got to thinkin' something else. Who might be collecting outside?

"All right, since you ain't cooperating, you'll have to get out now."

"I think we'll stay," Admiral said.

This wasn't playing out the way I'd hoped it would. Twenty of them gunslicks over at Mrs. Gladstone's, and the boss and his daughter in with me. I saw Rusty chewing on this too, and nodded to him to open them doors. If they wouldn't get out clean, they'd get tossed out on their ass.

I didn't waste time. The sawed off ten-gauge was right there, so I simply stepped over and jacked a cartridge in and swung it toward the gent, who was too busy glarin' at me to draw his own artillery.

"You wouldn't," he said.

"Obstructing justice," I said.

Rusty peered out, and then swung the door open.

"You got two choices. Leave now, or let yourself get frisked before you get taken to the boy. If you're carrying guns or tools or keys, I'll toss you in there with him."

I thought that feller was going to explode, but he didn't. He steered Queen out, and Rusty and me stood at the door a moment, watching the Braggs vamoose. They crossed the square and vanished somewhere.

"It ain't over," Rusty said.

"You mind watching the place? I'm going out there."

"You're crazy. They're fixing to bust King out."

"I think they were. But not now. Admiral thought he'd slip something to his boy. I'm going to wander into the Sampling Room."

Rusty stared. "You're crazy, Cotton. We're in the middle of a jailbreak. What if they grab you and hold you hostage? Trade you for King Bragg?"

"Don't do it. No trades. That's an order. No matter what they threaten, just don't."

Dusty sighed. "Good way to get yourself kilt."

"Where's DeGraff?"

"He's coming in at six."

"All right, you've got the afternoon to kill. Talk to King. Maybe you'll find out some things."

"He'll just tell me he's pure as the driven snow," Rusty said.

"He might be at that, Rusty."

The deputy started wheezing. He thought that was pretty rich.

"Truth to tell, Rusty, I'm kinda itchy about this. I wish the trial had got into things a little better. Maybe the Bragg boy's being hustled to a grave he don't belong in."

"He belonged in one by the time he was eleven," Rusty said.

Rusty let me out. Doubtful was pretty quiet. It sure was a nice May day. There was a knot of horses down at the end of Wyoming Street, and most would be Anchor branded. I started with a sweep around the courthouse square, thinking it would make sense to look for surprises. I poked down alleys, looked into mercantile windows, and checked brands of horses. But I sure didn't spot nothing amiss. I stopped in the courthouse, waved at yawning clerks, and peered into empty rooms, and then hiked out the main drag, Wyoming, toward Saloon Row. But I didn't go into the Sampling Room. Not yet. I wanted to see what else was going on there. Like maybe a bunch of horses at the hitch rail in front of the Last Chance. There was only two or three nags there; not much happening in Upward's watering hole. He was probably sitting on a stool there polishing the bar, which is what he did when there wasn't anything else to occupy him. I liked Upward. One of these days he'd pour me a free drink. It hadn't happened in three years, but it would. If Upward liked you, you could drink cheap.

Mrs. Gladstone's Sampling Room was long and narrow, with double doors in front and a skinny bar down the right side. There was a row of tables along the other wall, and a sort of poker parlor at the rear, with a door going out to the two-hole piss palace. Only her customers never got that far. They mostly leaked into the alley, which didn't improve the way things smelled around

Doubtful.

I pulled open the door and stepped in. It sure was dark. Mrs. Gladstone, she hadn't lit any lamps yet because the sun was still shining, and enough light got through the window in front to let her pour. She was behind the bar, not doing much of anything, wearing her usual white smock and one of them white thingamabobs on her hair to keep it from flying in all directions. But pretty near the whole payroll of Anchor Ranch was in there, all right. I didn't see Admiral Bragg, or Queen, but the rest was lined up in a long solemn row down the bar, one foot to the rail, and a few was sitting at the tables. Her dealer, Cronk, sat at the rear, presiding over an empty green table with a single lamp burning to supply light to players. But he sure didn't have no customers.

The place was uncommon quiet. Most of them slicks didn't even have a bottle of Valley Tan in front of them. They was just standing there: Alvin Ream, Big Nose George, Spitting Sam. They was carrying sidearms, all right. There was a lot of metal hanging off of one or both thighs. Well, there was no law against it in Doubtful.

They looked me over, and I looked them over, and one thing was clear. The whole bunch of them was waiting for something.

TEN

Well, they sure weren't missing anything about me. All them dudes was studying me like I was an anarchist or something. Their gazes was drifting toward my handgun, studying my boots for hideouts, checking the back of my neck for knives in easy reach.

Well, screw 'em. I spotted an opening between Big Nose George and Spitting Sam, and bellied up.

"Good afternoon, gents," I said.

Mrs. Gladstone, she sort of sidled toward me, like maybe she wanted to steer clear of any lead flying in my direction.

"Red-eye, ma'am," I said.

"Nice to see you, Sheriff. You hardly ever drop in."

"Orderly place, ma'am. Sampling Room's always quiet. Anchor Ranch folks are all model citizens."

I was layin' it on pretty thick, but no one smiled any. She brought the brown bottle and settled it in front of me, along with a tumbler and a pitcher of cold water. I thanked her.

"Looks like you got a full house this afternoon," I said.

"My best customers," she said.

But they weren't buying much this afternoon. It looked like sarsaparilla in most of them beakers.

I poured myself a generous shot, and added a splash.

"Here's to the Anchor," I said.

That got me more silence.

"You fellers don't want to salute the Anchor Ranch? What happened? You all draw wages?"

I couldn't get a rise out of any of them.

"George, how come you ain't toasting the Anchor? You got shut of the place?"

Big Nose George eyed me a moment. "Sheriff, Admiral Bragg, he's just the finest gent this side of St. Louis, and we'd all be glad to toast our excellent employer. But we're all going out on a picnic any time, and we'll toast Mr. Bragg and his beautiful daughter Queen when the time comes."

"George, that's a noble idea," I said.

Spitting Sam nodded solemnly. "We all love and respect Miss Queen, so it's gonna be sort of a Sunday School affair, soon as we get word from Mr. Bragg."

"Yeah, dat's it," said Smiley Thistle-thwaite.

"Well, here's to Queen," I said, and sucked on the red-eye a bit.

"She's a beautiful lady, Sheriff," said a gent down the bar. He was one of them in the hanging party, so I gave him a cold stare.

After that, things dipped into silence again, but all them fellers was watching me, watching me sip a little, and maybe calculating how much the hooch might slow me down if it came to that. The hooch wouldn't slow me down because I had no intent to pull the iron out of my holster.

This here was the strangest business I ever seen in a saloon. It was like a bunch of saints dropped in. They was all behavin' themselves mighty fine, for some reason or other. It reminded me of one of them billboards put up by the Temperance women that said, "Lips that touch liquor will never touch mine." I always figured them women deserved it. But here was a whole saloon full of gents with their bark on, sippin' sarsaparilla. Who was I to complain? Not a one of them was breaking any law, far as I could see. Mrs. Gladstone, she just nodded cheerfully and winked at me. I thought about arresting the whole lot and charging them with good behavior, which would have got them fined ten dollars and jailed overnight. No one in Doubtful wants cowboys around that are all behaving themselves. There ain't a nickel in it.

I polished off my red-eye, left two bits on the counter, and thought to quit the place.

But first I turned to Big Nose George. "You be kind to grandmothers and dogs now," I said.

"I kiss grannies and kick dogs," he said.

"I kick grannies and kiss dogs," Spitting Sam said, trying to raise an argument.

But it didn't fly. Them fellers standing along the bar, they just smiled and nodded.

There was no point hanging around the Sampling Room, so I pushed through the batwing doors onto the peaceful street, and wondered why it felt like the quiet before the storm. I howdied my way toward the courthouse square, and then I spotted that blood bay and palomino and another saddled nag in front of the Stockman Hotel. It wasn't much of a hotel, four rooms and a dining room, but Doubtful didn't need much of a hotel. It was mostly empty anyway, except for an occasional whiskey drummer peddling his sauce.

I'm always looking for ways to get into trouble. So naturally, I was wondering who belonged to that horse tied there beside the blood bay.

So I steered my aching feet — I'm enough of a cowboy so I hate to walk more than ten yards — over to the hotel. Riding boots, like most cowboys wear, are an invention from hell, and Western bootmakers ought to be hanged from the nearest hayloft. Sure enough, in the saloon and dining parlor on the left, there was Admiral and Queen, and with them was Judge Axel Nippers, the selfsame judge as sentenced the boy to be hanged. They was all chomping on filets of beef and mashed spuds. Last I knew, Judge Nippers didn't own a saddle horse, which made me all the more curious about this business.

I decided then and there to have me some lunch. "Howdy," I said.

Admiral, he nodded curtly, and Queen peered down her long nose at me, and the judge was too busy wolfing down beef to bother. No one was inviting me to the table, at any rate, so I continued on to another one within hearing distance.

Mrs. Garvey was all a-twitter. "Why, Sheriff, we've not seen you in here but twice."

I couldn't recollect when, but she knew more arithmetic than I did.

"I'll have what they're having," I said.

"Oh, you'll enjoy it. Sauteed filets in burgundy sauce, with pickled beets."

I smiled, since I was getting in over my head. I like chicken-fried steak, maybe once a year, and deviled eggs now and then.

Well, whatever the palaver was at the other table, it quit real sudden, and that threesome was busy patting lips with real cloth napkins, and hurrying through the chow. I was sort of hoping to pick up a notion or two of what was happening around Doubtful, but I saw it'd be a lost cause. That bunch wouldn't even talk about the weather.

I tackled them sauteed filets and pickled beets, and when she laid the bill on me, I pretty near fainted. It was about a week's salary. And all I got for it was a mess of silence at the next table. Them three lapped up their chow and retreated, so I was all alone in there, dining like I could afford the ticket. I took a gander out the window, in time to see the judge walk back to the courthouse and the Braggs ride off, leading the spare and riderless horse.

It sure was funny. There was the Braggs, the judge, a spare horse, and down the street was every gun-toting hand the Anchor Ranch could come up with. But nothing happened. Or maybe something woulda

115

happened if I hadn't been barging around town, lookin' after the peace. I thought I'd never know.

I couldn't make heads or tails of it. But the whole business was probably intended to bust King out of my hospitality and send him off to California or some awful place like that. Maybe they was gonna snatch the judge and then try to exchange him for King. Maybe this was some sort of jailbreak that I couldn't figure out. Maybe not. Maybe them Anchor Ranch rannies was going on a picnic, just like they said. Someday, I'd get the rest of the story. Something like this didn't just vanish into air. Someone would be babbling, and my guess was Queen.

I scraped the last coin out of my purse and laid it on the lady, and got out of there. It sure was a nice spring day. I didn't see no riot at the jailhouse, or hear shots being fired, so I walked over there, knocked, and this time DeGraff let me in and locked the door behind me.

"Anything perky around here?"

"No," he said. "I'm on catnap duty."

"There's something out there. A lot of Anchor men in town, at the Sampling Room. Admiral Bragg and his girl are floating around."

"So I heard."

"I can't get a handle on it."

"Maybe it's nothing."

We laughed.

I pulled a key off the wall and headed back into the cell block. There was four cells, two on a side, separated by an aisle. King was in the one farthest back and on the left. It was gloomy in there, with only a barred window high up tossing light anywhere.

King was pacing round and round his ten-foot exercise yard. There were thick iron bars between him and me.

"You all right?"

He stopped suddenly. "That's not a question that needs answering."

He had a disheveled look about him. First time I'd seen that. Somehow, he always kept himself neat.

"Your pa and sister came in."

"I heard about it from your deputy."

"I couldn't let them back here without them being searched."

"My father usually has a dozen plans all going at once."

"I think he wanted to bust you out. There's a lot going on around here I'm not smart enough to figure out."

King smiled harshly. "I'm not either."

"He was carrying. Maybe she was too. She

had more metal in her underwear than a tool and die maker."

"Don't talk about my sister like that."

"I figure he was going to slide you a derringer or two, and she had a collection of rat-tailed files and blank keys for you to work on."

"I wouldn't have taken them. I'm not interested in a breakout."

I wanted to laugh, but didn't. He was serious. His gaze fixed me intensely.

"You don't know me," he said. "I want one of two things. To be proven innocent and cut loose, or to die. I don't want to be called an outlaw or a fugitive or a criminal on the run. I'm a proud person, Sheriff. I won't go for half a life. I won't go for a life on the lam. If he'd laid all that stuff on me, I'd have turned it over to you the moment they left here."

He stared at me in a way that almost knocked me backward a step or two.

The thing is, darned if I didn't believe him.

"Tell me again what you know," I said.

"About that afternoon? I walked into the Last Chance for a drink. Yes, I was looking for trouble. I like trouble. I had a few drinks. Upward poured some red-eye, and I sipped, and heard some laughter behind me. That's all I remember."

"And?"

"I was on the floor looking up at several men. There was gunsmoke in the air. My six-gun, a Peacemaker, was in their hands, and every chamber was empty. If I did it, I did it. If I didn't, I didn't. I have nothing more to tell you."

"Upward says he didn't see it. He says he was in the storeroom getting a bung starter when he heard the shots. And he says the two witnesses, both T-Bar men, have drawn wages and vanished."

"Then there is no witness you can call a liar," King said.

"Was there anyone else in there?"

"A few T-Bar men."

"That's more than the court was told about. Do you know who?"

"I had my back to them, remember? I was buying some booze."

"King, if you was to tell me what to look into, who to talk to, what would you tell me?"

"Crayfish Ruble was having some rustling trouble. Some mavericking too. He was itchy and wanting to stop it."

"How do you know that?"

"Drovers talk, Sheriff."

"What should I ask Crayfish?"

"Ask him about the rustling."

King glared at me, wheeled away from the bars, and settled on his iron bunk. It was plain I wasn't going to get another word from him. I wanted to.

I didn't much care for him, but somehow, I was coming to respect the boy. I knew I shouldn't, but my pa was always telling me I've got no common sense.

ELEVEN

I hurried over to the courthouse, and found Judge Nippers in his office.

He turned toward me, scowling. "It's about time you showed up."

"What was that all about?" I asked.

"Admiral Bragg had some plans for my future," the judge said. He frowned until his weathered face looked like a creased prune. "But you changed his plans." He glared at me. "Sit! Why are you standing there like an idiot? What are you, my butler?"

I eased down into one of them oaken swivel chairs, and pushed my holster around some so it wouldn't jab at my leg. I never much fancied carrying six-guns all over. Them things are so heavy I'll probably end up with one hip lower than the other.

"A social visit, he said. Lunch at the hotel. When I saw that extra nag tied next to theirs, I knew what's what, and made sure I had my old pepperbox handy. You ever see one?" He pulled a pepperbox pistol out of his bosom. The thing had five barrels. By yanking on the trigger, one could move a loaded barrel under the hammer and discharge it. "Sprays a lot of lead, sometimes in my face," he said. "Damn thing. But it's a croaker, all right."

He put it away, for which I was grateful because them pepperboxes are famous for going off unexpected.

Nippers adjusted his gold-rimmed spectacles and eyed me like I was some sort of dead fish.

"Admiral Bragg had nefarious designs, Sheriff. He wanted me to vacate the sentence, call off the necktie party, and when I told him the hell with that, he suggested maybe he'd carry me off and then trade me for the boy. Hold me hostage, in case that doesn't quite sink into your noggin."

I never heard that word nefarious before, but I sort of figured it out. "How was he gonna do that, Your Honor?"

"The virgin Queen had some artillery aimed at my crotch beneath the white linen tablecloth, he told me, and we'd casually finish our delicious repast, and then the Braggs would cheerfully escort me to the third nag out there, and we would cheerfully ride away." He studied me to see if I was getting all this, and decided I was. "Only, you came in, which shifted the game a little. It no longer seemed like a good idea to shoot my balls off."

"What were all his men doing in town?"

"Oh, who knows? Maybe just keeping Ruble's crowd at bay. Ruble's gang wants to bust into your lockup and hang the boy just as badly as Bragg's gang want to bust him out. But I think that what happened today wasn't what Admiral Bragg had in mind. His first purpose was to spring the boy — arm him and help him get out. But you kept messing him up, Pickens, putting yourself between him and his plans. Now isn't that a thigh-slapper?"

I never could quite figure Nippers out, but I sort of wished Bragg had taken him hostage, just as an educational experience. Nippers had a lot more smarts than I ever would, but sometimes smarts ain't the equal of a six-gun.

"I ain't got much thigh-slappin' in me, Your Honor."

He cackled. I'd enjoyed that cackle. Nippers had cackled clear through the trial, mostly at King Bragg's claim that he didn't remember anything.

"What you gonna do now?" he asked.

"Arrest the pair of them. They were obstructing justice."

"Good luck. And who do you want to replace you?"

"King Bragg," I said, and wondered why I said it.

"Make sure he's hanged first. And if you value your privates, don't let Queen point a gun your way."

"She already has, Your Honor. And she didn't pull the trigger."

By the time I got outside and was walking the courthouse square, I could see all them Bragg cowboys were gone. There was hardly a horse hitched on Wyoming Street. I debated whether to ride out to Anchor Ranch right off and drag the pair of them into town. That didn't seem too bright an idea, but you never know. Hitting 'em when they least expect it is a good idea itself. But I let it pass. I'd toss them behind bars soon enough. I'd put the whole Bragg outfit behind bars if I had to.

I didn't know what to do. This sheriff business was mostly annoying me, and I wondered how come I wore the star. My ma, she always said, put your thinking cap on. I've seen a dunce cap, but never a thinking cap, and I wouldn't know one if I saw it. In my case, it wouldn't do me a lick of good anyway. Heating my brain would cook it but not cure it.

It was getting along to drinkin' time, so I strolled toward Saloon Row again, just to see what pot was boiling over. There was a few T-Bar men sipping suds in the Last Chance, but things were quiet enough for a weeknight.

"Want something, Sheriff?" Upward asked.

"Sarsaparilla," I replied.

He rolled his eyes like he was a long-suffering saint, and uncorked one for me. I laid a wooden nickel on the bar, which he snatched up.

"Lot of Anchor men over to the Sampling Room this afternoon," I said.

"That's a nutless bunch," Upward replied.

"I wouldn't want them busting down the door to my jail."

"That's what they were up to?"

"Could be," I said.

"You know what, pal? You worry too much. Why don't you just take a siesta and let it all work out? You've got good deputies. The jail's well guarded. The gallows go up in a few days, the kid gets a necktie, and it's all over. So quit worrying."

"Maybe it's the wrong necktie," I said.

"I give up on you. Don't come in here no

more. I don't want to hear all your worrying."

Upward, he was polishing the bar something fierce, so I knew he meant it.

"I'm not quitting," I said.

Upward stopped polishing and stared at me. "All right. I tried to tell you. You've been warned. Now I'm warning you again. A certain person told me to tell you to lay off. You did your duty, and that ended when the kid was sentenced. Now leave it lay. If you don't, well, you'd be pretty dumb."

"Who says?"

Upward, he just shook his head, and I wasn't gonna get more out of him.

"Who?" I snapped.

He just shook his head.

"Who?"

He didn't say nothing.

"I thought so," I said.

It had to be Crayfish Ruble.

Upward looked like he was about to reach for his sawed-off scattergun, but I just smiled, and he got aholt of himself.

"You tell Crayfish I'll keep on looking into this, and if he messes with me, he'll be in the next cell from the kid."

I was feeling blue, and got out into the fresh air before I did something I might regret. Upward was a friend, and now I was running out of friends. My pa, he didn't have any ideas about how to be a lawman, but my ma would have told me stick to what I know. And now Upward was in there polishing that bar and I didn't want to know what he was thinking.

The town was as quiet as a Quaker prayer meeting, so I took time to say hello to Critter. He sure was getting ornery, boxed all day in a stall, but I didn't have much choice. When I needed him, I needed him, and usually fast. He was lounging in the Turk livery barn down on Medicine Bow Street, so I hiked in there, enjoying the good smell of sunlight and horse apples. I wandered down the aisle, and there was Critter all right. He snarled at me and he plainly was fixing to commit murder if I stepped in there. A month in a stall for him was like life in the pen for other criminals.

But then I saw something that pretty near stopped me cold. Hangin' over that stall was a noose. It hung down from a rafter, and swayed softly, the noose a little over Critter's head. It was a well-done noose, neat and clean and the rope was fresh hemp, straight out of the hardware store. Critter, he snapped and snarled, but I didn't pay no attention. That noose got my attention real good. It was not just tacked on there on the rafter either, but wrapped around and tied down, like it was getting set to be used.

That made me madder than a stack of hornets, so I climbed the gate, pushed Critter back, and tried to untie the knots. But it was up there solid, and wasn't just stuck there, and I finally had to pull out my jackknife and whittle through that hemp until I could pull it away. It sure was a professional job, and it sure was there to say something to me, though I didn't quite know what. I didn't know anyone around the county could tie a noose like that. It was a real hangman's noose, so orderly and tight it sent a chill right through me.

Critter bit my arm, which got my attention.

"Cut it out!" I yelled. I was ready to bite him back.

I set the noose aside and curried him, but he was being ornery and kept crowding me into a wall, so I snarled at him and quit the currying. He thanked me by pulling my hat off, but I snatched it away. He was so barnsour I felt bad.

"We'll go out tomorrow," I said. "I got stuff to do."

He sawed his head up and down and would have taken a piece of my shoulder out, but I dodged, and slammed the gate shut. This sure wasn't my day to make friends.

I hid the noose in the stall a moment, and got aholt of the liveryman.

"Turk, you seen anyone around here with a rope?"

"Everyone's got a rope," he said. He sort of slurred his words because he didn't have many teeth, and all the gaps between them whistled.

"I mean, a big thick hemp rope, not some lariat."

"Hemp? You mean like the stuff in the Emporium?"

I nodded.

"If I did, I wouldn't tell you," he said.

He was a toothless grinning sonofabitch, and I wanted to shove a fist into his gums, but I didn't.

"Who's been hanging around here since yesterday?" I asked.

"Oh, the usual. Half of them too broke to pay their bills."

"Who's come by to pay you?" I asked, figuring that someone who could buy some hemp rope would have enough to pay the livery stable.

Turk just shrugged and smiled, licking his gums. "I don't keep any books," he said.

"How do you know when people owe you?"

"All in my head and on my fingers," he said.

"Does Admiral Bragg keep horses here?"

"Not regular."

"How about Crayfish Ruble?"

"Oh, he sometimes buys a week or two."

"Has he been around?"

"Not since the three killings and the trial."

"Who else?"

"None of your damn business."

Turk wheeled away, heading for the pen outside, and I let him go. I collected the noose and headed for Mrs. Gladstone's Sampling Room.

I found her in there, sweeping sawdust. The Sampling Room was a fancy joint compared to the Last Chance.

She looked up and I handed her the noose. She took it gingerly, staring at me.

"Give it to Admiral Bragg, and tell him I'm tired of nooses," I said. "Next noose I get, I'll make sure it fits his neck."

"Oh, Mr. Sheriff . . ."

"If we're going to have nooses around here, I'll make sure they fit any neck that deserves it," I said.

She peered at me with real fear in her eyes.

"Tell him that, or maybe I'll make one for

you too," I said.

She clapped a hand to her mouth.

I was plumb tired of nooses.

"Yes, sir," she whispered, plainly scairt.

I didn't care. Doubtful was up to its crotch in nooses.

I left her holding that limp rope, knowing word would soon reach the Anchor Ranch and into the ears of Admiral. I hiked back to the sheriff office and jailhouse, and sure enough, someone had tied a little noose, just a little feller made from cord, onto the door handle. It was hardly six inches long, something someone could stuff in his pocket and not be seen with, but there it was, tied tight around the handle, and dangling there.

I knocked. "It's me," I said.

"You all right?" Burtell asked.

"Good as gold," I said.

He opened. I pointed. That little noose was dangling from the latch.

He stared.

"Guess we ain't popular," he said.

At first I thought to cut it loose, but then I decided just to let her hang. That noose sent a message in all directions.

TWELVE

Next thing I knew, there was Judge Nippers steaming over from the Puma County Courthouse with something clutched in his gnarled fingers. I sure knew what it was.

"This, this insult to my divine spark, was hanging from my doorknob," he said, shaking the little cord noose that was a brother of the one hanging on our door.

"Guess someone's of a mind to string you up," I said. "You got any objections?"

I got to give credit to the old boy. He grinned at me like a snapping turtle. "Now and then," he said.

"You see anyone in the courthouse?" I asked.

"That mausoleum, you could fire grapeshot down the halls and never hit a live mortal during business hours," he said. "No, I don't have the slightest idea, and no one else over there does either. I asked the same question."

132

"There's been a few nooses put here and there," I said. "One real one hanging in my horse stall at the livery barn. Another hanging from the doorknob at my office."

"Hardly know which side's having all the fun," Nippers said. "But I'm ordering the gallows built for half a dozen. If they want hangings, they'll get more than they bargained for." There was something real bright in that old prune of a face. "You got any notions?"

"Admiral Bragg's crew was in town, but they're gone. There ain't a T-Bar man in sight."

"Tell me about your nooses," the judge said.

"One was hanging from a rafter above my horse. A real one, thick hemp, put there by someone that could climb up there and tie it down. These here little ones, anyone could slide them onto a knob."

"Which side, do you figure?"

"Admiral Bragg's outfit already threatened me if I hang the kid. They're just making sure I get the message."

"What about Crayfish Ruble?"

"Well, what about him? It's not his boy gonna stretch rope. He told me the other day, all he cares about is getting it done.

133

Justice. His men were kilt so he wants justice."

"Any threats from Ruble?"

"Not toward me or you. It's the Anchor Ranch they're thinking about. If Admiral Bragg's bunch bust the boy out, there'll be a war around here. But as long as the hanging goes forward, they're not getting their drawers in a knot."

"Get me some proof," he said. "By gawd, I'll string up the whole lot."

He sure was enjoying himself. He twirled his noose around like it was a trophy, and then stuffed it into the pants of his ancient suit, probably the only one he owned. Nippers patted the bulk bulging from his breast pocket.

"You think a pepperbox can't hit what it's aimed at?" he asked.

Actually, that was pretty much true to what I knew about them. I nodded.

"Well, I'll show you a thing or two!"

He whipped that miserable firearm out of some pocket down inside his bosom, and began eyeing targets.

"No!" I yelled.

But he just ignored me, and finally settled on some dodgers that had been pinned to the rear wall because I thought them fellers looked familiar to me.

"Judge, put that thing down!"

But he was squinting along the top of that handheld Gatling.

Bam! A slug cut through an eyeball of Lorenzo Baca. Bam! The lips of Rattlesnake Billy vanished. Wham! The forehead of Art Hammer was perforated.

Judge Nippers blew smoke away and smiled. "It's all in the practice," he said. "I'll leave two chambers loaded to give me fangs." And with that, he plunged outside.

"Don't know as I've seen the like," Burtell said. "Them things put lead everywhere but straight ahead."

Judge Nippers sure was an entertainment all by himself. The smell of gun smoke lingered in the office. I went and looked at them dodgers. Nippers hadn't missed a shot. He'd nailed Baca, sure enough. It occurred to me that Baca looked a lot like Rocco, one of them three that King Bragg had sent to heaven, or wherever. I thought maybe I'd write the sheriff down in Refugio County, New Mexico, and see if Baca ever used another name.

I'd had about enough of Admiral Bragg's meddling, and thought maybe to take a couple of deputies out there to Anchor Ranch and haul his skinny butt into town. The best place for the boss of the Anchor

Ranch was in the cell next to his boy. I wouldn't have no trouble rigging up a few charges to hold him on.

I headed into the cell block to make sure King Bragg was all right. He was lying on his bunk.

"I heard some shots," the boy said.

"Judge Nippers making a believer of me," I said.

"I wish he'd saved one for me. Get it over with."

"How come you went to the Last Chance that day?" I asked.

"Make some trouble."

"How'd you know there'd be any T-Bar men in there?"

"They told me."

"Who told you?"

He stared at the wall. "I don't know. I had too much to drink."

"Someone told you?"

"Yeah, someone said there was some T-Bar hands looking for a fight, and if I dodged it, they'd know what to think of me."

"A fistfight?"

He stared at me. "What does it matter? I walked into it."

"You went alone, looking for a brawl with that bunch?"

"I guess so."

"Something don't add up, King."

"You ever been called a coward, Sheriff?"

"Mostly, they call me lazy. My ma, she used to scold me —"

"Not what I asked."

He irritated me. "Yeah, a few times. Made me mad."

"I'm not one. I'm not afraid of dying," he said. "If you were in my shoes, would you be?"

"I'm not in your shoes," I said.

Then he turned his back to me. He was just counting the minutes and hours left to him. Or trying not to.

I kept wanting to palaver with him, but he clammed up, so nothing came of it. I hiked out of the jail and locked the door, and thought I'd patrol the town. Burtell would be on until supper, and then DeGraff would come in for the night.

"I'm going out," I said.

"Better than sitting around," he replied.

I opened the door and discovered a regular parade out there, a mess of horsemen all heading my way. And Crayfish himself was leading the pack, on a ewe-necked gray horse that should have been sold for wolf bait.

Them fellers was armed to the teeth. Most had a pair of six-guns strapped to their waists, and most of the others had rifles or shotguns sheathed or in hand. A few had regular bandoliers loaded with shiny brass hanging over a shoulder. This here was a regular army. Worse, they spread out in a way that looked like they was priming for action.

"Crayfish, if there's trouble, you'll be answering first," I said.

He knew what I meant. "That word, answering, is an interesting allusion," he said. "Actually, well done and interesting syntax. My congratulations."

I just about had a fit, but all I could do was snarl some.

Crayfish smiled easily. "We've appointed ourselves your posse," he said. "We are going to keep the peace in Doubtful until the hanging is over."

"What are you mouthing about?"

"A posse, we're a posse, Sheriff. We're an armed body of men acting in an official capacity on behalf of the legally constituted law officers of Puma County, Wyoming."

"You ain't nothing until I swear you," I said, "and right now you're not keeping any peace around here."

"Ah, Sheriff, you don't quite comprehend. Our town is under siege. Anchor Ranch, in all its power and glory, threatens to perform a lawless act. Namely, breaking the young multiple murderer spawned by its owner out of your lockup and spiriting him away from the majestic reach of the law."

"He ain't getting out, and I can take care of it myself," I said. "We don't need a posse."

Crayfish smiled. "Well, you've got one. I've leased the upstairs of Rosie's Parlor for the duration, and that will be the T-Bar headquarters until justice is done."

"Sounds more like the T-Bar's hindquarters, Crayfish."

"That too. My main worry is that my staff will be too weary to perform its duties adequately. We will need alert and ready men to patrol the streets, guard the courthouse and especially rim your jail with stouthearted stalwarts. A week or two upstairs at Rosie's might gravely weaken my force, but that is a risk to be endured."

"Some risk," I said.

"At any rate, Sheriff, the T-Bar posse will be patrolling Doubtful day and night. We will ensure good order at the Sampling Room and other watering holes. We will ensure that no illicit armies of the night sweep into your understaffed jail and attempt to spirit away the prisoner. We will, of course, frisk all visitors to the jail, making sure that lawyers and such don't smuggle instruments of violence within. And of course we plan to accompany you on your daily rounds. Henceforth, wherever you go, two of my best men will be serving as your deputies, lockstep with you. Two other trusted men will protect Judge Nippers and the courthouse. Nothing will escape their attention."

"Thanks, Crayfish, but I'll just handle it all myself. I don't need your posse."

He smiled. "Well, your thoughts are noble, and your skills are unquestioned, and your bravery is legendary, but we're here, and we're staying, and we're protecting Doubtful until justice is served, and you'll find me at Rosie's henceforth."

"How about you just get out of town and leave the peacekeeping to those that got a badge?"

He simply smiled. "See you around, fella," he said.

Well, that was the damnedest thing I ever did see.

He waved his hand, and all them horsemen wheeled around. A pair of them dismounted and posted themselves in front of the jail, two more headed for the courthouse, while the rest hightailed for the livery barn and Rosie's. I thought the ones ordered to guard my office and jailhouse drew straws and lost. The rest of that bunch was gonna get acquainted with Rosie's ladies. That was going to be a hell-raising time, but it was legal and there wasn't anything I should do about it except maybe try not to be envious.

Well, there they were, two ranch hands smiling at me like they was being friends. Only thing was, I sure didn't know what direction that pair of bores would be pointing toward.

"You ain't coming in," I said, and knocked.

Burtell opened a crack, and I slid in and bolted up.

"What was all that?" he asked.

"Crayfish's calling it a posse. I'm calling it trouble."

I filled him in on all that. He just stood there and whistled.

"I don't know what I'm gonna do," I said. "Crayfish says he's putting two deputies, that's what he called them, on me so I can't go take a leak without a pair of T-Bar rannies tagging along. It sure's a problem."

Burtell laughed. "We've been had," he said.

It was time to put my thinking cap on, which was a futile idea. Truth to tell, I didn't have no idea what to do. The town got took over. That smart-talking bastard was two jumps ahead of me.

Ruble had taken over. I was a prisoner in my own town. If I stepped out the door, there'd be men shadowing me, seeing what I was up to. If I rode out on Critter, there'd be some of Ruble's hands following me. If I tried to form a real posse from merchants in town, Ruble's men would scare them off. There were tough men, strong men in Doubtful, men I'd deputize any time, but no match for the gunslicks on Ruble's payroll. And it looked like this was going to keep right on for almost two weeks.

I decided I'd just keep on doin' my duty, do my rounds, keep King Bragg secure inside his cell, see to the safety of them workmen when they put up the gallows, and all. And if anyone interfered, someone was gonna eat some lead.

THIRTEEN

Burtell was shuffling through dodgers, them flyers that come in the mail with pictures of wanted men on them. It was one way of beating the boredom.

"Sheriff," he said, "you seen these?"

He handed me a couple of old dodgers, printed three years ago. They'd been sent up from Colorado. A sheriff down there was looking for a pair of rustlers and holdup men, Foxy and Weasel Ramshorn. I stared real hard at those drawings, and even if the ink was bad, them two fellers did look a lot like Foxy and Weasel Jonas, the pair that were lying out in the cemetery after King Bragg emptied his revolver into them. But it was pretty tough to say these were the same fellers. That was the trouble with dodgers. A few had photographs, but most had bad drawings and bad descriptions, and it wasn't easy to make any sense of them.

This pair of bad-asses was wanted for

rustling, for robbing a Denver and Rio Grande train, and for holding up a Pueblo state bank. They was also wanted for questioning in the death of a rancher down there named Jarred Bobwhite, who was found in four pieces on his front porch after he'd filed charges against them brothers. That happened in Sterling, out on the plains.

"You think that pair of saints is the same pair as got shot here?" Burtell asked.

"Danged if I know," I said.

They was described as medium height, dark, thin, and Foxy was missing an earlobe. They were considered armed and dangerous, and there was a thousand-dollar reward dead or alive for each one. That interested me some. I was wondering what King Bragg was going to do with two grand.

I took them dodgers back into the jail and found King Bragg pacing.

"These the pair you shot?" I asked.

He shook his head. "Sheriff, I've told you twenty times —"

"Yeah, I know. But do these dodgers remind you of anyone?"

He stared. I held them dodgers on my side of the bars, not wanting him to tear them up.

"Yes. Those are Ruble's men. I'm sure of it."

"There's a reward. You applying for it?"

He glared at me, and whirled back to his metal bunk.

"I guess that wasn't a good question," I said.

But he wasn't talking no more, so I let him stew back there. Maybe his old man would get the reward money if it could be proven. Maybe King Bragg did the world a favor, getting rid of them two Ramshorn brothers.

"I guess I better write that sheriff down there, Carl Cable is his name," I said. I dreaded writing a letter. I'd written only one or two in my life, and now I was stuck with writing another one. But maybe I could get Judge Nippers to do it. Nippers would know how to string all them words together.

But I thought maybe there was something else for me to do first. I stuffed them dodgers into my pocket.

"I'm gonna show these to Crayfish," I said. "You hold the fort now."

Burtell nodded. He was piling through more dodgers. Now that he'd discovered something real interesting in that stack, he was hell-bent to find some more. I knew he was looking for a dodger on that other feller King Bragg dispatched, the one called Rocco whose last name no one knew. He

145

was just Rocco and he was cold in the ground.

I let myself out, and Burtell locked up after me. It sure was a fine spring day. Them two hardcases guarding the place for Crayfish nodded, but didn't follow me. He'd put them there to keep Anchor Ranch men from busting in, and there they stood.

I was pretty sure I knew where to find Crayfish. He'd be upstairs in Rosie's Parlor House, along with most of his crew. I guess that was as good a place as any if you're going to take over a town for two weeks. Rosie's was actually behind Saloon Row, across the alley, and discreetly out of sight for anyone ridin' into town. You have to give Rosie credit for that. The less visible she was, the better for her business. Her place was another of them board-and-batten buildings that was so common in Doubtful, the kind of structure that can be gotten up fast, and could be ditched without no pain if Doubtful disappeared, the way most Western towns did. So it was just another weathered brown two-story building hidden away. But Rosie was always a little different. She had a big veranda on the front, and a mess of flowers growing in pots there, makin' the place look nice. Her front door was enameled bright blue, and had a little eyehole in it. There was only a couple of windows downstairs, mostly frosted glass to discourage peepers, but there wasn't much to be peepin' at downstairs. A barroom with a piano and red velvet drapes, a nice little parlor with a few stuffed chairs, and a small kitchen. A feller could go in there and have a drink and sort of meet the help, which drifted through there in little gauzy outfits.

There was a big old stairway going upstairs, and maybe eight or ten little cribs there, and Rosie's suite, which was two rooms nicely furnished. Like most places in Doubtful, you had to slip outside to the crappers behind there on the alley if you had the need. The ladies had one of their own sort of off to the side, in a private fenced yard. Rosie usually had half a dozen ladies engaged in the trade, plus herself and a barkeep and a clean-up boy or girl.

It was sure a fine day, bright warm sun, and I enjoyed my hike over there. There was a mess of geraniums in pots on that porch. I knocked on the blue door, and pretty soon it got opened up by a maid in black, wearin' a little white apron. She saw my badge, and hesitated.

"I'm just gonna palaver with Crayfish," I said.

"He doesn't want to be bothered, Sheriff."

"Well, I guess I'll bother him anyway. Where's he at?"

"Ah, I'm not supposed — well, you could find him in Miss Rosie's rooms."

She looked mighty worried.

I smiled. "I'll just go knock, and I won't say who steered me there."

She nodded, looking real worried.

I could see there was a few of the T-Bar Ranch hands lollygaggin' around in the parlor and the bar, sipping red-eye and looking bored. The girls was leavin' them alone. They'd likely had their fill, and was just passing time now. There was a few more of them hardcases upstairs. The doors to half them rooms was open, and about every other room had a T-Bar man lying buck naked in there.

I just waved as I passed, and headed toward Rosie's rooms, which fronted on the street above the veranda. Sure enough, Rosie's door was shut tight, so I just rapped.

"Whoever you are, beat it," Rosie yelled.

"It's your old pal Cotton," I replied.

"Come back some other time. I got a customer."

"I got to talk with Crayfish, and right now, Rosie."

Crayfish answered. "All right, all right, let me get out of the saddle."

I waited real polite, and finally Crayfish, he just says to come in.

The pair of them was lying side by side on that fourposter bed. They both had their south half covered with a sheet. She sure was pretty, even if she was twice my age. I'd heard she was on the shady side of forty, but except for some little crow's-feet around her brown eyes, you couldn't tell. Crayfish, he was just a mess of curly chest hair and arm hair and neck hair not worth a second glance. They was just lounging there, sort of smirky, waiting for me to present my business to them, and enjoying the whole she-bang. Me, I was getting annoyed, not knowing how to do my sheriff business with a half-naked gent and lady staring up at me.

"Well?" said Crayfish.

I could hardly keep my eyes off Rosie, but she was just smiling there, enjoying it, waiting for whatever would happen. I had the itch to escape and do my sheriffing some other day, but now that I was there in Rosie's Parlor House, I thought maybe I'd just get myself together and get her done.

"I come to show you some dodgers," I said, trying to be dignified, which wasn't easy.

"Well, you're interrupting a business conference I'm having with Rosie," he said.

"I got some sheriff business," I replied.

"I'm thinking of buying out Rosie. I always wanted my own cathouse," Crayfish said. "And you've got to know the merchandise. It's called due diligence. I've got to know the merchandise backward and forward, from top to bottom."

I didn't have no answer to that, so I just swallered hard and sort of got things pulled together in my head.

"I need for you to look at these dodgers," I said. "We found them in my office. It looks like these two fellers, the Ramshorn brothers, are the same as got kilt by King Bragg. Only here they was using a different name, Jonas. There's Colorado warrants on them for rustling and a few items like that. I thought maybe you could tell me for sure whether these fellers in the pictures are the same as got kilt in the Last Chance."

I handed him the dodgers, and Crayfish, he gets out of the bed and fetches his spectacles and has a look.

"I don't think so," he said. "Jonas brothers weren't so dark and skinny, and younger."

"They got the same first names, Foxy and Weasel."

"Well, half the drovers I hire have got strange monikers like that. I've got a Tiger

and a Blue and a Rabbit and a Bullwhip.
No, Sheriff, these are not my boys."

"Let me see," Rosie said.

Crayfish handed the dodgers to her, and
she studied them real good. "They all come
in here sooner or later, you know. I see just
about every drover and ranch hand in the
valley. And I've never seen this pair of Ram-
shorns. But all I can see on these dodgers
are the faces, and I hardly ever look at
faces."

She handed the dodgers back.

"I got wind somewhere that the Jonas
brothers, they were picking off a steer now
and then from you," I said to Crayfish.

"From me? They were good men. Reliable
men. I've felt the loss ever since the Bragg
boy killed them."

"You weren't losing beeves to them?"

"Go talk to my foreman, Plug Parsons.
Tell him I sent you. He's in one of these
rooms in here."

"You're pretty sure these Ramshorn boys
in the dodgers got nothing to do with the
Jonas boys?"

He sighed. "You're interrupting my business conference, Sheriff. I hoped to find out
whether to purchase this place."

I guess there wasn't much more to ask
Crayfish Ruble. Them two was mighty eager

for me to get out. The funny thing is, I didn't believe Crayfish. It was two Colorado rustlers and train robbers we got in the Doubtful cemetery, even if Crayfish wasn't admitting it. But there wasn't much I could do about that. If Crayfish wanted some outlaws on his payroll, that was his business. I thought maybe he was using them two outlaws to lift a few beeves off of Admiral Bragg's pastures. It sure made sense.

They was waiting there for me to get out, but just to be ornery I stuck around a little.

"Sure a sunny day," I said.

Rosie, she caught me staring at her, and smiled. "I'd enjoy your business, Sheriff," she said.

Well, I'd enjoy hers, no doubt about it. But right now there was this thing in my head. I wanted to find out whether Crayfish knew about them Jonas boys. In fact there was a heap of stuff I wanted to find out, and maybe I could worm a little out of Sammy Upward, even if he was some put out with me.

"I reckon I'll let you get back to business," I said.

Rosie, she winked at me, but Crayfish, he looked like he was just getting mad.

I sort of strolled slow to the door, not

wanting them to think I was in any rush to get out of there, and at the door I turned for a last glance, and they was just staring at me. So I got out, and started looking for Plug Parsons to see what he knew about them brothers. He was still around Doubtful after all in spite of what Upward told me. But Plug wasn't in the parlor house. I tried most every door, interrupting business here and there, but I never did find Plug. I thought he'd give me some straight answers on the Jonas brothers, and maybe he'd have a word or two for me about that other one King Bragg shot, the one called Rocco.

I got out of the parlor house and sucked in some fresh air. Too much perfume in that place. I headed for the Last Chance, hopin' to find out a little more, and when I walked in, I knew I was real lucky, because standing at the bar and talking with Upward was Plug Parsons himself.

FOURTEEN

It couldn't be better. There was Plug Parsons, the foreman, sipping red-eye along with Upward. Plug was the straw boss of the T-Bar, and also was one of the two witnesses that got hauled in to testify about the shooting.

Upward, he glanced at me like he was none too pleased to see me. But he gave me a fake smile.

"What'll it be? Sarsaparilla?"

"Naw, Sammy, I'll buy me a shot."

"You must be off duty, eh?"

"I'm always on duty, Sammy."

He set a glass in front of me and pushed the bottle toward me. It had been in front of Plug Parsons.

"Good to see you, Plug. Ain't hardly seen you in town since the trial."

Plug eyed me a moment, and then shrugged. "We're here for the hanging," he said.

I poured two fingers and sipped. That stuff, it was pure firewater, distilled maybe two weeks ago and left to cure maybe two days. That splash, it attacked my teeth, scraped my nostrils, sandpapered my throat, and needled me all over.

"Mighty fine," I said. "Best sipping whiskey I've had in a while. Probably won some gold medals somewheres. Guess I'll add a splash, Sammy."

They smirked. Watering down the booze was a sign of being a sissy, but I didn't care. Let them think I'm a sissy. It actually would give me an advantage if I needed one in a fight. I hardly had a hair on my chest neither. Not like Crayfish, who was the hairiest man I ever did see, with a mat of it all over his chest and arms and neck. I sure was glad I didn't grow hair like that. Some fellers thought hairy men was meaner and harder than smooth men, but I never thought so. But I'm pretty smooth myself, and don't need to scrape my face but once every two or three weeks. I like a little stubble anyhow just to keep the wind off my chops.

Upward, he added a little water while Plug got smirky.

"That'll be an extra two cents for the water," Upward said.

Plug got pretty tickled about that, and started watching me sip.

"You hear the old one about the feller who was dining, and he says to the waiter, 'There's a fly in my soup.' And the waiter, he says, 'That's an extra nickel for the meat, sir.' "

"You got a real sense of humor, Sheriff," Plug said.

"Yep, that's a knee-slapper," Upward said.

I studied Plug some. "I guess you fellers are gonna stick around for a few days," I said. "Well, that's fine."

"We're making sure that little bastard gets strung up proper," Plug said.

"Oh, he will be," I said. "But you know, he sort of did a favor around here, plugging a pair of outlaws like the Jonas brothers."

"They was outlaws, all right," Plug said.

"There are warrants out of Colorado on that pair," I said. "They were a pair of bad boys, for sure."

"What were the warrants for?" Plug asked.

I sipped a little, now that I had their attention.

"Oh, a mess of stuff. Rustling. Bank robbery. Train robbery. And they was wanted for questioning in the death of a rancher down there. Seems the rancher caught someone making off with his cows, so maybe them two kilt him. Stuff like that."

"Ain't that interesting," Plug said. "I didn't know that part. Crayfish, he thought he was hiring a pair of gunslicks to keep the lid on around here, with Admiral Bragg pushing and shoving the way he did."

"I ain't got anything on Rocco, except he was palled up with the Jonas boys," I said. "Maybe the boy did the world a favor."

"What do you mean?"

"I mean, King Bragg wiped out two real bad fellers and maybe one more, fellers that would have turned on their boss, and maybe were fixing to get real mean with Crayfish."

Plug, he suddenly turned real quiet. "No, nothing like that," he said. "Crayfish, he can take care of himself."

Upward smiled and nodded.

I sometimes ain't the brightest candle in the lamp, but I got some instinct, and I knew from how this was going that I was poking into places where them two didn't want me to travel. So I let it lay a minute.

"Them dodgers that come in the mail, half of them are so blurry they don't help none. I get them all the time. The good ones, they got a photograph, but most just got a sketch and some information that don't help at all. Like, the wanted man's medium, and light haired, and got a scar over the left eyebrow and shifty eyes. How am I supposed to do something with that? You got any notions, Plug?"

"I'm not a lawman, Cotton. Me, I like to hear about reputations. Someone wants me to hire them on the T-Bar, half the time someone else knows something about the man. The boss keeps his ear to the ground too. He knows who he wants on the place."

"I guess maybe he's plumb glad them three got shot," I said.

"Wouldn't know about that," Plug said swiftly.

Upward hastened to tell me how wrong I was. "Crayfish felt real bad about it, good men down, shot in cold blood by that punk kid. Crayfish, he paid for the burying and declared a day of mourning on the ranch, and I served free beer all that day of mourning. Sort of like a wake, Sheriff. Lots of T-Bar men in here, and a few tears. We hated to say good-bye to some T-Bar riders."

"That so?" I asked. "I sort of thought them three were about as rotten as they come."

"It don't matter," Plug said. "They was with the outfit, and we're loyal to the brand, every last one of us. When anyone in the outfit goes down, we all pull together.

158

Crayfish started a widow and orphan fund for them, put in ten dollars for starters, but no one claimed it. Them two Jonas brothers were loners, I guess."

"They'd have to be loners, rustling their boss blind," I said.

"Who says that?" Plug asked.

"It's on the dodgers from Colorado," I said. "They were makin' a dime or two on the side, and not telling anyone about it. But they got caught, and then escaped."

"You don't say," Plug said. "That's sure news to me. You sorta wonder about people sometimes."

"Was them two moving a few beeves out of the T-Bar?" I asked. That was sort of the jackpot question.

Upward and Parsons, they just glanced at each other. "Not as I know of," Plug said. "I'd have heard of it. Mr. Ruble, he never asked me to look into it."

"How come King Bragg put bullets into those two? Were they rustling beef from the Anchor Ranch?"

Plug, he just shrugged. "He just walked in, got himself a drink, and started pumping bullets. That's what he had in mind before he set foot in here. He just walked in and pretty soon there was three dead T-Bar men, good hands, bleeding on the sawdust."

"I don't get it. How did he know them three were here?"

"Someone must have told him."

"Who?"

"Beats me," Plug said.

This whole thing didn't add up as far as I could see. It all added up for the court, which is why Judge Nippers sentenced the boy to hang. But there were a lot of questions in my mind, and I sure wasn't getting any answers.

"Sheriff," Upward said, "you're sniffing around the way a dog sniffs at vomit. Why? Just let it go, all right? The whole thing was tried, there were witnesses including me, and the jury convicted King Bragg of triple murder, and the judged sentenced him. Just let her go now, and get back to keeping the peace."

There sure was an edge to Upward's voice. Almost like he was commanding me. Almost like he was threatening, even though there wasn't no threats that I could hear. He was just telling me to lay off, and I guess he was right. The thing had been worrying around in my head for days, and I needed to let it go.

But I knew I couldn't. Things didn't seem right. A boy was about to get himself hanged. And time was running out.

"Well, it's Rocco that interests me," I said. "I'm just not sure who he was."

"He was just a drifting bum from back East," Plug said.

"Why'd you hire him then?"

"For safety. Rocco never wore a gun. You never saw a short gun on him. But he's the one I'd like to have with me in a saloon. He could cut someone up so fast they'd be dead before they knew they had a knife in 'em."

"A knifer?"

"The best. You never saw a knife on him either, but he always had two: one sewn into his boot, and the other in a pouch hanging behind his neck under his shirt."

"Why would Crayfish Ruble want a knifer on his payroll?" I asked.

"Beats me, Sheriff."

"Castrating bull calves," Upward said.

"That takes a knife fighter? It didn't spare him from a bullet from King Bragg," I said. "Now why'd the boy shoot him too?"

"Let it go, Sheriff." That was Upward talking, and he was plain irritated.

"So why'd he die?" I asked.

No one said nothing. The question hung there. Plug Parson, he sipped his drink, and Upward, he polished his bar, and me, I just stood there waiting for some answer that didn't come.

"Did Rocco get crosswise of anyone?" I asked.

Plug Parsons, he swilled the last of the drink down his gullet. "I'm going back to Rosie's," he said. "I come here for a good time, nice afternoon, and next thing I know the damned sheriff's digging up old bones."

I watched the straw boss hike his jeans up and walk out.

Upward, he got the bottle of red-eye from me, and put it on the back bar out of my reach, and turned his back to me. Things was getting sort of unfriendly at the Last Chance.

I left two bits on the bar and headed into the sunlight of late afternoon. The town was peaceful enough, but all them T-Bar men was keeping it peaceful. Maybe too peaceful. I got to thinkin' about that little visit. Plug wasn't even curious when I told him the Jonas brothers had a record. He must have known it. He didn't ask to see the dodgers either. I wondered if Plug knew they had changed their name from Ramshorn to Jonas. Plug sure was not surprised. Sammy wasn't surprised. And strange to say, I wasn't surprised that they weren't surprised.

Back at the jailhouse and sheriff office, I seen that Rusty had taken over from Burtell and that things was peaceful enough.

"You been running around to bars and cathouses, I hear," Rusty said.

"It sure was an education. Over at Rosie's, Crayfish and Rosie were having a horizontal business conference, and over at the Last Chance, Plug Parson and Sammy Upward weren't very happy when I started talking about them three that King Bragg shot. But I don't know much else. You know anything?"

"Yeah, King wants to ask you a question."

"I'll go talk to him."

The kid was peering through the bars.

"How many drinks does it take to knock someone out?" he asked.

"I sure don't know," I said. "Some fellers, they can drink all night and never even get fuzzy. Other fellers are flat on their ass after a couple."

"One drink?"

"I never heard of one drink knocking anyone out," I said.

"I only had one drink of ale at the Sampling Room that night," he said.

"You sure?"

"One drink. Then I went over to the Last Chance, and Sammy Upward served me."

"And after that?"

"I was lying on the sawdust. I think I got hit on the head."

FIFTEEN

Critter was mad at me. When I entered his stall, he fired a left rear hoof at my groin. He sure knows how to hurt a guy.

"Cut it out. We're going for a trip," I said.

I started to brush him, but he leaned into me, pushing me against the plank wall, intending to break a few of my ribs.

"You're dog food," I said.

I kneed him away just before he splintered my whole rib cage. He laid back his ears and clacked his teeth.

"Try that again and I'll leave you here," I said.

That subdued him. He hated cooped-up life in there. He suffered in there. He rolled his eyes upward like a helpless wife in there. And in between, he plotted murder and mayhem. But the threat to leave him there wrought a new cheerfulness in him, and he settled for a swat across my face with his dung-soaked tail.

"That's better," I said.

I brushed him real good, threw the blanket on, and my saddle over that, cinched it up, wary of another hoof, and then I stuffed a bit in his mouth and slid the bridle over his ugly ears.

I backed him out into the aisle. He sighed, farted, dropped some apples, and we were ready to travel. Critter and I had been friends for half a dozen years.

The town would take care of itself this day. Rusty and DeGraff would man the sheriff office and jail, with shotguns at the ready. But I didn't expect trouble. All them T-Bar men wanted was to make sure there was a hanging, and the prisoner didn't get stolen away from us. But that wasn't gonna happen.

I steered Critter out on Wyoming Street, and soon put Doubtful behind me. It was a nippy spring day, with a few razors in the wind, but that was fine with me. I get tired of city life pretty quick. I wasn't sure I'd stay in Doubtful for long, but the pay was pretty fine and I got to sip some red-eye now and then, and look at horseflesh, and sometimes female flesh, which was better than once-a-month ranch paydays. I buttoned my canvas coat up tight and pulled my hat low against the gusty wind out of the snowy mountains.

Critter and me, we were going on a little exploration. As long as most all of them T-Bar men and Crayfish Ruble were camping in my metropolis, I thought I'd just go have a look at the T-Bar when there was no one but a couple of caretakers around there. I just wanted to see a few things. It wasn't that I thought King Bragg was innocent, but things didn't add up, and I'd hate to hang a feller who didn't do what he was said to do. I still had a few days before the big event, so I thought I'd just poke around and see what could be seen. I didn't much like it that the only witnesses to King Bragg's killing spree of T-Bar men was other T-Bar men.

Critter, he was so happy to get out of jail that he was almost frisky. He kept wanting to run, but I reined him in.

"We got ten miles each way, feller," I said.

But I let him settle into a jog that was easy on my ass-end and still ate up time. The T-Bar was up the valley, farther than the Anchor Ranch owned by Admiral Bragg, which was a bone of contention. Crayfish ached to be closer to town, and had designs on Bragg's property so he could ride into town most any time and entertain the ladies. But Bragg had got here first, and had nabbed all the best land, which even had some well-watered hay meadow and a creek or two, leaving latecomers like Crayfish to settle the dry hills and long gulches.

It sure was peaceful. Even if the wind had an edge, the sun was bright and warm. I like to get out of town and see the crows flying when I need a little time away from people, who are usually at each other's throats. Not that nature is peaceful. That hawk circling over there was pretty quick going to land on a vole or some such critter and have him for dinner. Nature's the same as people when it comes to spilling blood, but I like the country better than the town anyway.

I steered past a mess of Anchor Ranch cattle. Bragg had started with them red shorthorns, and was trying to breed closer to Angus now. I steered toward a bunch that was all wearin' the Anchor brand unmistakable. I continued up the road a piece and saw a horseman heading my way. Only it wasn't male, judging from that big straw hat and the way the party sat the horse. I sort of dreaded what was coming. I guess Queen Bragg was the last person I wanted to see. She was a huffy sort, and probably would've tried the jailbreak her pa was cooking up, and besides, she was ornery and uppity too. But I thought I'd put up with it, seeing as how she was closing on me fast.

Sure enough, it was Queen, riding a blooded mare and wearing one of them split leather skirts so she could ride astride. I never did understand why women ride sidesaddle, and I sort of secretly was pleased to see Queen showing some sense. Well, she sailed right up and smiled.

"Howdy, Miss Bragg," I said.

"Howdy yourself. You looking for something here?"

"Nope, just riding through."

"Off to the Crayfish empire then."

I wasn't gonna tell her my business so I just stared.

"You want company?" she asked.

"No, miss, I'll just go her alone."

"Well, you've got company," she said, steering that blooded horse in beside me.

"I'm doing fine alone, miss, so you just get along now and take the morning air, and I'll be on my way."

"You're stuck with me."

I surrendered a little. "Only until we get to the T-Bar range," I said. "This is your turf, so I'll somehow manage to survive the next mile or two if I try real hard and you don't try no more jailbreaks."

She laughed, damn her. How do you chase

off some woman like her without threatening to shoot her and the horse? She had me roped and tied, and she knew it.

She settled in beside me, and I could tell she was eyeing me out of the corner of her eyes, but I just stayed real stony. I wasn't gonna bend an inch.

"I'm sorry about what happened in town," she said. "It wasn't my idea or my will, but my father made me."

"Made you what?" I asked just as cold as I could.

"Made me smuggle."

"Smuggle what?"

"A loaded two-shot derringer, a hacksaw blade, a file, a knife, and a ball of cord."

"You had all that stuff under . . . down there?"

"In my skirts. I was a walking arsenal because I also had a spare revolver if my father needed one."

"You was hauling iron, miss. I should have pinched you." I didn't like how I said it. "I mean, arrested you."

She smiled. "Maybe pinched would have been better."

"Now see here, Miss Queen, I'm a proper sheriff."

She laughed, and I was plumb pissed off.

"I should have arrested you and had you

170

searched."

"You could have searched me without even asking, Cotton."

"Lady, you stop your nag right there and I'm riding ahead, and don't you follow."

I never got invited to search a woman before, and I don't have the smarts to deal with it, so I just got huffy, which seemed to work, at least for a few moments.

She followed, and then caught up, pushing her nag until it was beside mine. I scowled at her some, but what's a feller to do. Queen, she had a faint smile twitching her lips a little.

"Is King safe?" she asked.

"I think so. All them T-Bar riders just want to make sure he's, ah, sent away. They ain't trying to bust in. Truth is, Miss Bragg, they're making sure you and your pa don't spirit the boy away."

"He's innocent, you know."

"No I don't know. But I'm poking around some."

"Is that what you're doing now?"

"I don't think it's your business, miss."

"If you are, maybe I can help."

"No, when we get to the T-Bar line, I'm crossing and you're staying put."

"I ride the T-Bar range all the time. No one ever bothers me. That's because I'm me. I know some things to show you."

"Like what?"

"Unmarked graves. New brands that aren't registered in the brand books."

"No, that don't have any bearing on King shooting three T-Bar men."

"But they do. The brands are all on mavericked calves."

"What's that got to do with anything, girl?"

She absorbed my tone, and rode quietly beside me, saying nothing. Critter, he didn't like that blooded mare beside him and snapped now and then. But the day was too fine for anyone to stay ornery, including a horse who'd been pining for sunshine and grass.

We got to the T-Bar line. This was still pretty much open range, but there was a gate and a drift fence here. I got down and opened the gate. She rode through.

"Hey! This is where we part company," I said.

She didn't budge.

I turned Critter, reached down and grabbed the bridle of that blooded horse of hers, and led it through the gate. Then I got off Critter to close the gate, but next I knew, she was back on T-Bar range. This was getting tiresome.

"You head back or I'll head back. The pair of us ain't going forward," I said.

"I wish you were more forward, Sheriff," she said.

She was sitting her saddle and smiling at me like a cat that just gulped a mouse. I just don't know how to deal with ballsy women.

"Oh, all right," I said, feeling grouchy. The best I could say for her was that she was different away from her pa. Around him, she was mean and always lookin' down her nose at me. Here she smiled some when she looked down her nose at me. This Queen Bragg was a lot more pleasant to be around than the version of Queen when her old man was lording over her.

"Well, you show me the stuff, and then go hightail out of here," I said, not wanting to surrender easily.

I pulled the wire gate shut and dropped the loop to secure it. I sure didn't know whether this was a good idea, her along with the sheriff on T-Bar Ranch land. There wasn't no one in sight; just a lot of grassy hills, greening up in the spring, and blue sky, and puffy white clouds that could betray a feller and dump snow or ice or cold rain in a moment.

I guessed we wouldn't see anyone, what

with all but two or three of them T-Bar men in town. But I pulled my badge from my pocket and pinned it on my coat. That badge could put me there on the ranch proper. But I didn't have no badge for her.

It sure was quiet. The wind had slowed to a whisper and the midday sun had warmed things into a fine day. I didn't see one steer or cow or calf or bull. Nothing but a golden eagle, wings spread out to every last feather-tip, patrolling for mice or rabbits.

We began to ride among T-Bar cattle, grazing peacefully, their brand burned into their left flank. Crayfish wasn't much interested in breeding up, so his cows were a motley bunch, every color I could think of and then some, and showing a lot of horn, like there was some Texas longhorn in the lot.

We rode onward, and then hit a bunch of young stuff, yearlings mostly, and this bunch interested me because it had a Two Plus brand burned into their left flank, instead of the T-Bar. I steered Critter close to have a look, and sure enough, the brand was one I'd never seen, and I could see how easy it was to turn a T-Bar into a Two Plus with a running iron. But there the bunch was.

"I guess I'll have to look in the brand book to see who owns those," I said. "Maybe

Crayfish does."

"Maybe he didn't but does now," she said.

"What do you mean by that."

"They've been mavericked. You can call it the Two Plus if you want. I'll call it the Double Cross."

That sure was a revelation.

"I guess I'll look for some answers," I said.

"Now I'm going to take you to the cemetery," she said.

"What's there?"

"You'll see."

She took the lead, riding toward ranch headquarters located in a broad gulch a mile ahead. We still didn't see a soul, what with all them boys in town. But long before we reached the ranch buildings, she turned into a side gulch, and we followed it completely out of sight of the main buildings. It was a brushy gulch, and we scared up deer and skunks and various critters, working through red willow brush and whatnot. The gulch divided into three branches, and she took the rightmost one, which wound deep into grassy hills.

I sure got to wondering where she was going, and how she knew to come to this silent notch in the foothills, but she kept right on until she suddenly stopped.

There, on a clay flat, were four long

mounds, that sure looked to me like four graves. They weren't marked, and one of the mounds was pretty much disintegrated from flash floods running over it.

"Dig," she said.

But I didn't have a shovel.

SIXTEEN

There sure wasn't a shovel anywheres except maybe at the T-Bar headquarters, and I wasn't planning to borrow one there. But the more I thought about it, the more I began to itch.

"How do you know these are graves?" I asked Queen.

"What else would they be?"

"Ranchers bury lots of critters."

"No, we mostly drag dead horses or dogs or sheep into brush and let nature take care of itself."

"I don't know of anyone come up missing. Them cowboys come and go, riding the line, and I don't know of any one that's gone and got himself killed."

"Not cowboys. Women," she said.

"Now what the devil are you mouthing about?"

"Women in those graves. The ones who vanished from the Red Light District."

There were some of those. A few of them fancy ladies had up and vanished, and the madams told me about it. But mostly everyone figured they got hooked up with some cowboy promising to marry them and live in eternal bliss forever, and so they just took off.

"There were a few," I said.

"Crayfish Ruble's women."

Crayfish Ruble was a veteran of every parlor house in town, and I'd heard a thing or two about him and the girls. He had favorites, and once I heard he'd bought one from a madam and hauled her off. That's the last anyone saw of her.

"Why do you say that?" I asked.

"It's common knowledge," Queen said. "And here's where they ended up."

"You got proof?"

"Sheriff, I know things without what you call proof."

I wasn't following all this very well. "What's this got to do with your brother?"

"Crayfish."

I sure wasn't following her logic, if that's what it should be called.

"I ain't gonna borrow a shovel from the T-Bar. I'm not sure I'm even gonna dig around here without some good reason."

"I knew you'd say that," she said.

She was making me itchy again. "Let's get out of here."

She was smiling at me, as if she knew exactly what I'd do next. I ignored her and steered Critter down the gulch, wanting to get off of T-Bar range and then get shut of her. I was getting tired of uppity local aristocracy. She was worse than Admiral when it came to lookin' down a long nose at me.

We rode out, our backs to the wind, and watched the new grass weave in the blustery wind. The farther we got from that burial ground, the better I felt. Them graves were probably real old, not fresh, and probably went back to Indian times. She kept grinning at me, sort of out of the corner of her eyes, and I didn't feel much like jabbering with her, so we just rode across big pastures with cattle like tiny black dots here and there. It sure was big country, the kind that lifted the heart and made a man feel complete. I opened the gate at the fence line, and she rode through and I closed it behind us. We were on Anchor Ranch land then, and the funny thing was, she sort of shrank down, like it was her pappy's land and she was back under the thumb of her master. I watched her. She even rode different on that blooded horse. I thought maybe she'd turn mean on me, but she just rode quietly until we got to the place where the road to her headquarters turned off.

She turned to stare at me. "He's innocent. Time's running out. Please try to save him."

She reached across and placed her hand on mine, where I was holdin' the reins, and just pressed for a moment. It sure was nice and made me almost forget she was Queen Bragg, snotty daughter of Admiral Bragg, and was confessing to smuggling jailbreak tools a while before. Then she steered the blooded horse up the road to her place and left me there.

I was sort of wondering whether she really liked me, or if she was just using some of that female stuff to try to help her brother. I decided it wasn't me. She was just tryin' to spring King. If King got loose of the hanging, Queen's nose would be back up in the air whenever Sheriff Pickens rode by.

Still . . . I figured I'd better put her out of mind. My ma, she always warned me not to believe anything a woman under eighteen said. I plumb forgot how old Queen was, but just to be cautious, I'd start calling her seventeen.

The bad thing about all this was how I kept wondering whether King had killed them three T-Bar men after all. The doubts just kept sneaking up in my head, and when I thought that King had been tried fair and true, and had him a good lawyer, and there was two witnesses saw him do it, and when he hadn't no defense except he was looking for trouble, drinking, and didn't remember much, why, that should be enough. The court had spoken. The sentence had been given. And in a few days now, the gallows would go up in the courthouse square.

But that whole thing was clawin' at me, and I didn't know what to do next.

Critter, he settled into a slow walk back to Doubtful, not wanting to get penned in a box stall again, and when I put my heels to his ribs, he snarled at me, farted, and slowed down all the more. Well, I hated to put him back in prison. I run a jail, and get to see how bad it is for people caught inside of one, helpless and hurting. Maybe some deserved being in there, but I never did like to take freedom away from anyone. I guess I'm just softheaded. If I had a harder head, I'd just say get in there, you crook, and suffer for what you done.

I penned up Critter in Turk's livery barn after brushing him down, and he snapped at me with those big buck teeth of his, getting a nip into my shirt.

"Better luck next time. I was ready for

181

you," I told him.

He just clacked his teeth and laid his ears back, but I closed the stall door and left him to repent for a day or two.

I checked in at the sheriff office and jail, and Rusty said all was quiet, so I patrolled the town, finally landing in the Sampling Room, thinking maybe to talk to Mrs. Gladstone. She'd served King his drink just a little before he left and kilt three men, so maybe I ought to just find out what he was tossing down his parched throat.

She was in there all right, but she had no customers since Anchor Ranch men were steering clear of town, with all those T-Bar men everywhere. I guess Admiral Bragg didn't want to pick a fight and was keeping his crew out at the ranch.

Her place, the Sampling Room, had always been a little different. It was the cleanest saloon in Doubtful. The glass shone. The floor was shiny and waxed. The spittoons were emptied daily. Like the rest on Saloon Row, she had an outhouse on the alley, but she limed it regularly, and it didn't stink the way the others did, all summer long. She had put them pen and ink drawings of thoroughbred horses on the walls, along with etchings and such like. And she'd gotten mail-order furniture in, some chairs that were almost comfortable. There even was a brass rail at the bar, like a proper saloon in the cities. It was too fancy for me, but some people liked that sort of place, I guess. I always got a little itchy in there, like I didn't belong in a saloon like that.

She eyed me from a rocking chair, where she was sitting in a shaft of sunlight, knitting a scarf.

"You're the first person I've seen today," she said. "My customers seem to be staying away from town."

"They don't want trouble, ma'am."

Her needles were clacking away. I could never figure out how anyone knit anything. I've tried to watch them hands at work, makin' little knots of yarn, the fingers going here and there. It sure ain't men's business for sure. But them scarves were welcome, and she gave them away to people she cared about. I sometimes wished she'd knit one for me, but I guess I wasn't a regular customer.

She rose. "What can I pour you, Mr. Pickens?"

That was another thing. She always called me that. It didn't matter that I don't like either my front handle, Cotton, or my rear handle, because that's what she set her mind to calling me.

"Some red-eye. I'm done for the day," I said.

She frowned. "I'm sure you wouldn't sip on duty."

"I'm always on duty, ma'am."

"Well, it's your prerogative," she said.

There was another of them big words no one ever taught me. "My what?"

"Your choice, your privilege. You are privileged to do what you wish."

"I never heard that one before. Where'd you get a carpetbag full of words like that?"

"I was an English teacher in the Minnesota Normal School before I came here."

"English? You?"

"This is better. I earn a living here. Don't ever go into English, Sheriff. People who work with words don't get a wooden nickle for it. People who write starve. People who teach reading and writing and spelling can't make ends meet."

"So you came out here?"

"Mr. Pickens, I make three times more money running the Sampling Room than I did teaching English to students who intended to be teachers. And in the Sampling Room I serve a better class of customers."

I got to chewing on that for a while. I thought maybe to chew some tobacco too, but thought better of it. The Sampling

Room had its own ways, and I was probably crosswise of half a dozen of them.

She set the bottle of red-eye on the bar, along with a tumbler.

I poured two fingers, being real careful not to get too enthusiastic.

She watched me with approval. At least she'd sell one drink this slow day.

I sipped, wheezed, let that first firewater slide down and start some trouble in my gut, and then sipped again. You had to ease into red-eye, and not take her all at once. Once it numbed your tongue and throat, then you could swaller a little more, but only after it scoured your stomach and started south from there. It took skill to drink red-eye whiskey, and not many fellers ever got the hang of it. It you took it too fast, it'd make you crazy, and if you took it too slow, it would poleaxe you.

She studied me to see if I measured up. I'd just flunked her English lesson, and was fearful I'd flunk whatever else was coming along the pike. But she sort of smiled. She had a lovely smile, even if she was sort of too soft for me. I prefer women who ain't too soft-lookin'. My ma, she always told me to mind my knitting, and I never did understand that until now. But Mrs. Gladstone was a real pleasant lady, maybe twice my

185

age, and maybe I'd come to like her some as soon as she stopped scaring me.

So we sort of hung there at the bar, she behind and me in front, with a boot on the rail.

"Is there something you wished to see me about, Mr. Pickens?"

"Well, ah, yes, ma'am. I want to talk about King Bragg."

She sighed. "I can't bear it. Talk about anything else. The sands of time are running through the hourglass."

I could never understand talk like that. I'd just say he was gonna croak pretty quick, but she got it all tied up with sand and hourglasses, and I never got the hang of that way of talking.

"I'm sort of looking into it a little," I said. "Do you remember how he was acting around here — before he, ah, got himself in trouble down the street?"

"He was always a little youthful and impetuous, Sheriff. And he was that evening."

I figured I'd just pretend to know what that word impetuous meant. I wished she'd talk plain English.

"Was he drunk as a skunk?"

She eyed me real patiently. I don't think I had said that in any way she approved of.

186

"He had sipped one ale, Mr. Pickens. Just a little ale, made in Wisconsin and shipped clear out here. I keep a little on hand for him and his father."

"That's all — some ale?"

"It's a very gentle drink, Sheriff."

"Why did he leave here and go over there to the Last Chance?"

"A man pushed him into it. A gentleman came in and told King Bragg that the cowboys over at the Last Chance were saying bad things about him and his family and the Anchor Ranch, and if he wasn't a coward he'd come and settle their hash."

"Someone goaded him into leaving here?"

"Goaded is a good word, especially coming from you, Sheriff. Yes, a sort of heavy gentleman came in, goaded him, and finally King drained his ale and stepped out into the dusk."

She wiped her eye. "I didn't want him to go. I knew something bad would come of it. And it did. That was the last I saw of the young man."

"Do you know who that man was, the one that goaded him?"

"Why yes, I knew him slightly. It was the T-Bar foreman, Plug Parsons."

SEVENTEEN

I found Judge Nippers in his office, nipping a little amber stuff from a flask.

"Come in, boy, and join the party," he said.

He handed me the flask. "I'm on duty," I said.

"Well, so am I. A little hooch improves duty."

He sure was an ugly cuss, who reminded me of a bullfrog, except bullfrogs look nicer and got no hair. Nippers had hair going in the wrong direction all the time, which he oiled down with lamb fat or something. It sure made the top of his head look slippery, which is probably how his mind worked too. I never met no one with such a slippery mind as Judge Nippers. He made most of the county lawyers look like virgins.

I took the flask, since he was wavin' it before my eyes like I had some duty to perform, and sipped a little. It sure wasn't red-eye; it was something smooth and fine. He must have got it sent to Doubtful, because there wasn't stuff like that served in any saloon I knew of.

"You've come to talk about the hanging," he said. "You're going to tell me you're not up to pulling that lever and sending that brat to his fate. You're going to tell me to bring in a professional hangman."

"Well, it crossed my mind," I said.

"You don't enjoy hangings."

"Well, it ain't high on my list of pleasures."

"It beats having a woman, but isn't as good as a satisfying trip to the outhouse. A good trip to the outhouse is the most under-rated event on earth."

I sure didn't know how to talk to a judge talkin' like that. He nipped another sip from his flask and smiled, revealing yeller teeth between crusty lips.

"You nip your way through a trial?" I asked.

"A good nip improves the sentence. I never lay a sentence on anyone until I've refueled a little."

"Improves?"

"You bet, young fellow. Justice is sublime. It takes a keen understanding to fashion a sentence that fits the crime. A good nip will inspire me to improve the sentence by two or three years."

I hardly dared ask which direction. He smiled cheerfully, and scratched flakes of dry flesh off his jowls. "I believe you repaired to my chambers to discuss something," he said.

"I don't need to repair nothing."

"Repaired, to make one's way."

"You sure got a few years of school on me, Judge."

"You can cure that with a sip or two."

"I guess what I come to ask is whether you can stop a hanging."

"Yes, I can stay it."

"What would that take?"

"New and compelling evidence."

"Otherwise, you just let her rip?"

"Otherwise, you the sheriff will pull the lever, and our young prisoner drops about ten feet and dangles with a broken neck, and justice is entirely done, and the world is made whole again."

"I've got an itch about this, Your Honesty."

"Your Honor."

"My honor's fine. Doing a hanging's about as hard as it goes, but there's one thing worse."

"Worse, worse? How could anything be worse?"

"Hanging an innocent man."

"Ah, you're getting soft. I thought you were a tough sonofabitch, Pickens. You've gone soft on me."

"I do what I have to do, sir."

"I can see it. About ten minutes before you're required to pull the lever at eleven in the morning, and drop King Bragg, you'll resign. You'll say you're not up to sheriffing anymore, so here's the badge, and you're on your way to California or the Fiji Islands or someplace like that where you can eat coconuts, and sun on the beach. Fess up now, Pickens. I've got the measure of you."

"You calling me something?"

He smiled. "Nothing you wouldn't call yourself."

That sure hurt. I sorta had to admit to it, all right. I just ached not to say another word, but I made myself. "I sorta think maybe the Bragg boy's innocent."

"Innocent? Just by carrying the name of Bragg, he's guilty as hell."

"Well, I'm not sure he done it. I think something happened in there and I don't know what, and I need to find out."

"This is pure cotton."

"Well, that's how I'm called, all right, but I've learned a few things."

"You can tell me, but it won't budge me one iota." He took a hearty sip of whiskey, just to make his point.

"Them three that got kilt, the Jonas brothers and the one called Rocco, they was bad apples, with some dodgers on them for rustling and stuff."

"Good riddance then."

"Yeah, well, there's some calves out on the T-Bar with altered brands, like they'd been mavericked. And I was sort of wondering how Crayfish Ruble is dealing with that. Maybe the Jonas brothers were nipping calves from their boss. And Rocco was in there somehow."

Nippers smiled. "Why, obviously Crayfish arranged for the Bragg boy to come into the Last Chance and blow them off."

He was chortling, but damned if that wasn't what was gonging in my head these times.

"Judge, they sort of goaded him to go over there to the Last Chance. He was drinkin' an ale nice and peaceful over to the Sampling Room, when Ruble's foreman, he come in and began working on the boy, getting him to come next door because they was saying stuff about Admiral Bragg."

"Well, Admiral Bragg deserves everything they say about him."

"So the kid went over there, ordered a drink, and someone hit him and next he knew he was on the floor holding his hot revolver, and there's bodies around."

"Yes, yes, that's all in the trial record."

"What if the boy didn't do it?"

Nippers stared. "You got even the tiniest shred of evidence?"

"King Bragg don't remember it."

Nippers guffawed and wiped more flaky flesh off his jowls. "You got to do better than that, boy."

I could see how it was going, and I was getting mad myself. I've got a temper, and that judge was working it. "I'll keep looking, and if I find out something, I'm coming back here and I'm going to ask you to stop this hanging."

"Fat chance," he said, and nipped another.

I got out of there. Nippers had already hanged the boy in his mind, and wouldn't be changing anything before the necktie party. Maybe the boy was guilty as hell; that's what the jury said. But Nippers wasn't going to help much even if I found some new evidence.

I knew who I wanted to talk to. That dirt-bag foreman Plug Parsons, him who lured King Bragg over to the other bar, and testified that the boy killed three men there. Plug was always sort of smirky, and I never much cared for him, but now I cared even less. He'd either be at Rosie's or at the Last Chance Saloon, so I hightailed it over to the saloon and looked around in there, but I didn't see him. There was a mess of T-Bar men in there, whistling at me when I walked in, and makin' jokes, but no Parsons. Upward, he just stared at me and then watched me leave. I wasn't welcome around there, but where is a sheriff ever welcome?

So maybe it would be Rosie's. I walked right in, past the unlit red lamp, it being afternoon. The place stank. The T-Bar men smelled worse than hogs. Parsons, he wasn't in the parlor or kitchen or nowhere downstairs, so I tried all the doors upstairs, and checked out a couple of snoring males, but Parsons wasn't in there either. I guess I just would have to wait. Truth to tell, I was itching to grab a fistful of shirt and hammer on Parsons until he talked. But first I had to find him.

Doubtful ain't a big place, but a man could still hide himself in town for a while if he wanted to. I didn't see anyone resembling Parsons, who was pretty solid beef from head to toe, so I decided to check on Critter. I hiked over to Turk's livery barn and found Critter gnawing on the gate, which was bad. You don't want a gate-chewin' horse around.

"Cut it out," I yelled.

Critter just yawned.

"You'll wear down your teeth and die young," I said.

"You talking about me?" someone asked.

It was Plug Parsons, standing in the aisle behind me.

"I've been looking for you."

"So I've heard."

"I got some questions to ask about that night that the T-Bar men got shot."

"I've already testified, Sheriff."

"I got a few more ends to tie up. Did you go into the Sampling Room and dog the boy some?"

Parsons yawned. "I thought maybe you wanted to talk about something else. That was weeks ago. Forget it."

"We're gonna talk about that, and I want some answers. What did you tell the boy? Why did you lure him over to the Last Chance?"

Parsons hoisted his gun belt around a little, and I didn't miss it.

"You trying to spring that little killer, Sheriff?"

"Maybe he should be sprung," I said.

He grabbed a handful of my shirt and yanked me tight. It didn't surprise me. Some foremen are like that.

"You're a two-bit punk with a shiny badge," he said. "Grow up."

"My ma says I'm big for my age," I said.

He kneed me but missed. His ham fist swung around behind me, but I shoved him down fast and hard. He landed in manure, and sprang up quick, reaching for his Peacemaker. But he was slower than me; mine was out and pointed. He saw that muzzle aimed between his eyeballs and sort of settled down some. His hat rested on a pile of fresh green apples.

"Now answer my questions, and do it right," I said.

He just stared at me.

"What happened when King walked in?"

Plug was beet red, hotter than a boiler.

"Who was in there? You and Upward and who else?"

Plug, he just glared.

"What knocked that boy into the sawdust?"

Plug was steaming now, and a little blood oozed from a cut lip.

"Who shot those three T-Bar men?"

Plug's eyes gave him away. He wasn't very good at hiding things. But neither was he talking.

"Whose gun kilt them men?"

This time he answered quietly. "It's all in

my sworn testimony."

"Your testimony's a lot of bull."

He was standing there, wondering which way to jump.

"Lean against that wall," I said. "Hands high."

He was slow about it, but he obeyed, and I grabbed his revolver.

"All right, I'm locking you up. Walk in front of me."

"For what?"

"I'll think of something," I said.

I could see he was about to try something, so I buffaloed him. That barrel made a dent in his skull, but it taught him a little respect.

"Walk," I said.

He wobbled out of the livery barn, me behind him, and headed along the street, making a spectacle. But no one stopped us.

There was a couple of them T-Bar men lounging around the sheriff office.

"I've got an itchy finger," I told them.

Plug shook his head and they got the message.

Rusty must have seen me coming, because the door swung open and I jabbed Plug into the office. The door swung shut behind us.

"What'd he do?" Rusty asked.

"I'll figure it out," I said.

Rusty opened the iron door to the cells,

and we patted down Parsons and then shoved him into one and slammed the door. Across the aisle, King Bragg was staring at us.

Parsons had a lump on his head, and rubbed it. "What to know something?" he said. "I'm going to kill you. Maybe not now, but soon. You can count on it. And if I don't, my men will. There's not a one wouldn't plug you on sight. You and everyone you hire. You know what, Sheriff? You just bought the ranch."

EIGHTEEN

I let Plug cool down a couple of hours, and then headed into the cell block. He was standing with those ham hands on the bars, glaring away.

"You can go," I said.

It sure startled him some.

"You ain't done nothing much except grab my shirt and cuss me out. I guess I can forget that fast enough."

He simply dead-eye glared at me so much, I thought to go real easy. I was ready — just in case.

I unlocked the cell door, and he bulled through hard, maybe to knock me off balance, but he saw I was ready, with a billy club that I knew how to use hard and fast.

Instead, he simply stopped and fixed me with that glare. "I'll kill you soon as I can, Pickens. I'll kill you and kick in your face and hang you from the nearest tree. It don't matter whether I kill you face-to-face with a short gun or shoot you in the back with a long one, because either way, you'll be cold meat."

"You go cool down at Rosie's, and stay quiet. I don't want to see you runnin' around Doubtful for a while."

He clenched those ham hands, and I stepped slightly back. I was waiting for him, and he saw it. He knew what a billy club could do, which made him halfway smart.

"Punk kid wearing a star. You'll pay, Pickens. You'll be horsemeat before you know it."

"Get along now," I said, edging him toward the front door.

"I won't forget this, you punk. As long as I live, I'll remember this, and I'll come kick manure on your grave."

Plug was sure fussing at me, but I eased him through the sheriff office, while Rusty watched real careful, and then I pushed Plug out the door and locked it.

"You didn't charge him? You let him go?"

"Oh, he'll get past it."

"You coulda charged him with a dozen things. Haul him in front of Nippers. Put him behind iron for six months."

I laughed. "He got whupped. Not many foremen ever get whupped."

"He was madder because you let him go

200

than he was when you dragged him in."

"He's the big bull, and you know how them bulls are, Rusty. Now he don't have much to bitch about. I let him go! Only thing he's really mad about is because I got the drop on him and hauled him in."

"You better watch your back."

"It's a gamble," I said.

I figured it was better for Plug to be outside of the jail than in. I didn't have the manpower to keep twenty or thirty T-Bar men from busting in, grabbing Plug, and killing King too.

Rusty eyed me like I was plumb loco, but I made my choice and now I'd live with it.

We watched Plug race down Wyoming Street toward the Red Light District, and I knew that within minutes the story, Plug's version anyway, would be spreading around there.

"We better fort up," I said.

Rusty, he spread the spare shotguns at the barred windows and we dropped the bar on the door. We had boxes of buckshot shells that could make nasty holes in crowds. It would be Rusty and me against them T-Bar men, and I thought we'd do pretty well. We'd get help too, soon as Burtell and De-Graff heard the banging.

I headed back into the cell block, and

found King Bragg standing just behind the bars.

"You enjoy that?" I asked.

He shook his head. "I thought he'd tear those bars apart and kill me before he killed you."

"You talk about anything?"

"I asked him a few things. Like, what happened after I walked into the Last Chance, with him dogging me."

That caught my attention for sure.

King smiled suddenly. " 'Wouldn't you like to know,' Plug said. And I said I would because I sure don't know what happened. All I know was, I walked into the Last Chance and there were a few T-Bar men, and Crayfish, and Upward served me a redeye, and I waited to see what they were gonna say to my face."

"And then?"

"I'll never know, Sheriff, and I'll hang for not knowing what happened next."

"Who else was in the Last Chance?"

"Foxy and Weasel Jonas, and Rocco, all bellied up to the bar, sipping whiskey."

"And somehow you shot them."

The look in his face was about as sad as any I ever did see.

There was something about this that was nagging at me, but I sure couldn't figure what, so I changed the subject.

"I'm expecting some visitors," I said.

"Armed and ready to break in, kill you and Rusty, and then kill me."

I hesitated. "If it comes to it, I'll free you and give you the means to defend yourself. But I want your word of honor —"

He snapped, "I won't give you my word of honor, so forget it. If they catch me in here and kill me, that's how it'll be."

He was some riled up. I sort of admired him, but I didn't know why.

"You want anything? Water?"

"You want to take my pisspot out and empty it?"

"In a while. Right now, I got to deal with Plug. He sure had some heat in him."

"Nothing'll happen," King said.

I wasn't so sure. I locked up the cell block and slid the key into my pocket. Rusty, he was studying the streets, but they looked calm enough. It wasn't yet dark, this being late spring with lots of long light. I decided not to light the kerosene lamp. Not this eve. We were gonna sit there in the dark and watch the streets and close the shutters if lead started flying. But the seven-day clock in there just kept ticking away, minute by minute.

"You think they'll try midnight or later?"

Rusty asked.

"I'm thinking maybe dawn, when they figure we've drifted off."

"Go to sleep, Cotton, and I'll watch."

"I couldn't if I wanted to."

It sure was a long dark night, and I was askin' myself what I was sheriff for. It wasn't any job I wanted, but I got stuck with it when the city of Doubtful had a hankering for my services, seeing as how most everyone else was dead that wore their star. But there wasn't any point in grousing about it. Sheriff is what I was and would be.

The night was real quiet, and we saw no one hunkered down out there. With dawn, Burtell and DeGraff showed up, and I was glad to see them. We filled them in and left them in charge, while I headed back to Belle's boardinghouse where I had me a little room. I didn't need much from life. There was an iron bedstead in there, a blanket and pillow, a place for a trunk, and a place to hang up a few clothes. Maybe someday I'd have a woman to care for, and I'd want a little cottage somewheres, with some rambling roses around, but there weren't no prospects. I thought some about Queen, but she wasn't thinking about me, and I didn't like her anyway, except when she smiled a little, which wasn't very often.

So I walked home through empty streets, since the merchants weren't up and around yet. Belle's boardinghouse sure was quiet. I was ready for a good sleep, having spent the night awake, waiting for trouble at the jail. My room was up on the second floor, at the rear, where the sole window looked out on the alley and the outhouses. It was fine in the winter, but a feller didn't want to sleep with an open window in the summer. I went down that hall, feeling them planks creak under me, and then I noticed the door was ajar a little. I whipped out the .44 without thinking twice. My ma used to tell me I was a little slow, but made up for it by being quick. I never quite figured that one out, but it didn't matter none. That door was not tight, and I thought I might meet a hail of lead if I opened it more. In fact, there wasn't nothing but a skinny layer of veneer between the killer in there and me, and that creaking hallway gave me away. So I just paused, wondering what to do, thinking maybe I should get flat on my belly.

"Do come in, Mr. Pickens. I've been waiting most of the night for you."

I fear I recognized that voice straight off.

"You alone in there, Mrs. Gladstone?"

"Certainly. Three's a crowd at a rendez-vous."

"A who?"

"A lover's meeting, my dear."

This was getting worse than being shot.

I edged the door open, ready to shoot, and saw she was alone, sitting in the one chair I possessed. I slid my revolver back in its holster and eyed the lady. She sure was nice-lookin' wearing a white wrapper, with her hair down and falling over her shoulders. The dawn light from the window seemed to flow like gold over her. She had some slippers on too, with a hole in the side of one for her bunion. Them bunions are awful. My ma and pa both had bunions, mostly from buying bad shoes.

"Come in, dear boy," she said. "We'll have a little tête-à-tête."

This was making me plain itchy. I didn't dare ask what them words meant.

She motioned me toward the bed, where I sat down real gingerly. She sure was pretty, all soft and gentle, with a brightness in her eyes. I'd never seen a lady in a white wrapper before. My ma, she pined for a white wrapper all her life. Pa got her a gray flannel one with purple petunias on it, and I never knew that wrappers came in other colors until I was off on my own. This white wrapper flowed over the Widow Gladstone in a way that didn't quite hide much.

But I couldn't think of a blasted thing to say, and if I tried I'd just babble out a mess of words, so I swallowed real hard and settled on the bed and tried to make sense of this.

"Now then, we'll just talk a little. I might have some information for you. I know you're looking into that whole tragedy. You've been asking questions. I'm hoping you'll save the dear boy. I'm very fond of him."

The way she said that sure stirred up stuff in my head.

She waited a moment, while I studied her white wrapper. I couldn't keep my eyes off that white wrapper. That wasn't much under there. Her dress and all that other stuff, all them thingamabobs women wear, she had folded them all into a stack sitting on my dresser. So I was stuck with staring at her wrapper, because I didn't know what else to do.

"My information might lead you to the truth about King, and might free him from the awful fate that awaits him," she said.

"Well, what is it, ma'am?"

"Oh, I'm not going to tell you. Not unless I have my way with you."

This sure was getting peculiar. I tried to run that through my head, and it kept bucking like Critter in a bad mood.

"Mind you, what I know might not change anything. I know nothing about what happened next door, after King left along with Mr. Parsons."

"Well, seems to me if you're keepin' stuff from me, then you're going against the laws," I said. "Someone told me that once. You've got to fess up all you know."

"Well, that's for you to decide," she said. "I have a price."

She had a price, all right. That there white wrapper was just the butcher paper on the package.

"We would have a lovely time," she said softly. "I am an experienced woman."

Well, I sure didn't have a clue about what to do.

"You got to tell me what you know, how you know it, and why you're telling me," I said, trying not to look at that wrapper, which was sort of sliding down her shoulders a little.

"Just say Open Sesame, and magic will happen," she said.

"Now what's that supposed to mean?"

"Ah, dear boy, I'm looking forward to teaching you."

She sure was pretty. She might be older, but she was just fine, sitting there, smiling, looking like an angel in the dawn light, making life sweet in the town of Doubtful, Wyoming Territory. I sort of figured she was trying to save King Bragg's life, and maybe she'd worn that white wrapper with King Bragg as her company. Who could say? She was like some loving angel lookin' down on us poor mortals.

"Ma'am," I said, real firm. "I've got a headache."

"That's very familiar," she said. "You may turn your back."

I did, and when she told me I could turn around, she was dressed, with a small sad smile on her lips. She leaned forward and kissed me softly, and left my boardinghouse room.

My ma always told me I'm a little slow.

NINETEEN

That timber cutter Lemuel Clegg and his boys were waiting for me when I got to the office. I sort of halfway knew what they would tell me even as DeGraff let me in. I motioned them three to follow, and closed and locked the door behind me.

The county hired Lem Clegg to build the gallows. He had a mill up in the forest out of Doubtful, where he cut posts and planks and such. When it came to hiring someone to build the gallows, I told the county supervisors, Reggie Thimble and Ziggy Camp, I didn't have no money in the budget for it. They said, hell, man, hang King Bragg from the nearest cottonwood limb. They thought that was pretty funny until Judge Nippers had a fit, and told the county to have a proper gallows and pay for it. So one way or another, the Cleggs got hired to do the job. I knew they were out there cutting timbers and squaring them up, and getting plank lined up, and such. And now, with a week left before the big event, I knew they'd be putting it up on the courthouse square, and we'd soon be seeing a proper gallows.

"You met my boys? This here is Barter and this other is Wage. I give 'em names to set them in the right direction when they get growed up some."

"Oh, I got a miserable name hung on me too," I said. "I never did cotton to Cotton, but I got stuck."

Lemuel pursed his lips some, not caring for that. He had a scraggly gray beard and his lips were a little orange purse in the middle of it.

"Sheriff, we got robbed. Highwaymen. We was driving the first of the timbers into Doubtful, and half a dozen masked men surrounded us and all we saw was the muzzles of big revolvers."

"What did they want?"

"Not my purse. They didn't even ask for my purse." Lem pulled it from his pocket and dangled it before me so I could see it was fat with bills and coins. "It was the wood they wanted. They plumb stole every stick off our wagon, carried it over to their own, and sent us on our way."

"You know who?"

"Sure I do. I'd recognize that blooded

211

stock anywhere. That gang was Anchor Ranch or I'll eat my shirt."

From the looks of his shirt, I thought he'd be eating a lot of grease and slobber and road dirt if it came to that.

"You say they were masked?"

"Yep, every last one. But if you put all them Anchor Ranch men in a line, I'd be able to finger a bunch. I think I saw Spitting Sam, Big Nose George, and Smiley Thistlethwaite, but I wouldn't make a bet on it."

"What was the lumber?"

"The uprights, the crossbeam, four angle braces, and some two-by-fours to start framing the platform. I'd say a hundred dollars of good wood. I gotta tell you, Sheriff, we'd put our best into it. The uprights, they were ten-inch-square posts of lodgepole pine, planed smooth and no knots. The crosspiece was ten-inch-square Colorado spruce, finest we could buy, full of resin to give it plenty of bounce. Why, you could drop a four-hundred-pound fat lady from the Barnum and Bailey Circus from it, and it wouldn't even shiver. You can drop a hundred people from that spruce, and it wouldn't hurt the spruce a bit. Why, you could drop a thousand and it'd not show a sign of wear. When Lemuel Clegg builds something, he builds it to last a century. That's me. We'll build a gallows for that Puma County Square that'll last long after our grandchildren have come and gone. The county can put that gallows in a warehouse and bring her out and put her up any time, and it'll be just as good as the day we built it. Yep, at least a hundred dollars of fine wood in there."

"The good wood's not why they stole it," I said.

"No, I guess it ain't. Looks like we'll have to cut some more and get us an armed guard to bring it in."

"Can you put up the gallows in time?"

Lem sighed. "I suppose so, if we work night and day, and we don't get any more wood stole from us. But it'll be cheaper wood. Lodgepole planes faster than spruce, so the whole thing will be lodgepole, which isn't the best wood for this sort of thing. A good gallows should be made to hang people for a century or two."

"I know a hundred or so fellers deserve a hanging," I said. "One long-life gallows might save the county a pile of money."

"Well, you can start with that fiend King Bragg," Lem said. "If he'd been out cutting trees like my boys, he wouldn't have gone bad."

I got more details, time and place, descriptions, anything that Lem and his boys could think of, and then they hightailed out. There sure was some question whether Puma County would have a proper gallows up and ready for the day of the hanging.

"All right, you go cut some more wood, and next time let me know before you bring it in, and I'll make sure you've got a guard," I said.

They took off.

DeGraff eyed me. "Going out to Admiral Bragg's place to pinch a few?"

'I'm thinking on it. I'm also thinking just to send them a message. King Bragg's gonna get his neck broke on the right day, even if there's no gallows. I'll hang him from the flagpole if that's what it takes. So they may as well cut it out."

"Want me to go tell Admiral?"

"Yeah, do that. Tell him we're not waiting for a proper gallows. That boy's gonna hang, and that's the whole story."

"All right. I'll ride. See you tomorrow — if they don't shoot me."

"Or make a hostage of you," I added.

He grinned.

"Keep a sharp eye out," I said.

DeGraff headed into the afternoon, and a little later I saw him ride up the road toward the Anchor Ranch. It would be a long, lonely trek for him, and not without danger. But he'd do the job, all right. I had good deputies. Some of them, like Rusty, had started down the owlhoot trail but saw how it would end, and came on over to the sunlight side of life. That just made them better deputies. They knew how the others lived, what they thought, what they believed they could get away with, and all the ways they were foolish as well as smart. My deputies were handy with guns, but not as fast as all those gunslicks on the ranches. But Rusty and Burtell and DeGraff knew enough to know that the one that aims good is the one that wins a gunfight, and speed don't matter much if the lead flies past its target. All three of them was pretty happy too. They was getting regular wages, had enough for a few beers after work, and the whole town of Doubtful admired them. Our mayor, George Waller, even told me that Doubtful was lucky to have me and them three keeping things quiet. It was good for business, he said.

Things weren't so quiet lately, though.

I went back into the cells to see about King, who was staring at the ceiling.

"Anyone going to feed me this week?" he asked.

"You didn't get fed?"

"Not since yesterday. And that pot —"

He didn't have to say any more. It stank. That was the trouble with my deputies. Rusty and DeGraff hated to feed any prisoner or take the chamber pot out, and I'd told them a million times to do it, and take care of the men behind bars.

"How'd you like it if you were behind bars and no one fed you or got you water or took your stinking crap out?" I'd asked them.

Rusty, he just smiled. "No way I'm ever gonna be behind bars again," he said.

Well, they weren't perfect even if they was good men.

I beckoned, and King handed me the chamber pot, and I took it out and emptied it in the crapper, and then I pumped a pail of water and splashed it over the pot, and threw it toward the geraniums the Doubtful Women's Club had planted. I took that back to King Bragg.

"I'll get you some chow. It ain't right, starving you."

"In a week, it won't make any difference," he said.

I stopped. "I'm still trying to find out what happened in there. Tell me something. Did Mrs. Gladstone hear what Plug Parsons said to you?"

"She was right there."

"And what did Plug tell you?"

"He said Crayfish was next door and wanted to see me, and wanted to send a message to my father."

"Crayfish was next door?"

"That's what Plug told me."

"And was he in the Last Chance Saloon?"

"No, I didn't see him. So I just ordered a drink from Sammy Upward while I waited."

"And where was Plug?"

"I guess he went to get Ruble."

"And where were the ones that got killed? The Jonas boys and Rocco?"

"Beats me," King said. "I had my back to the room, and was facing the bar, getting a drink."

"And then?"

"Then I was on the floor staring at the ceiling with Ruble and Plug standing over me."

"With your gun in your hand?"

"No, in my holster. They took it out and told me every chamber was empty and I'd soon hang."

"Why didn't your lawyer, Stokes, go into this?"

The boy stared. "What's there to go into?"

I sure had a prickly feeling in me. "All right, I'll go over to the café and get you a meal. You want something in particular?"

"What's this, my last supper?"

I didn't feel much like answering. I locked up and headed down the street to Toady's Beanery, where we sometimes got our chow for our prisoners. We had a regular account with Toady, and he billed the county. He also kept some of our tin bowls on hand, so he could dish up a meal real quick.

Toady was a one-eyed Civil War veteran, and he didn't wear a patch either. Beans was all he made, but some weeks the beans would have bacon, and some weeks beef, and some weeks other stuff, like tomatoes, just for variety.

"Wondered when you'd come," Toady said. He reached for one of them mess bowls and filled it. "You still have that boy in there? You feeding him somewhere else?"

"You mean he hasn't been fed?"

"Not this morning or last night."

I got angry. Half the time my deputies forgot to feed the prisoner, and I'd told them about it over and over, and now the boy was starving once again. It was one hell of a way to treat someone caged behind iron bars and helpless.

"Make it double, Toady," I said.

The man ladled another round of the beans and handed it to me, and I headed back through the quiet afternoon to my jailhouse. You'd think Doubtful was the peacefullest town in Wyoming. There wasn't no one in sight, not even them T-Bar men of Ruble's keepin' an eye on my office. I unlocked and took the bowl straight back to King Bragg, who accepted it with both hands, like it was a communion plate.

He sat on the bunk with the bowl in his lap and clasped his hands together.

"I thank you Lord for these thy gifts. Amen," he said.

He glanced at me, saw me standing there, and turned his face away from me and kept on praying. I didn't know what he was saying, but a boy who's gonna be hanged in a few days might have an awful lot to say to God. I didn't know whether to stand there or get out and give him his privacy, but somehow I just stood there and watched while he said whatever he had to say. Then, finally, he was done.

He took the metal spoon I'd given him and dug in, and I noticed his face was wet with tears, and those tears just kept flowing and flowing down his cheeks even as he downed the beans. It was so bad I could hardly look.

TWENTY

Judge Nippers was parked in his swivel chair, drunk as a skunk, so I rattled his shoulder some to fetch him awake.

"Huh? Huh?" he said, and grabbed for the little revolver he kept in his desk drawer.

"It's me," I said. "Put that piece back."

He did.

"You up to talkin'?"

"I'm up to whatever the world throws at me. I am a sterling public servant, and won't abide your insults."

"You mind if I hang King Bragg from a cottonwood limb?"

"Mind! Of course I mind! The boy's gonna be hanged proper, from a scaffold, by the Territory of Wyoming, just as fine and fitting as can be done. And no short-cuts. No tree limbs. This'll be done in a professional fashion."

"Ah, there's a little problem," I said. I told him about the Cleggs comin' to town and getting their timbers stolen.

"Admiral Bragg's work," Nippers said.

"The robbers were masked, and we can't prove it."

"Well, it's perfectly obvious. You tell Admiral Bragg to cease and desist or I'll hang him from the same gibbet after he watches his boy swing."

That was booze talkin' and I let it pass. "It may take the Cleggs a while to get that scaffold up, if we keep running into trouble. It may not be ready in time."

"Well, then I'll issue a brief stay. When it's up, I'll give the go-ahead."

"There may be a lot of delays. Depends on how much Admiral Bragg wants to slow it down."

Nippers eyed me coolly. "Then spirit the young punk to Laramie. Armed guard, middle of the night. Let Laramie enjoy the hanging."

"Our merchants won't be happy with that," I said. "They're already stocked up for crowds of people having a party. George Waller, he says most every merchant in town's laid in food and picnic stuff. There'll be people from all over Puma County coming in for the show, and they'll spend good money. If we move the hanging, you're gonna have Mayor Waller and every mer-

221

chant in town mad as hornets. It ain't just the merchants either. I've already employed Doc Harrison to declare him dead. And Sammy Upward's advertising half-price drinks after the show, and free hard-boiled eggs."

"Tough beans," Nippers said. "If I say spirit the prisoner out, you're going to spirit the prisoner out. If I say hang the bastard in Laramie, you're gonna hang the bastard in Laramie. And if the merchants whine, I'll tell them to elect someone else next time. I'm tired of being a magistrate anyway."

"Well, don't do that until I see whether we can get the scaffold up. I'm going out there and escort the Cleggs next time they're hauling wood."

"You do that," Nippers said. He'd found his flask, and was losing interest in me.

I abandoned the Puma County courthouse and headed back to my jail, only to run into Crayfish Ruble, standing right there with Plug Parsons at his side, grinning at me like he wanted to spill a little blood.

"Hold up there, Sheriff," Ruble said.

"I got no business with you," I said.

"We got word that the Cleggs got held up by Admiral Bragg's men, and they made off with the gallows timbers."

"Where did you hear that?"

"From Old Man Clegg. He was on his way out of Doubtful."

"I'm on it. And it's not going to happen again. I've sent a deputy to tell Admiral Bragg that ain't gonna stop a thing and he's obstructing justice."

Ruble just laughed. "Fat lot of good that'll do."

He riled me some, and Plug was itching for me to take a swing at his boss, but I just stood real quiet.

"Here's the deal, Sheriff. We're going to escort Clegg and his boys and those timbers into town, and if Admiral Bragg's men try anything, they'll be leaking blood into the ground."

"No, you won't," I said. "You're not going to do that. I'm a peace officer, and I'm not going to let a gang war start in Puma County. If you try that, I'll throw your ass in jail."

Plug, he just wheezed happily, like he could hardly wait for me to try it.

Truth was, the odds were pretty bad, but I was the law, and I wasn't gonna let a bunch of gunslicks shoot it out.

That evening, Barter Clegg slipped into Doubtful and told me his old man was ready to haul wood in the morning. He said they'd worked real hard out there, and got the timbers ready, and wanted to leave before dawn, figuring they could get the timbers into town before anyone was up for the day. I told him I'd be there, and the kid slid away. I hoped no one was looking, but in Doubtful these days I never knew who was spying on me.

I found Rusty and DeGraff inside. "I'm going out to Clegg's lumber mill, and I'm escorting the wagon in. They've cut some new wood. We're driving back here before dawn."

I stared real hard at them both. "Now you're going to take care of the prisoner, feed him, and do it proper, because if he ain't fed and cared for, you're going to be looking for some other job."

DeGraff got riled up. "Don't blame me," he said.

"I'm not blaming anyone. I'm just warning you that anyone fails to treat that boy proper, he'll answer to me."

"I don't know why you bother when he's gonna be cold meat in three days."

"He's gonna be taken care of proper until he hangs," I said.

In fact, I think DeGraff was the one who wasn't feeding the boy or cleaning his slop bucket when he was on duty, and I was thinking maybe I'd get a new deputy if he didn't shape up real fast.

I went to the gun cabinet and looked things over, and finally selected a double-barrel twelve-gauge shotgun and some shells loaded with buckshot. The one I took with me had an eighteen-inch barrel, just right for making a good cone, but not so short it sprayed lead all over. I never thought much of shotguns, but that's what I wanted this time. With my revolver I could put a pill through the ace of hearts at ten paces. That took some practice, and I took some pride in it, but this time I'd be alone against three, four, five of Admiral Bragg's best. I respected all of them, especially Big Nose George and Spitting Sam, and I'd carry whatever advantage I could.

I got up in the middle of the night, when it was quiet and cold, and went to get Critter. He was dozing and had a fit, kicking his stall hard until I quieted him down.

"We're going for a night ride," I said, "so cut it out."

He got the message, and didn't even try to break my ribs by squeezing me into the wall, and pretty soon I got him saddled and bridled, and led him into the quiet night. He sniffed the air, snorted, and decided he was going to enjoy the trip.

Lemuel Clegg's mill was about two hours

away, so I started out there around three and rode in about five. There was enough moon so I could make them out. They had a draft horse hooked to the wagon, and on the bed were two more uprights, a cross-piece, and support timbers. They was loaded and ready, and we set out. None of them was armed, and that was good. I didn't want some amateurs getting themselves kilt just because they was hauling metal.

It sure was a nice night. I didn't try to talk none with the Cleggs, because I wanted to listen to all the night sounds. But we made two, three miles without trouble, until we come to a narrow place where the hills cramped the road some, and there was room enough for the road and the dry gulch running alongside.

I felt Critter tighten, and could just make out his ears rotating off to the left some. I didn't wait for anything to unfold. I put my spurs to him, and he bolted left so hard it pretty near pitched me off the saddle, and sure enough, there was three or four horse-men waiting up ahead. I pulled the shotgun and barreled right in, and by the time they got wind of me I was on them, and I aimed one barrel at a knot of them. The shot must've caught men and horses too, because some of them nags, probably good blooded stock belonging to Admiral Bragg, were bucking and screeching and pitching their riders. I sure was curious to see who might show up in town wearing a few bandages.

It only took that one shot. One rider picked up a downed rider, and the mess of them hightailed away. I had my shotgun at the ready, but that bunch was gone. I pulled the empty shell and reloaded, and rode back.

"We'll likely have no more trouble," I said. The old man whupped his draft horse to life, and we creaked and groaned our way into Doubtful.

Them Cleggs unloaded the timbers on the courthouse square and took off for their mill. They needed to bring in another load of planks and two-by-fours for the platform, and I worried about them getting ambushed on the second trip. But I couldn't be every-where at once.

A lot of people studied them big timbers, but no one touched anything. I thought the timbers would be safe enough there, out in front of the whole town. But the presence of those timbers changed everything. Doubtful would soon be a place where a big crowd would watch a criminal boy get hanged, and a sort of brooding settled over the town. Them timbers did it. The timbers made everything real.

I found Judge Nippers and County Supervisor Reggie Thimble eating lunch at the beanery, and told them I thought the Cleggs would get the scaffold built proper, and tested proper, before the big event. Lem Clegg claimed to have built one before, and knew all about it, and knew how to test it out, with a weight on the trapdoor, so when I pulled the lever nothing would go wrong, and King Bragg would drop hard and fast. That would be exactly at eleven in the morning, in three days.

"Well, that's fine," Thimble said. "Build it to last. I'm all for it. If we can hang five or ten a year, pretty soon we'll have the cost down to a few dimes a drop."

I sure wasn't enjoying the thought of hanging anyone, but I was the sheriff and I'd do what I had to do. But I kept wishing some piece of evidence would come along that would free the boy. I wasn't sure he killed anyone, even if he once swaggered around Doubtful, making the most of being his father's son. But boys are like that. He was a different boy now, back in the cell where he was going to spend the last hours of his life.

I kept an eye out for anyone with a bandage wandering around town, but no one like that showed up, and I knew that anyone injured by my buckshot was staying out at the Anchor Ranch, and not coming into Doubtful to get himself arrested by me.

The Cleggs made another round trip, this time with a heap of planks and studs and a cask of ten-penny nails. They unloaded the whole shebang in the courthouse square, and come over to the jailhouse to ask me just where to put up the gallows. I walked over there and had a look. It had to be in a place where everyone could see real clear that justice was done. I decided on a place fairly close to the Puma County Courthouse steps, so the crowd would gather down from the courthouse some. There sure were a mess of people around there, and I noticed the T-Bar men were sort of guarding that pile of lumber. Crayfish Ruble was making sure that nothing stopped the hanging of the killer of his three ranch hands.

It was a real quiet night, and the next morning the Cleggs were hard at work. They bolted the foot timbers to the uprights, and then bolted in the angle pieces so that each upright stood on a base and wasn't gonna tip none. Then, while them uprights was still lying on the grass, they bolted down a spruce crossbar good and solid. And then the Cleggs got some big ropes and tied them to the crossbar, and began to tug the whole thing up in the air, so that by the end of the first day at work, they got the framework up and braced into place. It looked mighty solemn, and a lot of people stopped to stare at it. The merchants liked it because all them folks stayed right around town and went shopping. A few of the ladies bought spring bonnets they could wear for the hanging.

I told the Cleggs they could sleep in the jail if they wanted, and I saw Lemuel talk a little with Wage and Barter, and then they turned me down without sayin' why. But I knew why. They didn't want to bunk in any cell next to the condemned boy. So they drove out to their place that night, and planned to come back in the morning. If they stayed on schedule, they would frame the platform tomorrow, and put in the hardware, and spend the last day before the hanging testing it to make sure there was a good drop once I pulled the lever. I wanted a good drop for the boy too, so he didn't just dangle there and choke to death real slow.

I didn't know nothing about making a noose, but DeGraff said he did, so I was going to leave that to my deputy. I went over to Waller's hardware and bought twenty yards of one-inch hemp rope, tough rope that wouldn't bust when it took some weight, and I told DeGraff to make a noose, and we'd get her up there as soon as the Cleggs were ready.

Things were coming right along, all right.

TWENTY-ONE

Lem Clegg and his boys was putting up the gallows in fine style, taking real pride in their work. I kept an eye on them, but no one was bothering them none. They'd got the hanging part of it up, good and solid, and now they was working on the platform and the trap. They'd put in posts and stringers, and soon they'd be running plank across. They sure knew what they were doing, and I wondered if they'd built a few other gallows in their day. It felt real good to have some professionals doing the job.

There was a mess of people watching them work, most all the time. A lot of Doubtful mothers, they'd bring their young ones over for a look, and tell them kids to behave themselves or they'd get themselves hanged just like King Bragg was going to in a couple of days. Some of these boys, they got real excited by it and wanted to get real close to see it when the moment came along.

Mrs. Cadbury, the schoolmarm, she brought the fifth grade over to see the gallows going up, and told them all how it would work. Them little kids were impressed, and I thought they'd stick to the straight and narrow rather than get their necks broken. When she came back with the seventh graders, they all begged her to watch it when the time came, and she promised them she'd let them out of school so they could see justice done and take part in the hanging of a mass murderer. I thought that was pretty good myself, and it'd keep the peace around there real good. The more people saw King hang, the better, when it came to stopping crime in its tracks. She told me it was better than reading the Bible to them every morning, and since the gallows had started to go up, she'd had no trouble in class and not even much truancy. So that gallows was sending a message, all right.

Doubtful didn't have no high school, just grades one through eight, so there weren't any older children seeing the gallows go up. That was too bad, because the older ones, they'd see that King Bragg was eighteen, about their own age, and that would make some sort of impression on them. The more that came to the hanging, the better off

Puma County would be, and of course the merchants were expecting a big day in their shops too.

It sure was a nice spring, and I thought if the weather held, King Bragg would get himself hanged on a fine, warm, sunny day, and that would be good. I'd hate to hang a feller on a cold, mean day.

There was a mess of T-Bar men floating around, but the Anchor Ranch outfit was staying away. That suited me fine. Admiral Bragg, he'd tried everything from a fake hanging to scare me to smuggling stuff to his boy, and only a couple days earlier I'd stopped them from robbing the gallows timbers and trying to slow down the hanging. So I wasn't very fond of that one, him with all them airs. And his daughter Queen was just as bad, except once in a while when her pa wasn't around. I felt sorry for her, under his thumb like that. But maybe she deserved it, being so snotty like that.

Crayfish Ruble was whiling away his days over at Rosie's, and I hardly saw him. But I knew he was around, and I knew he was pulling strings. His gunslicks were all over town, almost patrolling it, like they were the lawmen and not me. But it was peaceful enough, and as long as they didn't bust any laws or cause trouble, I had no reason to mind. Maybe it was even to the good, because it kept Admiral Bragg and his bunch out of Doubtful so the hanging could go ahead real peaceful.

After watching the Cleggs saw planks and hammer them down, I headed out Wyoming Street, thinking to have a visit with Sammy Upward. He might still be mad at me, but I didn't care. I was as itchy as ever about what was going on in my town.

The moment I walked in there, Sammy starting rubbing the bar with his rag, and I knew I wasn't very welcome. There was a bunch of T-Bar men in there, and it was like I'd walked into their private club and they didn't like it none.

Sammy just slapped a bottle of red-eye on the bar, and a tumbler, and told me it'd be a quarter. "I'm charging one bit now," he said.

It had been a dime. I didn't object, and laid out two bits.

"I'm looking for a few things," I said.

"You got something to tell me first?"

Sammy was back in his trading mood. He'd tell me something if I told him something.

"Sure," I said. "Admiral Bragg tried to stop the scaffold going up. I put some buckshot into the ambush."

"That so?" Sammy seemed impressed. I hadn't told anyone about that predawn fight when I rode with the Cleggs. "You know who took some shot?"

"Nope. Anyone that got hit's staying out at the Anchor Ranch. I'll pinch anyone with a bandage on him just now."

Sammy polished away at the bar, and finally decided it was okay to cut loose with something I might need. "Well?" he said, sounding irritated.

I peered around a little. All them T-Bar men had quit their talking and were listening to me. They wanted to know what the sheriff was askin' about, so I decided to give them an earful.

"This fellow Rocco, the one that King Bragg shot. I'm just curious about him. I got some flyers on the two brothers, so I know they were up to no good, but I don't know a thing about Rocco. Crayfish hired him, and he didn't seem like one of the regular bunch out there. You gonna help me with that?"

"What do you want to know for?"

"I was sort of wondering if maybe King Bragg did the world a favor."

Upward thought about that a little, polishing away on his bar, and then said, "He didn't do the world any favor. Rocco, he

236

was different all right. He wasn't a regular cowboy living in the bunkhouse like the rest. He lived up at the house like Mr. Ruble. He was Mr. Ruble's manservant, you know? The gent that kept the big house and got whatever Crayfish needed and took care of things. Mr. Ruble, he has no woman, you know. So he had this Eastern gent, Rocco, do all that stuff."

"What stuff?"

Sammy eyed the silent crowd, and then leaned forward, almost whispering to me. "Crayfish Ruble sure liked his women, and once in a while he'd send Rocco to town, with the black buggy, to fetch him a woman. Rocco would go rent one from one of the parlor houses. He'd go to Rosie and rent one for a week, and bring her out to the ranch, so Crayfish could enjoy her for a few days."

"Then he'd take her back?"

Upward shrugged. "I only know what I heard. That's all I'm telling you."

"Rocco, did he spend time with the rest of the T-Bar men?"

"Naw, he was a loner. He was real well educated, and talked different. He never talked about cattle or guns or anything like that. When he came in here with Crayfish, they would talk about good wines, or how to cook venison, or what women in Paris were wearing."

"Rocco was from where?"

"How should I know? But I once served a man from that hellhole called Brooklyn, and this Rocco, he sounded like that. I couldn't place it if I tried. But he was smart."

"And Crayfish employed him as a manservant? Anything else?"

Sammy sighed. "Maybe an informer. I think he was Crayfish's eyes and ears. Now that's all I'm gonna say. I'm done. I told you more than you told me."

He stalked off to serve one of the T-Bar cowboys, who was wanting another shot. I just waited real quiet. I wasn't done with Sammy.

Pretty soon I had another crack at it. "How come King Bragg shot him?" I asked.

"I don't know or care. King Bragg shot Mr. Ruble's best friend and two of his best hands in cold blood. Crayfish Ruble told me a dozen times, Rocco was the most valuable help he had, and them Jonas boys, they was harder working than most everyone in the bunkhouse. I'll tell you something, Cotton. When that boy killed three of his best men, Crayfish broke down and pretty near cried some. He'd hate me for saying it, because men don't shed tears, but I saw

Ruble kneel over those three murdered men and fight back a tear or two, not wanting anyone to see how bad he felt."

"Were they baiting King?"

"Naw, it was cold-blooded murder, an execution if you ask me."

"The kid simply pulled his gun and shot the three of them?"

"He did. They was all in a row next to him while he was sucking red-eye, and next I knew, there was all this gunfire, and I was in the storeroom. When I stuck my head out for a peek, there they were. Three dead men on my sawdust, leaking blood and coughing their last. Oh, man, Sheriff, that was a bad moment."

"Must have been," I said.

One of them T-Bar men came up to me. It was Carter Bell. He had witnessed the shooting and testified at the trial. So he was still around town.

"That hanging going to happen like it should, Sheriff?" he asked.

Carter Bell had a real nice-sounding name, but he reminded me of a rodent. I swear, every time I looked at him, I thought of rats. He had that rat-face on a skinny body, and if I didn't know he was a live person, I'd of thought him to be a big old alley rat. He didn't have rat whiskers, but he had little buck teeth at the end of a long snout, just like one of them big gray rats. You sure couldn't always tell a person by his name.

"Everything's going just as the court directed," I said.

"Well, if it ain't, there's going to be a hanging anyway," he said.

"You planning on doing it?"

He smiled, his little rat-mouth widening. "Count on it, Sheriff."

"You got the itch to string up the boy, do you?"

"I got that itch so bad, I'd like to bust in there and do it all by my lonesome before anyone else has the chance, Sheriff."

"How come? What did the boy do to you?"

"He killed three T-Bar men in cold blood, and I saw it."

"I guess you and Plug Parsons were the two that saw it happen, with Sammy here."

Then this lobo wolf Bell, he said, "if you don't hang that punk proper, watch your back, Sheriff."

"Well, my ma, she always said I needed an eye in the back of my head."

"You ain't hearing me. I saw the Bragg boy shoot our friends deader than buzzard bait. The court settled it weeks ago. So drop it now, damn you. You gonna quit sniffing around or not? Answer me, dammit."

He was standing there, hand hovering over that sidearm of his, looking for an excuse to yank it out.

"Bell, cut it out," Sammy said.

Bell sure got himself riled up. He was crowding me, and if he'd try to pull iron he would have gotten a knee right where it hurts. Maybe I'm a little thick in the head, but I'm fast with the rest of me. But the steam sort of hissed out of him, like maybe Sammy was giving orders, and pretty soon he backed off. But he was hot and stayed hot and looked like he'd go for iron any moment.

"Just 'cause you're wearing a star don't mean you're bulletproof," he said.

I turned my back on Bell. "Thanks, Sammy."

"Don't thank me. He's right. Quit sniffing around and get on with the hanging."

I got out of there and wondered whether to go visit Rosie. But hell, Rosie's place was full of them T-Bar boys, and Crayfish himself, so I thought maybe I'd go talk to Big Lulu, who ran the Home Comfort, where one could hire several temporary wives.

Big Lulu was a rival of Rosie, and half a block away, but Lulu had a different clientele, mostly shopkeepers, bankers, tent preachers, traveling salesmen, piano tuners, and folks like that who wanted all the comforts of home, especially when there weren't any comforts of home available to those fellers. And Crayfish was there as often as he was at Rosie's, singing fine old hymns around the parlor organ, joking with one of them wives that made the gents comfy, or taking tea and crumpets in the parlor with a few of the gals.

I had in mind a little conversation about Rocco.

TWENTY-TWO

Big Lulu's was sure a nice place, with a homey parlor where lots of swell folks gathered. I went in there, and felt right at home. Big Lulu herself was at the parlor organ, wearing a gray wrapper with purple petunias on it, just like my ma's. She was a little on the plump and curvy side, but lots of fellers preferred that to skinny and bony.

She was playin' "Rock of the Ages," and some fellers were singing away. I saw George Waller, the mayor, warbling away so that his Adam's apple sort of wiggled his red bow tie. After that, Big Lulu paged through some other music and started in on "Nearer My God to Thee," which was real nice. It was a good song for tenors, but was all right for baritones.

She had horsehair sofas and chairs in there, and ivory lace curtains, and some Brussels carpets on the plank floor, so it was all fixed up good. After a bit, one of them young ladies of hers, all dressed up in lavender gauze, came out with a tea cart and began dishing up hot tea from a blue pot. She smiled and offered me some, but I was waiting to talk to Big Lulu, so she turned to a drummer that was in town selling schnapps, and offered him some. He licked his lips and smiled.

Finally, Big Lulu, she wrapped up her concert, and everybody was feeling real uplifted, and she turned to me.

"You want something, Sheriff, or shouldn't I ask?"

"Well, yes, I'd like to talk with you private."

"Well, that's five dollars, same as everybody."

"No, I mean talk with you about stuff."

"Boy, my mouth isn't where the action is so I'd want six dollars."

"No, I mean just ask questions."

"I get schoolboys in here all the time asking questions."

"All right, I'll just ask them right here at the organ."

"I charge extra for public performances, Sheriff."

I sure was feelin' slow. I couldn't get the right words to tell her I was there on sheriff business. So I just decided to plunge in.

"You know Rocco, the one that King Bragg shot?"

"Do I know him? Did I know Rocco? I knew him from top to bottom."

"What I want to know is, did he rent some of your nice girls for Crayfish Ruble?"

She frowned. "He rented them but didn't return them. He always said they decided to catch the stagecoach to Denver and Crayfish paid for the tickets. I lost a couple of my best temporaries that way. He'd come in and offer me thirty-five a week plus board to rent a lady, so I didn't have to feed anyone, and I thought Crayfish was cheap, but who was I to complain? Long as he fed the girls, that was fine with me."

"So Rocco would rent girls for Crayfish, and sometimes not bring them back?"

She sighed. "Is that news to you?"

"Yep, it's news. What did you think of Rocco?"

She smiled. "Woowoo," she said.

Danged if I could make sense of that.

"Do you miss him?"

"Honey, he was my favorite gentleman."

"You any idea why King Bragg killed him?"

"I never believed the Bragg boy did it," she said. "Honey, I got customers, I gotta go now — unless you want to join our

245

Special Tuesday Half Price Happy Hour, including drinks and ladies."

"No, no, I'm heading for the square," I said.

I hardly got clear of her before she was playing "Down by the River."

I got out into the sunlight. I sucked in some fresh air, and kept on doing it. Truth is, I was glad to get out of there. I was about ready to suffocate in there, so I gulped in lots of fresh springtime air on my way back to the courthouse square where the gallows was going up.

When I got there, it looked pretty near done, and the Cleggs was just winding things up with a little stair they'd built that would take me and the prisoner up to that platform. There sure was a bunch of spectators. Some young mamas was holding their little tykes up so they could see the gallows, and telling the little fellers to behave themselves.

Lem Clegg spotted me and came on over. "You're just in time, Sheriff. We've got to put up the noose and test the whole shebang. You say your deputy can tie the knot?"

"DeGraff, yep, he says he can."

"And I need some canvas bags and some rocks. How much does that boy weigh?"

"Oh, maybe a hundred twenty, thirty."

"Well, we'll test it out with some canvas bags with that much stone in them. Make sure everything works. We wouldn't want anything to go wrong now, would we?"

"No, sir, I ain't counting on it."

"Well, you get the noose and we'll fill some sacks with rock."

"I've got some canvas bags," a feller said. It was Alphonse Smythe, the postmaster. "Good stout mailbags," he said.

"Those'll work," Lemuel Clegg said.

Smythe hightailed to the post office to fetch a couple of them bags. A bag full of rocks should test her out all right.

"I'll get DeGraff and the rope," I said.

I found both in the office. "You got to make Clegg a noose now," I said.

"I can do that," he said. "I've made a few."

We got the hemp rope and headed back there. DeGraff, he knew what he was up to, and it made me wonder some about how he'd spent his earlier years. He laid out the rope on the platform, and made a sort of N with one end of it. I sure didn't know how that would get turned into a noose, but he went right ahead with the loose end and pretty quick he was making them coils, six in all, and then tied it up. It was a noose, all right.

"I thought them nooses had thirteen

coils," I said.

"No, that's just superstition. They'd be too hard to handle. Six coils is about right. The coils keep the rope from going in reverse. Once she tightens, it's real hard to pull it loose. That makes sure the condemned gets strangled good and proper. That rope just slams the airpipe shut. The knot is always put a little to the left, and that snaps the neck. Some say the knot itself does it, but I think it's just the twist, it being off-center, does it. Anyway, done right, the condemned is totally ruined. Not a twitch, except they soil their britches."

He fetched him a ladder and climbed up to the crossbar and slung the rope over it.

"Now that boy's about five seven or eight, right?"

"I guess that's right."

"I'll fix it for a four-foot drop. That's enough. Too long a drop, and it pulls the head clear off. That's not being respectful of the deceased, even though the spectators like to see it. You get a hanging where the head comes off, and them schoolchildren talk about it for a week. So a shorter drop, that's better. Too short, though, and it doesn't snap the neck. So it's got to be done just right."

"We don't need the mailbags," Clegg said.

"My boy Barter, he's the same size as King Bragg, and he can just step in here."

"You sure you know what's what?" I asked.

"Oh, sure," Clegg said. "Barter, you fetch yourself up here and stand right on that trap there. Right smack in the middle."

The boy, a grinning fool, just hopped up there and stood on that trap.

"Now, Sheriff," Clegg said, "This here trap will drop when you pull that lever over there. It's nothing but a stick on a pivot, but when that stick clears, the old trap will drop right smart. Go pull her slow and steady."

"But your boy's standing on it."

"He's not connected to a rope. Just pull her."

"Are you set, Barter?" I asked.

"Good as gold," he said.

"All right then." I yanked the stick, and sure enough, the trap swung down and the boy dropped straight through that hole in the deck and landed in a heap on the new green grass of the courthouse square. He laughed, and got himself up. There was lots of whistling and cheering around there. I hadn't realized that there was plumb fifty people watching.

"All right, I'll push that trap up and swing

the lever back," Lem Clegg said. "It sure works good. That kid of mine dropped like a ton of bricks."

He put the trap up and the lever in place and ducked out from under the platform.

"All right, Barter, you stand here on the trap and let Deputy DeGraff fit the noose to you. You and the condemned is just about a perfect match," Clegg said.

The boy stepped out on the trap, and De-Graff was about to drop that big old noose over his head, but I didn't like it.

"Whoa up. Barter, boy, you get off that trap. The deputy can fit you out with a noose without you standing there."

"Nobody's pulling any levers," the boy said. "I ain't afraid."

"Well, I am."

I guess he took me serious, because he did step back off that trap onto solid platform, and DeGraff dropped that noose over his neck and then began adjusting the length of the rope from the crosspiece. He had simply wrapped the rope three or four times from the crosspiece, and now he pulled the coils tighter until he'd taken some of the slack out. He left two or three feet of slack in there, so I'd have some wiggle room when I laid that noose over King Bragg, but pretty soon he had it all rigged up, and the rope tied down tight on the crosspiece.

"All right, Barter, you can pull that thing off now," his father said. "And let that be a lesson to you. Make an honest living and you'll never wear a necktie."

Barter smiled like some fool, and did a little jig, dancing real close to the trap, and then doffed the noose. It sort of swung there, in the wind, twisting and turning with the spring breezes. I thought it was a mighty fine job.

That's when Smythe returned with a couple of mail sacks.

"I guess we won't be needing 'em, Alphonse," I said.

Smythe sure looked disappointed. "I was hoping to see one drop," he said.

"Well, if you want to see a mailbag drop, we'll just do her," I said.

We hunted around for some rock. There wasn't much on the square, but a bunch of fellers did come up with a few dozen stones after scouting things out, and we filled the mailbag and drew the strings shut.

"Weighs a good hundred pounds, Alphonse," I said.

The postmaster eagerly dragged the bag onto the trap and centered it precisely.

"You want to pull that lever, Alphonse?"

"Sure do," he said. "I'll send the U. S. Mail to Eternity."

By now there was some crowd, all right, taking it all in. I seen some rotten boys whistling and cheering. There were half a dozen ladies too, in summer bonnets and straw hats.

"Now this here's serious business," I said. "We're making sure justice is done, so you mind your manners."

Them brats just grinned at me. I knew half of them and told them I'd be talking to their pa if they didn't behave. But they just snickered like it was the funniest thing they ever heard.

Smythe took hold of the lever and looked around real solemn. He was pretending that the mail bag full of rocks was the real thing. He stared at the rocks, and then at everyone hanging around there, and then slowly, majestically, he inched that lever along until suddenly that trap dropped and that bag of rocks hit the turf. He grinned. Them rotten boys all whistled and cheered.

"Now it's my turn," a redheaded kid said.

"No, it ain't your turn."

"How come?"

"Because you ain't old enough. And it's none of your business."

"I'm almost as old as you are."

He had me there, but I ignored him.

Smythe, he dragged his mailbag out from under the platform and began doling out rocks to that pack of boys. "You put these back where you got them," he said.

"I'm keeping mine for a souvenir," said that rotten redhead.

"This show's over," I said loudly. It wasn't just them boys I was talking to. It was half the town of Doubtful, seemed like. Pretty soon they all drifted off, except for a few fellers who thought they knew everything, and were pointing at the noose, or at the gallows, or at the platform and the trap, sharing all that stuff they had in their heads with anyone in sight.

DeGraff picked up the spare rope and carried it off to the sheriff office, and the Cleggs cleaned up their stuff and left, and then I was alone on the square, with that dangling noose, and wondering whether what was gonna happen in a couple of days could be called justice at all — or a mistake.

TWENTY-THREE

Things was real quiet. No one was trying to bust into the jail to hang the boy, or to bust him out. I told DeGraff to keep a sharp eye out anyway.

"We got two more days to guard him, and then it'll be over," I said.

"Over for the kid, that's for sure," he said.

My deputies had done a good job. They'd worked long hours, night and day. They were forted up and ready for trouble. And I made sure the prisoner got fed and cared for, which was something I plain insisted on after I found them fellers were ignoring the boy's needs. Still, I sure wished it was over. I didn't like the tension in town, like a ticking bomb, with all them T-Bar men of Ruble's running around, drinking too much, and scaring the people half to death. They was all armed, some of them with two guns, as if they were just itching for trouble. But it wasn't illegal for them to carry, so they did.

I unlocked the jail door and went in there to King Bragg's cell, and found him staring at the ceiling. He barely acknowledged that I was standing there. I guess when a feller knows he's gonna get hanged in forty-eight hours or so, he's got a lot on his mind.

"You all right?" I asked.

He stared at me as if that was the dumbest question ever asked. Lot of people stare at me like that. My ma used to say you could learn more from the way people looked at you than from what they were saying.

"Tell me again how it happened you went into the Last Chance that day," I said.

He just stared at me and said nothing.

"Tell me, boy. I want to know."

"I went in because I was stupid," the kid said. "All it cost me was my life."

He'd about given up; I could see that. There weren't any tears, any anger, any hope left in him.

"Well, just so I know, what did happen?"

"There's a record in the courthouse. I was tried, remember?"

"I want you to tell it, King."

"Why?"

"Just tell it."

255

He stared silently at the ceiling, but then he did talk. "I went in there — the Sampling Room, because that's where all the Anchormen go, and that's where we were welcome. I got a drink from Mrs. Gladstone. She always said I was too young for hard liquor, so she'd give me a draft beer, like I wasn't grown up yet."

"You were wearing your sidearm?"

"Of course. My father gave it to me. I'd practiced until I was good. I burnt more powder than anyone in the valley. It was for the Anchor Ranch. For my father. We had the oldest and best place, and we're not going to let someone like Crayfish Ruble drive us out."

"There was more to it, wasn't there?"

He glanced at me and then away. "I wanted to be the top dog."

"That was a dream, wasn't it? Being the fastest gun, the one no one could ever beat?"

"Stupid dream," he said.

"So she poured some suds for you, and you were sipping real quiet, and then Plug Parsons come in."

"Yeah, he walked in. He spotted me right off. Said he'd been looking for me all afternoon. Mrs. Gladstone told me Plug had been checking every few minutes to see if I was around town. The T-Bar outfit wanted to talk to me, or something."

"What did Plug do?"

"He's a big man, sort of all chest and shoulders, with a neck as thick as a gate-post. He came over, looked me up and down, and said, "Kid, if you think you're man enough, come next door. Talk to Crayfish.""

"That all?"

King Bragg shut his eyes. "That's all."

"You followed him out?"

"No. He left. I finished my beer. I checked my loads and made sure my holster was loose. Then I went over to the Last Chance."

I wanted to tell him that was the dumbest stunt a kid could do, but I guess he'd figured that out. So I just let him lie there. Maybe he'd say some more.

"There were a bunch in there," he said, "and they were waiting for the son of Admiral Bragg to walk through the door."

"Who?"

"Who cares now?" he replied.

"I care."

"I looked around pretty close. If they were going to rag me, I wanted to know who I was up against. They were looking for trouble, and I'd give it to them." He eyed me. "That's why I've lived so long."

"And there was Upward behind the bar,

and Plug Parsons, right?"

"And Crayfish, and Carter Bell, and those three I guess I killed, Rocco and Foxy Jonas and Weasel Jonas."

"I count seven, unless I got more fingers than I thought," I said. "But in the trial, Upward said he didn't see nothing because he was in the storeroom; Plug Parsons and Carter Bell, they were the witnesses against you. What happened to Crayfish himself? He was there?"

"Yes. Sort of licking his chops."

"You ordered a drink?"

"Red-eye. That's a man's drink. Mrs. Gladstone had gotten to me, serving beer. So I ordered some firewater."

"Then what?"

"Someone hit me. That's all I know. I woke up in the sawdust with an empty gun."

"You have a bump on your head when someone hit you?"

"No. I don't remember. I had a headache."

"Where'd you get hit?"

The boy just shrugged and turned away.

"Kid, I'm going to look into some things. You get some rest now."

"I'll get more rest than I want in a few hours."

I left him staring into the low ceiling, locked the jailhouse door, and headed out.

Crayfish had been there. That didn't come up at the trial. Crayfish Ruble was there, with Plug Parsons, and them two brothers that was mavericking calves, and Rocco, who was sort of pimping for Ruble and maybe stirring his own pot a little. And they goaded the poor kid into going in there.

Doubtful was a different town now that the gallows was up and a noose was twirling in the breeze. People no longer stopped to stare at it, but hurried past, not wanting to see it. All the brats that hung around there had vanished, and the only person I saw was a poor old grandma in black, sitting on a bench and staring at that noose. Some crows settled on the crosspiece and crapped on the platform, and I thought I'd clean it up real good. I didn't want any bird stuff on there when the day came. I wanted the gallows to be real clean, spotless, like a gallows should be.

I headed for the Last Chance Saloon, but Sammy Upward hadn't opened up yet. It was still morning, and none of the joints on Saloon Row had opened up. I rattled the door, but no one came along. I walked around to the back door, on the alley, where it stank all to hell, and that was open. I walked right into that place and yelled, but Upward wasn't around.

Maybe I was trespassing, but I didn't let it worry me none. There was a whole book of laws I was supposed to know, but I never could get 'em figured out, so I just ignored 'em and did what needed doing. What needed doing this time was a real careful search. I wanted to know if there were bullet holes in the walls, and where the bullets came from. If the Bragg boy had pulled his revolver while standing at the bar, he'd have shot away from the bar, or at least along it. So I kept looking around for holes in the wood, and I found a few. That T-Bar bunch cut loose now and then, so there was holes every which way. It didn't do me no good to try to pick out the ones that the Bragg boy put there. The other thing I wanted to see was what Upward saw when he was hiding from all the lead flying around after King Bragg started pulling the trigger. So I got over to the storeroom, and looked out at where Bragg was standing, and at the rest of the place, and then I stepped back, just as Sammy Upward would have ducked when them six-guns started spitting lead pills.

I also wanted to see what Upward kept under the bar. He had a sawed-off double-barrel shotgun resting there, a billy club, and way back in a dark corner, a little blue glass bottle with an eyedropper top on it. I reached for that, since I'd never seen the like. It didn't have any label on it, but it was a blue bottle just like pharmacists use, and there wasn't a thing that was telling me what it was. I got real curious about that bottle, and slid her into my pocket. I thought I'd see what was in there, and maybe try it out. Maybe Upward had the measles or something, and needed a dose of laudanum, or whatever they give for measles or mumps or the pox.

It fit into my pocket. If Sammy Upward was missing his medicine, he'd probably start asking his customers who done it, and meanwhile I'd find out what I could about the stuff.

I sure didn't learn much of anything in there. I didn't see any bullet holes in the bar itself, like maybe someone was shooting at Sammy. Maybe no one shot at Sammy because of his scattergun down there. He sure had a way of keeping order in the Last Chance Saloon. Anyway, I nipped that blue bottle, figuring I could get it back in there about as easily as I took it out, if I came early enough. So I slid into the alley. It was quiet and smelly back there, after the usual night's piss had been cut loose, and now there wasn't a soul anywhere.

That suited me fine. I eased out to Wyoming Street, and headed straight toward the square, with that big gallows sitting there waiting to be put to good use. The Cleggs sure done it right. Them uprights was straight and true, and the crossbar, it just laid flat up there and supported that rope. But I turned off to get to the sheriff office and jail, and passed by a couple of T-Bar riders lounging there, making sure Crayfish knew everyone that went in or came out. It wasn't illegal for them to sit there, but I didn't like it.

DeGraff opened up and let me in, and I was glad because he was the one I wanted to talk to. He sure knew a lot of stuff. He'd been a crook once, but went straight, and there was nothing better for a deputy than someone who knew how all that stuff worked. That was a lot more than I knew.

"I got a riddle for you," I said. I pulled the blue bottle out of my shirt pocket and handed it to him. He looked it over, noting there wasn't no label on it. "What's that stuff?"

"Beats me," he said.

"I got to tell you I lifted it out of the Last Chance, and if it's nothing, I got to return it."

"You stole it?"

"Well, I sorta borrowed her. It was down under Sammy Upward's bar, hidden in a corner, near his scattergun, way out of sight."

"That makes it real interesting," he said. "A little blue bottle hidden under a bar."

He unscrewed the top and sniffed, and sniffed again. "I'm not sure. We'll have to try it out."

"Try what?"

"Knockout drops. Chloral hydrate. About two drops of this stuff in someone's drink, and he's flat on his ass."

"Like being hit over the head?"

"Sort of. It'll drop you like you was poleaxed. Sip it, and bam, you're down for a while, and you don't know what end is up until it wears off. This is Sammy's?"

"He's the only one tending bar there."

"I could be wrong," DeGraff said. "It could be laudanum or something like that. Pain killer. Women buy laudanum in blue bottles and put a couple drops in water or tea to sleep good."

"Maybe that's all it is," I said. "I wouldn't know a drug from a dog turd."

"We'll find out," DeGraff said.

"Don't you go killing any dogs," I said.

He grinned. "I like cats myself. Cats clean the rats out of my cabin. But I won't try this on dogs. I got a better idea."

"You're making me itchy, DeGraff."

He had a quart bottle of sarsaparilla sitting on the desk. He went to the door and found them two T-Bar riders sitting on the steps, taking the sun.

"You boys want some sarsaparilla?" he asked. "You're looking hot. And it's a long time until King Bragg swings from that rope."

"Don't mind if I do," said one.

"Sounds fine to me," said the other. "Crayfish posted us here and we gotta stay, and sometimes I think I'll resign and take some other job."

"I'll bring some out," DeGraff said. "Can't let you in."

He found a couple of cloudy tumblers that hadn't been washed since Noah built his ark, and poured a little sarsaparilla in each, and then unscrewed the eyedropper and put two drops of that stuff in each tumbler and swirled it a little. Then he added a little more sarsaparilla until he had himself the cocktail he wanted.

"You sure that's the right amount?" I asked.

"I've done this a few times," DeGraff said.

You sure have to wonder about a deputy like that.

He took them two tumblers out the door and handed one to each of them riders, and they each took a good swaller, and another. Nothing happened. They just sat there for a little bit, sipping the sarsaparilla until they both tumbled over like ten pins getting hit with a ball.

"You sure they're alive?" I asked.

DeGraff laughed. He wasn't a laugher, but this time he laughed until all I saw was a row of yeller teeth. "It's chloral hydrate," he said.

I couldn't even pronounce it, but it sure worked real good.

TWENTY-FOUR

Judge Nippers was parked at his desk, soaking up spirits, which he sucked from a little flask he held tenderly in one beefy hand.

He eyed me from under bushy brows. "You've come to beg off. Forget it. Hang the bastard," he said.

"Well, I think we shouldn't, or at least until we get it looked at some more."

Nippers sucked cheerfully awhile, and exhaled, and sighed. "I knew it. You're going to give me some sort of flapdoodle excuse."

"Well, sir, I don't think the kid done it. And until we find out, I'd like to put off the big event."

He cocked a fat eyebrow. "You got evidence?"

"Sort of," I said. "Enough to put her on hold a little."

"Do you know what evidence is?"

"Well, sir, it's facts, I imagine."

266

"Relevant facts. That's good. I never would have thought you had it in you. Have you ever read the Territory of Wyoming Code?"

"No, sir."

"Or Blackstone's Commentaries?"

"No, sir."

"What have you read?"

"McGuffey's Reader, sir. To the fifth grade."

"Ah, now we're getting somewhere. You want me to stay the execution. Why?"

"I don't think he's the right feller, Your Honor. Here's what I think. The T-Bar bunch lured him over there to the Last Chance, and the barkeep, Sammy Upward, he fed the kid some knockout drops, and then someone there pulled King Bragg's revolver and shot them three crooks and put the gun back into King's hand when he woke up, and everyone testified he done it."

Nippers' beetle brows crawled upward and downward and upward, and a rusty laugh belched from his chapped lips. "That so? That's the evidence?"

"We tried out the bottle of knockout drops, DeGraff did. We knocked out the two T-Bar men."

"And where did you get this delicious concoction?"

"I was poking around under Sammy Upward's bar."

"Without a search warrant."

"I heard of them things once or twice."

"I'm glad you're educated, Sheriff Pickens. Now, where's the evidence?"

"That's it, sir."

I gave Nippers the bottle. He uncorked his flask and sipped and corked. "The ordeals a judge has to go through," he said. "It's enough to bring on gout." He waited for the yeller stuff in the flask to take hold some. "Now, then, did Upward confess to doing this? Or has a witness come forth saying he did it to the Bragg boy? Did Upward confess to owning the blue bottle you purloined?"

"What's purloined, sir? That's a new one."

"Stole, filched, nipped, snatched, swiped."

"No, he don't even know I snatched it."

"Now, let's see. Is there now a witness saying someone in there who wasn't King Bragg pumped lead into the deceased? And with King Bragg's revolver?"

"Nope, not yet."

"So there's no evidence for this baroque theory of yours."

"It ain't broke yet, sir, but it's swaybacked some."

"Swaybacked law. Now that's a corker,"

the judge said. "Pickens, you're a master of swaybacked law. Now so far, there's not a shred of evidence. Not a scintilla."

"A what?"

"Oh, never mind. You think this is enough to stay the execution?"

"That's what I'm thinkin'."

"You taking to pitying that little fart?"

"He ain't little at all, sir. Maybe it's because he's in his father's shadow he seems little."

"Speaking of his alleged family, Sheriff. First of all, this punk wanders around Doubtful with his shiny new six-gun looking for folks to plant in the local cemetery. Then he exterminates three gents from the rival outfit. Then, when we finally convict him with a proper trial, what happens? His old man shoots you in the outhouse and stages a mock hanging so that you get the message: If the twerp dies, so do you. And then this Admiral Bragg and his nefarious daughter Queen show up in your jail with enough hardware under the cloth to start a Cuban Revolution. Then they take me to lunch, and she's got a revolver aimed at my crotch, and they're planning on kidnapping me so they have a hostage they can trade for the twerp. Only, you wandered in and foiled their plot. Then his daughter starts

workin' on you, using wiles and charms —
Don't sit there blushing, Pickens. I got eyes.
If they can't spring the twerp one way,
they'll try another. She's got no shame, and
Admiral Bragg's got no shame, and they're
playing you for a sucker."

"Well, she took me to some graves on the
T-Bar I'm going to look at, sir."

Old Nippers, he cocked one of them
woolly brows and snorted.

"McGuffey Readers, fifth grade," he said.
"Here's what you do. Read the Territorial
Code. Get someone to help you with the
big words. Now get that blue bottle back to
Upward and apologize to him for poking
around in there. And get yourself ready for
a hanging, because that's what's going to
happen in a little while. You understand,
Sheriff?"

"I guess you ain't gonna postpone it any."

"No, and if you pester me again, I'll probably speed it up."

I escaped from there. Them fumes was
giving me a headache. It sure was nice
outside, where the air was fresh. That
reminded me. I hadn't looked in on Critter
for a few days, and I'd better get over there
before he had a fit.

He was in his stall at Turk's livery barn,
just like always. When he seen me coming,

he kicked the gate. I thought I'd been shot. He put a rear hoof into that wood so loud it sounded like a cannon. Then he did it again, splintering the planks some, by way of greeting me.

"I guess you been missing me," I said.

He kicked the side of the stall and snorted. Then he kicked again just to make the point.

"I guess I better back you out before you kill me," I said. I wasn't going in there when he was feeling a little unhappy. So I opened the stall gate, expecting him to pile out of there, but he just stood there, his ears laid back, his head turned just enough to keep an eye on me. I knew what he wanted. He wanted me to slide in beside him, so he could kill me.

"If you don't want to come out, I'll just shut the gate on you," I said.

He hammered both walls with his hooves, and then reared up and piled his front hooves into the head of the stall, for good measure.

That brought Turk. "Judas Priest," he said. "Give me a new barn when it's over."

"He's a friendly nag," I said. "He just takes it personal when he's penned up."

"Well, take him somewhere else."

I turned to the hoss. "Critter, you're dog food," I said.

Critter sighed, and backed out quietly.

"It takes some persuading," I said.

"That horse should be shot," Turk said. "You owe me."

Critter yawned. Turk stared, itching to get his knife and slit Critter's throat, but then he wheeled away.

"Critter, you gotta stop annoying people," I said.

Critter licked his chops and waited, while I brushed him down and threw a blanket and saddle on him, and bridled him up. The truth of it was, I just wanted to escape town a bit. It was getting so I didn't want to hang around Doubtful, and maybe a good ride would quiet me down some, and maybe quiet Critter too. I was strung tight as a piano wire, and maybe Critter was reading that in me. He was pretty quick to pick up how I was feeling, and truth to tell, I was so tight-strung that I didn't know how I'd get through the next two days, and maybe the next week because I didn't know how I'd feel after dropping that boy, who might or might not be guilty. Truth to tell, I was feeling real bad. I never thought when I took the sheriff job I'd be dropping people off a gallows and my hand would pull the lever that would send them to hell. It didn't seem the same as meeting someone in a fair fight.

It just seemed real bad, and it was gnawing at my gizzard all the time now.

I took Critter up Wyoming Street, and he was so happy he was prancing along. But then Sammy Upward came bounding out, and I reined up.

"Hey, you leaving?"

"Just for some air. This town's tight as a drum."

"I got a prowler."

"A prowler? Something get took?"

"Well, maybe."

"What're you missing?"

"Just some stuff — nothing to worry you about. But if you see anyone poking around my bar, let me know quick, eh?"

"You're missing something, Sammy. I gotta know what it is and what it's worth."

"I'm not missing a damned thing," Upward said. "I just got some suspicions, is all."

"I can't look for something I don't know what it is, or why it was took."

"Forget it. Just some loose bar stuff."

"Well, I'll keep an eye out for loose bar stuff, Sammy."

"I shouldn't have bothered. It was nothing," Upward said, and ducked inside.

Now that was sure saying something to me. He wasn't owning up to what was missing, and that was real interesting to me.

"Well, Critter, that was like a confession," I said. "Sammy should've just kept his trap shut, but he didn't think of that."

Critter, he just yawned, and headed for the open country up the road. He sure was one happy horse. It was a fine June day, not too hot, and he was kicking up his heels and thinking thoughts about mares, but that was all he could manage, the way he was fixed. I think about women all the time, and I'm not fixed. A year or so ago, I'd met a real sweet one named Pepper Baker, with big blue eyes. But her pa sent her off to finishing school back East, mostly to finish me. Still, me and Pepper weren't done, and when she came back we'd see about a few things. So I was in the same mood as Critter, only more so.

We loped up the valley a mile or so, and I was just thinkin' about turning back, when up ahead, coming over the brow of a hill, was a mess of horsemen, like an army of beetles. Twenty, thirty, maybe even more, and they wasn't in a hurry, just walking quietly toward me. Now that made me real curious, so I just reined in Critter, and let that bunch approach me. By the time they got within shouting distance, I knew what that crowd was. It was the whole damned

Anchor Ranch, on the move.

It sure smelled like trouble.

Sure enough, there was Admiral Bragg on that blooded horse of his leading the bunch, and next to him that Queen, riding astride shamelessly. And first thing I noticed was that every manjack of them was armed to the teeth. Admiral, he had a matched pair of sidearms. Behind him came an army, including Big Nose George, wearing a sidearm and carrying a longer one. Next to him was Alvin Ream, with a bandolier over his shoulder and a pair of irons hanging from his hips. And sure enough, there was Smiley Thistlethwaite, and his pal Spitting Sam, the pair of them looking like they was ready for trouble. There was a bunch more behind them, mostly riders for the brand, some of them well outfitted with one or two irons.

I didn't know what to make of this march upon Doubtful, but I knew who I was and what I am. I'm a peace officer. And this bunch looked like an army.

I sat Critter, who laid back his ears and waited to bite and kick all them animals coming his way. I might have enjoyed that. Most of them were blooded horses, because Admiral Bragg liked good horseflesh. Me, I like whatever thrives, and I don't much care how the beast looks.

So I sat there and waited, and before long Bragg pulled up, and Queen beside him.

"Afternoon, Sheriff," he said.

"You wouldn't be heading for Doubtful, would you?"

"Free country," he said.

"We're not going to have any fights in Doubtful," I said.

"We've come to say good-bye to my boy," Bragg said, pretty solemn.

"You're welcome to do that, but not with weapons. There's gonna be no weapons on anyone day after tomorrow."

"Is there a law against it?"

"Disturbing the peace," I said.

"Peace! You call the day when they break my boy's neck the peace?"

I felt a little sorry for the man; I didn't want to do what I had to do, and he didn't want me to do it. But things were in motion that I couldn't change, and we'd just have to live with it because that's how it was.

I saw how Queen was sort of hiding her hands in all them hiked up skirts she was wearing, for a change. I thought she'd shoot a sheriff if it came to that.

"Miss Queen, you'll want to put your hands in plain sight," I said. "I get plumb itchy."

She didn't move a muscle, and it wasn't hard to figure where that muzzle under there was pointing.

"Miss Queen, you just smile now, and I'll smile back."

She didn't smile none.

I decided to make up some rules as I went along. "There's gonna be no weapons at the hanging. Neither you nor any of Crayfish Ruble's bunch neither. We'll see to it. You're going to leave all your arms at the Sampling Room, and the T-Bar men are going to leave all theirs at the Last Chance Saloon. That's what you can expect. We're going to see to it that justice is done proper by the Territory of Wyoming."

I got me a snicker from Spitting Sam, and a few smirks from some of the others.

"All right," I said. "Anyone wearing arms, both sides, that day is gonna get tossed into my pen. And you'll stay there for a while."

"You done, Sheriff?" asked Admiral Bragg.

"For the moment," I said.

All them riders whirled by me, with little glances my way, and a few little gestures, and a few smirks. And then me and Critter were standing in the lonely road, watching that army head for Doubtful.

TWENTY-FIVE

It sure was tempting to run ahead of that bunch and try to stop the bloodbath when they rode into Doubtful. There'd be two gangs, one in favor of the hanging and one against it, and ready to kill one another, and maybe half the town in the process. It sure looked like real bad business.

But then I sort of took stock. They weren't there to fight each other. The Braggs, they were there in sorrow and grief. The T-Bar bunch was there to see justice done. They would probably settle down for the long wait, while the sands of time ran out for the Bragg boy, and then they'd just pack up and leave. I hoped so anyway.

There was something else on my mind. Now that both outfits were going to be in town, I had the whole countryside pretty much to myself. I had a little business out there, on Crayfish Ruble's range. Queen had shown me some graves in a side gully of a

278

nameless gulch, and it was time to find out what that was about. But that ranch was a long piece away.

"Critter," I said, "are you good for a run?"

He yawned, chewed on his bit, and dropped a few apples. That meant he was bored, and a run would make life real interesting in the day of a horse.

"All right then, we're going on a round trip to hell," I said.

He took off so fast he almost pitched me out of my saddle, but I got upright again, and reined him in a little. He steadied into a rocking-chair lope, so easy it was like walking for any two-legged critters. He wasn't even breathing hard, but just to play it safe, I tugged him down to a trot once in a while. A trot is the most infernal tail-banging gait on earth, but it rests a horse if he can stand the hammering of a hind-end on his backbone. I kept to a trot only long enough to give him a rest, because more than five minutes of it turned my butt into hamburger.

We kept at it, through country so big it was beyond the imagination of folks living cramped lives back East. Here was land as far as the eye could see, land without a building on it, land enough for everyone. The West was land, lots of land, land for the poor, the people starting out, the helpless, the brave, and everything in between. The trouble came when some fellers with a lot of self-importance wanted all the land and then some, and began pushing others out. Those fellers wanted the best valleys, the best water, the biggest ranch house, and a private army besides, just so they could be the biggest rooster. Admiral Bragg was like that. Crayfish Ruble had different goals. He wanted to get rich and get out. He wanted to run cows until there was no grass, make his pile, and head for the biggest town. If he left a land that was gnawed down to dirt, that didn't bother him none, so long as he got the last dime he could get out of the place.

Neither of them fellers was the sort to admire, in my book. Bragg had tried to scare or push me into letting loose of his boy, and that didn't sit well with me. But this trip I was going to look at Ruble's place, because there was something real bad going on, and I sure wanted to find out what, and whether it had some connection to this hanging that was coming up.

Critter, he began to darken around the neck and withers, so I slowed him down. I didn't want him to get too sweated up. We had a long ride back to Doubtful coming pretty quick. Besides, I wanted a little time to enjoy the air, the puffball clouds, the snowy mountains off to the west, and the greened up pastures, mostly giant wide gulches, that shone with spring wildflowers and emerald grasses. I sure didn't know why I was being a sheriff in Doubtful when I could be out in this, riding the range for some outfit. We never know why we make choices, and I still didn't know why I'd stuck with the sheriff job. I wasn't even qualified for it. Judge Nippers had just reminded me I didn't even know the law.

Critter and me, we rode into the yard at Ruble's headquarters and sure enough, we was met by Rudy Beaver, a shotgun-toting old boy I knew a little. He was a bearded old coot, a real cowman and not a gun hawk. He was grimy, and water-eyed and I don't think he'd washed for a year or so. He'd be the one to leave behind, looking after the place and the cows, making sure there was feed and water, and the dogs got fed, and the coyotes got shot, and lightning didn't burn down the barn.

He hobbled my way, cradling a shotgun in his arm, and I settled down Critter and waited for Beaver to come closer. I didn't know much about him, but I'd heard he had done some hard time somewhere long ago, and was mean as horseshoe nails.

I was wearing my star, which caught the sun and made my visit official. He just hobbled up, with the muzzle of that scatter-gun pointing low, like it should. He seemed peaceable enough.

"Sheriff? You need something?" he asked. "You ain't at the hanging?"

"That's in two days," I said. "No, I'm just looking around, and I'm hoping you'll answer a few questions for me, since I just don't know much of anything about this outfit."

He nodded, sort of wary, and laid a gob of spit at Critter's hooves.

"Your bunch is in town waiting for the hanging, and they're behaving themselves, far as I know."

"Far as you know," he said, a wicked twinkle in his eyes.

I sort of thought I might like the old boy. "Your boss is living in Rosie's. Half your crew's in there too. That and the Last Chance Saloon."

"Yeah, that's him all right. He's gotta have a woman every hour of every day. Me, I got weary of that about age thirty, and I've been happier ever since."

"Crayfish likes some women more than others?"

The old boy grinned. "Yep."

I waited a while. The old guy was happy to have someone to talk to. They'd left him alone on the place for days and he was feeling the itch to flap his gums a little. "He wants women that have never seen the inside of a church and don't ever plan to," he said.

"What doesn't he like about church ladies, Rudy?"

The feller just wheezed. "You're a dumbass, Sheriff," he said.

"Is it true he rented a few and brought them out here?"

Rudy Beaver stared into space. "I didn't hear what you said, so it never was asked," he said.

"I heard that his man Rocco rented some gals and brought them here."

Rudy, he worked up a gob and spat it into the clay. "You looking for something, Sheriff?"

"Yes, there's four graves out there." I pointed toward the lonely hills to the north. "They're girls Rocco brought here. Girls that never returned. The madams were told the girls hopped a stagecoach to Denver."

Rudy Beaver was turning real quiet.

"You know something about it," I said. It wasn't a question.

"I didn't have a thing to do with it. You done, Sheriff?"

"No, not done. Until this is cleared up, everyone on the place is under suspicion, and that includes you."

"How'd you find out about it?"

"How'd you know about it, Rudy?"

"Rocco. He liked hinting at things."

"Like killing girls?"

"I don't think Rocco did it. I think the boss himself got tired of them and did it."

"How'd they die?"

Rudy Beaver shrugged. "I never wanted to know."

"Why did you hide this from the law? Why didn't you come to town and tell me?"

"You don't know nothing, Sheriff, and you didn't learn a thing from me. Zat clear?"

"Did Crayfish kill Rocco?"

"No, that Bragg kid did it."

"Why would the kid do that?"

"Beats me, Sheriff. But that Bragg kid solved all of Crayfish's problems for him, including the calf-rustling of those Jonas boys."

"Sure is wonderful, how King Bragg solved all of Crayfish's problems, ain't it?"

Rudy, he just wheezed and laughed and winked at me.

"That Double Plus brand I saw on some

calves, is that Crayfish's new brand?"

"It is now, because the Jonas boys sort of surrendered it."

"So when we hang King Bragg, it'll all be over. The killer got hanged. Crayfish won't have anyone rustling his calves, and there won't be anyone blackmailing him either."

Rudy Beaver wheezed. "You're a real card, Sheriff. Watch your back!"

"How do you know this stuff, Rudy?"

"Because I'm deaf and read lips mostly."

"So nobody cares what they say around you?"

"Naw . . . Lookee here, Sheriff. I'm crazy and I made all this up."

"Just imagining it, I guess."

He peered right into my face. "Just thinking stuff up to pass the time. It sure is slow, nothing happening on the place. You get the picture? Just thinking stuff up. I'm crazy as a loon."

"Crayfish, he's a fine fellow, right?"

The old boy eyed me. "Nobody pays attention to a crazy old loon like me. Don't you either. I'm half blind, half deaf, and half crazy, so what I think don't matter none."

"You see any of it? You see Catfish do anything to them girls?"

"Don't even know what you're talking

about, dammit. Now you're trespassing on private property. This is the T-Bar ranch, mister, so you just turn that horse around and get your skinny butt off the place."

"How did Crayfish kill them women out there?"

"How should I know!"

"You like to imagine things. That's what you said. So in your mind, when you're thinking about stuff around here, how did Crayfish do it?"

"Bullwhip."

That sure startled me some. I got so I could hardly sit on Critter. "Bullwhip? Whipping those girls he rented from the parlor houses? Whipping them to death?"

"Just my notions floating around in my head," Rudy said. "Don't matter none."

"But you saw it happen? Saw Crayfish —"

"Naw, I'm the hear no evil see no evil do no evil monkey." He laughed, and suddenly lifted the shotgun until its twin bores were poking straight at me.

"Okay, okay, I'm going," I said.

"You never was here. I just think up things to pass the time away."

"Okay, I never was here. See ya."

I slowly wheeled Critter around, before he kicked Rudy to death, and we edged away. Them black bores of that scattergun sure

286

made my back itch.

The shotgun blast startled me bad; Critter began pitching and screeching. I was lifted out of the saddle a couple of times, and then Critter started to whirl and fishtail and rear up and land hard.

But Rudy Beaver, he was wheezing and slapping his knee, and waving that shotgun all over the place. I looked around for bright red blood on me or Critter, but didn't see nothing at all, just brown horse and a lot of me sitting on him. That buckshot had splintered some rough-sawn wood of a shed nearby.

"You ha! Hoo we! Har de har," Beaver was yelling. He had pulled his ancient, sweat-stained hat off, and was flapping it as fast as he flapped his gums. "I bagged a sheriff!"

It didn't take any encouragement from me for Critter to bolt out of there. I peered back, fearful that the old boy would be lifting that shotgun, and I'd have to shoot him, which I knew I could do. But Rudy Beaver had settled down, and was watching the sheriff of Puma County, Wyoming, skedaddle away from there.

If this was evidence, I reckoned that Judge Nippers would have no part of it. But it was something I'd sure tell Nippers about if he was sober enough to listen. I thought a little about sliding back there and nabbing the old boy and hauling into Doubtful and making him tell his story to the judge, but I knew by the time I'd gotten Rudy Beaver in front of the judge, he'd either act crazy or claim he didn't know a thing. Which, come to think of it, might just be true.

TWENTY-SIX

Critter was really dragging when we got back to Doubtful late in the evening. This time, his box stall would look pretty good to him. I steered him up Wyoming Street, wondering whether I'd find bodies stacked like cordwood, and blood blackening the street, but everything looked peaceful. There was a few lanterns still lit on Saloon Row, and I figured them riders were all celebrating.

This was Christmas for some of them boys. Two rival outfits, looking to kill each other, both in town, maybe sixty men all with itchy trigger fingers, drinking red-eye and working up to some fun. Some fellers dream of lollipops at Christmas, but these men dreamed of powder and bullets and having a fine old time.

But it hadn't happened this night. I turned Critter toward the livery barn, rode him straight into the aisle, and slid off. It was dark, so I scouted out a hurricane lamp in the office, lit it, and hung it on a peg in the aisle. I pulled Critter's saddle and blanket and bridle off, haltered him, brushed him down some, let him drink at the trough, and then led him to his stall. I swear, he trotted right in. Usually it's all pull and haul, but this time he was ready for some oats and sleep. I fed him some of them lousy oats Turk kept around there, and forked some hay in, and closed the gate behind him. Critter and I had come to an understanding. He wouldn't kill me and I wouldn't kill him.

That was more than I could say for half the men in town this night. I strolled through the darkness toward the square, and saw the gallows sitting there, the noose dangling in the moonlight. That noose was now the center of the whole town. Everything in Doubtful radiated outward from that noose. A night wind started it swinging, back and forth, twisting this way and that. There was no one else around there, so I hiked over to the sheriff office and knocked. Burtell let me in.

"Everything quiet?" I asked.

"Sort of," he said. "I think every rider for the Anchor Ranch rode up to that gallows and studied it some."

"The prisoner is all right?"

"Last I looked. His pa and his sister want to see him, and I said they should talk to you in the morning."

"I guess they have a right to, tomorrow being the boy's last full day," I said.

He grinned. "I'll make sure Queen is clean."

"No, we aren't going to search them. We're going to let them in back there."

"Not pat them down? After all they done to bust him out?"

"I'm going to let them go back and see the boy without us staring at them or waving a gun at them. That's how it'll be."

"Well, I don't want to be here when they come out of the cells shooting."

"Bragg loves that boy. His sister does too. They got a right to spend some time back there on his last day."

"After we remove all those derringers and hacksaws and shotguns she's got in her skirts."

I sighed. "That's how I want it. Leave her and her pa alone. Tell the rest, if I'm not here."

"You're nuts, Pickens."

"I think the boy didn't do it. I think he got roped into something, and I think I'm going to be hanging a boy who didn't shoot anyone."

Burtell stared at me like I was loco.

"I've got to talk to the judge." I said.

"Now? Middle of the night?"

"A witness I talked with says it was Crayfish that killed the three T-Bar men."

Burtell whistled. "That could change things some," he said. "Who was it?"

"Rudy Beaver."

Burtell, he started laughing so bad I just wanted to get outside.

I hiked over to Judge Nippers' house through pitch-dark streets and knocked. I knocked again and again, and nothing happened. Pretty soon a lamp glowed in the back, and then the door creaked open and the judge stuck a short gun into my ribs. He was wearing one of them nightshirts. You'd never catch me in one, dead or alive. I've always been a pants man. He eyed me up and down while I stood there, and finally decided I was the sheriff.

"Next time, I'll shoot first," he said. "This better be important, or it'll be your neck in the noose."

He motioned me in, closed and bolted the door, and led me into the kitchen, where the lamp burned.

"This better be important," he said again.

"I was poking around on the T-Bar, and

got to talking to that old cowboy Rudy Beaver, who's guarding the place. He told me all about how Crayfish tortured and killed the girls that Rocco rented from the cathouses and took out there, and he said Rocco was going to tattle on Crayfish, so Crayfish shot him and shot the Jonas brothers that were mavericking calves. Only then the old coot turned around and said he was just inventing it all, and he didn't say any of it and I didn't hear it. Is that good enough evidence for you to stay the execution?"

"Evidence? Did anyone see Crayfish shoot those three? What evidence? Pickens, you hang that boy good and proper, no matter whether he did it or not. We're going to have justice here. You understand me?"

"I sorta don't."

"You bring in evidence, someone who actually saw Crayfish shoot those punks, and I'll cancel the show for you."

"Yes, sir."

"I want evidence. I'll spell it out. E-V-A-D-E-N-C-E."

"I understand, Your Honor."

He turned down the wick. "And don't wake me up in the middle of the night again. Especially for this nonsense."

He let me out, and I heard the door thunder shut and the bolt drop. It sure was dark. I'd never seen it so dark. There were stars up there, but nothing to guide me and I hardly knew where to go. Back to my room at Belle's boardinghouse, I supposed, but I didn't want to sleep. I didn't know what I wanted to do, except pull this case wide open and find out for sure what happened there in the Last Chance that evening. I had a day and a half to find out, and after that it would be too late. I didn't know how to stop this freight train that was roaring down the rails.

I found my way to the boardinghouse in the blackest night I'd ever known, and climbed the creaking stairs to my room, mostly by feeling my way. I was just at my door when I sensed it was ajar, and when I slid my hand out, it was ajar, all right. I pulled my Colt .44 out, and jammed the door open with my boot. At the same time I jumped aside, waiting for the assassin bullet to sail by. But it didn't happen.

"I don't bite," she said.

I wasn't sure who was in there, but a flaring lucifer resolved that for me. The match revealed Queen, sitting on my bunk. She was dressed proper all in blue, but I wasn't sure she intended to stay that way, from the brief smile she flashed at me. She lit another match and put it to the kerosene lamp and replaced the chimney, and stared at me primly.

"You can put that away," she said, staring at my piece.

"How do I know you ain't got a mess of hardware on you?" I said. "Last time we knocked heads together, you must have been carrying more metal than a hardware store under all them skirts."

She pouted a little. "Well, I'm not," she said. "I'll prove it."

She stood up and started undoing all them buttons down her front.

"Wait!" I said, wondering why the devil I was trying to make her stop. "Wait!" I said, real weak. I had to say that just for the record, so no one could accuse me of not slowing her down, but she was a spitfire and ignored me, so I quit whispering it.

She wasn't in a stopping mood, and pretty quick she had that blue dress undone and was pulling it off, and I was too interested in all that to tell her to get it back on again. Then she was in her chemise and petticoat, or whatever all that stuff is called, and this time she did stop, sort of. She ran her hands all over herself, showing me that she didn't have any derringers or howitzers or Gatling guns or mortars or torpedoes or grenades hidden in there somewheres.

"Happy now?" she asked.

I nodded. She sure was pretty.

"Then you can put your revolver back where it came from."

I obeyed her. I'm danged if I can understand why I'd obey her and why she could boss me around, but that's what she was up to.

"Am I pretty?" she asked.

"Miss Queen, you don't need to ask."

She smiled. "That's the first civilized thing you've ever said to me."

"I'm not used to smiles. When you're with your pa, all I get is cold stares."

She sighed. "When I'm with my father, I'm under his big thumb. I can't escape it. I'm his wind-up toy. You know what he tells his friends about me? She's a pistol. That's what he calls me." She smiled again. "But right now, I'm not under anyone's thumb. And he thinks I'm sound asleep in the hotel. And the only pistol I'm interested in is yours."

I was sure getting sweaty. "See here, miss, I'm a peace officer," I said, because I couldn't think of anything else.

"I like you, Cotton. That's one reason I'm here. The other reason is to find out about my brother. Whether there's anything new —"

"I knew it. You think you can tempt me into cutting him loose."

She stared at me so bleakly I felt bad.

"I didn't mean that," I said. "I sure don't have women figured out yet. My ma, she always told me I needed a sister."

But the coldness was back in her face again. The other Queen. She rose, and reached for the blue dress.

"I'm trying to save your brother," I said. "I don't think he did it. I get little pieces together, but the judge, he just hits them with a flyswatter."

She stared, and sat on my bunk. "You don't think he did it?"

"No, I don't. But trying to stop this here execution is like trying to stop an express train. I can't even slow it down."

She sat there in the lamplight, her gold flesh glowing, the blue dress crumpled in her lap. She looked to be at the brink of tears. If there's anything that scares me, it's a woman crying.

"I got this here blue glass eyedropper bottle out of the Last Chance," I said. "Sammy Upward had it hid under the bar beside his sawed-off scattergun. My deputy, he told me it was knockout drops, so we tried it on a couple of them T-Bar men outside the sheriff office. Sure enough, they

297

keeled over. So I sort of figured Upward put some of that stuff into King's red-eye when he went over there."

"What happened to the T-Bar men?"

"They come to, after dozing a little in the sunlight, and thought they'd had a nap."

Well, I told her the rest of the story. How I'd talked to Big Lulu about them women that Crayfish rented, and about Rocco, and about riding out there this long day and talking with that old loco coyote Rudy Beaver. I told her how Beaver spilled a lot of beans and then said it was all talk, and didn't mean a thing, and he was just thinkin' up stuff, and I should forget he ever said it. I told her what I think happened; Crayfish had a few executions in mind, for them two Jonas brothers that was altering brands on the ranch, and for Rocco, who was gonna spill the beans on him unless he got a lot of money. And how Crayfish got the idea of pinning it all on her brother, who was always wandering around with that shiny gun looking for someone to bury six feet under. And I told her I just now got back from waking up Judge Nippers and telling him the whole shebang, but he said I ain't got one piece of evidence, real evidence, and it's all just notions and thin air, and he told me not to bother him no more, not unless I got a real witness, someone who saw Crayfish kill them three T-Bar men in the Last Chance Saloon.

"We knew he didn't do it," she cried. "We knew it."

"I ain't got any proof yet," I said. "And now I got one and a half days. Tomorrow, and the next morning before eleven o'clock."

"He didn't do it, he didn't do it," she said.

"I don't know, one way or the other. But I'll keep trying to shake the truth out of someone. There's a few witnesses. Plug Parsons, Carter Bell —"

"You'll try, Cotton?"

"What do you think I've been doing?"

"Oh, Cotton." She clutched me to her and hugged tight, and next I knew she was crying hot tears into my cheek, and I held her for a long time, till she finally pulled free, wiped her eyes, took my hand and kissed it, got into her blue dress, and slid into the night.

TWENTY-SEVEN

I sure didn't want to get up the next day. I just wanted to pull my blanket over me and stay in the sack until the day went away. And if I thought that day would be bad, the following day, Doomsday, would be far worse. It was too late for me to escape now. I'd do my job, or brand myself as a coward the rest of my life.

So I made myself put my two bony feet on the planks and get up. It wasn't Saturday yet, so I had a few days to go before I would head for the tonsorial parlor and rent the tin tub in the back room while Billy the Barber poured a few buckets of warm water into it. I was feeling more dirty on the inside than the outside anyway. I wanted to stop this freight train, and I couldn't even flag down the engineer. I wished I was ten times smarter, but all I got is what I was born with. My pa used to say a man's hands were worth more than his brain anyway, which is about the only thing I had in my favor.

I finally got myself together and headed into the streets of Doubtful. There sure was something in the air. No sooner did I step outside than I could sense it. The town was strung tight as a fiddle string, and there wasn't no shoppers or women or such on the streets. What with two rival outfits in town, both armed to the hilt, and a hanging, most everyone figured there'd be a lot of flying lead and it would be better to stay behind walls. After my morning trip to Belle's outhouse, I took a look around. There were a few gunslicks around, for sure, most of them lounging in the shade of them storefronts. I knew the sort. They was just itching to start the ball rolling. They pretended to build themselves smokes, standing there, but they were looking slit-eyed at everything and everyone moving around, especially anyone from the other outfit. And most of that wolf pack was wearing a sidearm, but two or three was openly toting around scatterguns. They sure were itching to spill some bright blood onto the clay of Doubtful.

I spotted Big Nose George blowing snot out of one nostril, and Smiley Thistlethwaite leaning against a storefront. And I watched Plug Parsons deliberately walk down the middle of Wyoming Street, bullnecked and mostly bald, and not wearing a sidearm at all just to show off. Carter Bell was lounging in front of Toady's Beanery, like he would decide who'd go into the place for breakfast and who wouldn't. He had twin Peacemakers poking from low-slung holsters tied down to his thighs. I thought that was sort of dumb, but that's how Bell wanted it.

I decided to hold off on breakfast. Right now, there was a few things that needed doing. I walked toward Rosie's whorehouse, and knew that every one of them gunslicks was watching my progress, and a few were thinking it might be the day's entertainment to shoot me in the back. But I had a task to do. I was the peace officer, and my business was to enforce the peace, and I would do it one way or another.

Rosie's was over on the next street, on Red Light Row, but now there was no lamps burning and the girls was all snoring away. They hardly got up before noon unless there was some urgent customer with a lot of cash in his britches, in which case they came awake fast.

Rosie's was where I'd likely find Crayfish Ruble. I was gonna talk to him, and to Admiral Bragg, first off. So I walked up the wooden steps to Rosie's in broad daylight and knocked. Pretty soon, the door opened up, and Street let me in. Street was some sort of Hell's Kitchen hooligan from back East, and Rosie paid him good to keep order in her parlor house. I've always liked Street. He could hammer someone to pulp and break a few bones and never get close to homicide. And besides, he was as good as a spare deputy sheriff if I needed him. His only vice was emptying the pockets of customers now and then, when they was off doing what they came to Rosie's to do. But no one ever complained about Street.

He nodded, licked the gap where he was missing three front teeth, and let me pass.

"I need to talk to Crayfish."

"He's busy now, Sheriff."

"Right now."

Street sighed. "He ain't gonna like it."

I watched Street lumber up the stairs toward Rosie's suite at the rear, and knew that he'd have Crayfish in tow when he returned. But it took a while, and when Crayfish showed up, Street wasn't with him, and I found myself wishing I'd come a few hours later. Crayfish was buck naked, walking down them stairs to the parlor. Bare-ass naked and yawning.

"Well? This better be good," he said.

It ain't easy being sheriff sometimes, and

this was one of them. Somehow, he was forcing me to think up what I wanted to say.

"I'm here to tell you that no one wears sidearms or carries any sort of weapon at the hanging tomorrow. Any of your men are carrying, my deputies will throw them into my jail and they'll stay there until they pay the fine for disturbing the peace. And it'll take a month before I'll give them their sidearms back. Get that?"

Crayfish, he just scratched his hairy chest with his hairy arm. "Good luck," he said, and smiled.

"You got the word," I said.

He yawned. "You shouldn't have got me up. Now I'll go pester Rosie, who likes her beauty sleep, and the whole day will be off to a bad start."

He started up the stairs, and I watched his skinny butt vanish, and got out of there.

Next stop would be the hotel. I started up Wyoming Street, and I swear there was a mess of eyes focused on me, stares coming at me from shadowed doorways, windows, alleys, and from the plank walks in front of the stores. I never felt so looked-at in all my days. That was all right. Let them see the law walking up Wyoming Street. Let them know the law was still keeping the peace in

Doubtful. For the moment anyway. That was the thing about this day. Peaceful one moment, but what about the next?

Still, it was sunny and cheerful, so I walked past all them lounging riders and gunslicks, and pretty quick I was at the hotel. I found Admiral Bragg and Queen in the dining room, like I'd hoped. They was just finishing up so I headed for their table.

Queen gave me a cold stare and lifted that chin of hers a notch or two. This was the other Queen, the one when her pa was ruling the roost. I didn't see the slightest nod, not the smallest signal that she remembered the night before, and the hug, and the tears she shed that flowed down my cheek.

"Want to talk to you, Mr. Bragg. Tomorrow, I'm forbidding sidearms at the courthouse square and anywhere else in town. We're gonna keep the peace here. Any rider wearing a sidearm or carrying a weapon, he's going to get pinched by my deputies and kept in the jail until he pays a fine for disturbing the peace. And it'll be thirty days before he can collect his guns."

"Are you quite through, Sheriff?"

"And that goes for you too. It goes for Crayfish Ruble. It goes for anyone in town. My job is to keep the peace, and it's going to be kept."

Bragg smiled. "Except for the violence done to my son. When the peaceful noose peacefully ends his peaceful life."

"That's justice, and it'll be done proper, and there'll be no arms on anyone in this town. And now you've been told. So see to it."

"Thank you, Sheriff. Your advice is always entertaining."

Queen was staring at me. And this time, there was no ice in it, only something close to tears. I nodded slightly.

"I think it is a good idea," Queen said.

Her father stared at her, his face reddening, steam rising in his boilers.

"Bullets have a way of finding the wrong targets," she said. "Please, Mr. Pickens, do what you can."

Well, I pretty near had a fit. Her sticking to her guns, and her pa looking like the safety valve was gonna blow on his boilers.

He smiled suddenly. "She takes after her mother."

"Mr. Pickens is doing everything he can — for us!" she snapped.

That done it. He arose swiftly, yanked her up, and steered her toward the rooms in back.

She refused to budge, and he dragged her

across the dining room and finally out the door.

Our eyes locked just as he propelled her into the lobby, but in that split second I saw something I can't rightly put words to. Sorrow and triumph and iron will, I guess.

"Now then, what were you saying, Sheriff?" Bragg asked.

"I'm saying that if you or your men disturb the peace in Doubtful I'll lock you all up, you especially, and toss out the key."

He smiled at that. He grinned so wide he bared some teeth, and then patted me on the shoulder.

"Give it a try, sonny boy," he said.

Meanwhile Queen, she was roaring back into the dining room, and headed straight for me, and before her pa could collect his wits and drag her off again, she came right up and kissed me square on the cheek. Then she stood there, daring her pa to have himself a heart attack.

"I'll deal with you later," he said to her.

His fist knocked me flat on my butt. I wasn't looking for it. I wasn't trying to get in the middle of a family fight. I come up hot and piled after him, but he was ready with a kick to my groin and some moves that told me that this man had some serious training. But I didn't care; I was young and hot and went after him until he pulled my .44 from its holster, and then I was so mad I knocked him across the room, spilling tables and chairs, and landed on him just about when he was getting his arm around to point my piece at me. The shot hit the ceiling. Someone screamed. I got the best of him then, and twisted his hand until he dropped the iron, and then yanked him up and hit him again.

"You're going to spend some time as my guest," I said, shaking him until his teeth rattled.

I pushed him hard, scooped up my revolver, and marched him off toward my executive suite in the jail.

Queen, she stood there dry-eyed.

"Tell your riders. If they show up armed tomorrow, they'll all go where your pa's going."

She nodded. I don't think she liked that any. But she'd do it. Word was going out to the Anchor Ranch's riders and gunslicks, so maybe something got done this morning.

"I suppose you know we'll tear your jail apart," Admiral said.

"Walk or I'll drag you."

He walked, soon resuming that disdainful way of his, as if I weren't clutching his shirt and holding my six-gun in his ribs.

Now the whole town was watching. A lot of folks had heard that shot, and they were buzzing around Doubtful like hornets on the loose, looking to see who croaked. But no one croaked. What they saw was me, dragging the boss of the biggest ranch in the valley off to my iron cages, and it sure started the mouths flapping. We got to the sheriff office and jailhouse where a couple of them T-Bar men was lounging as usual, and they sure got an eyeful, me marching the biggest cheese in the valley through my doors.

Rusty, he saw me coming and let us in.

"Book him," I said.

"For what?"

"I'll think of something," I said.

"Discharging a firearm?"

"That'll do. Anything'll do. Throw the book. Find enough stuff to keep him here for a few months."

Rusty whistled.

"Pat him down," I said.

Rusty went to work, and pulled out a double-barreled derringer from Bragg's breast pocket, and a hideout ankle knife he kept for insurance.

"You'll get these back when I feel like it," I said. "Which I don't."

I steered Admiral Bragg through the jailhouse door and then into a cell opposite his boy. The door clanged shut behind him, and he turned to stare at me so hard it looked like murder was pouring out. Which probably was about right.

He saw his son across the aisle and stared.

"Queen disobeyed me," he said to King.

King absorbed that some. "I'm glad someone finally did," the boy said.

I sure hated to have to do what I would have to do on the next day.

Admiral Bragg, he just stood there, absorbing that, and not believing it could happen to a fine feller like himself. He clasped them iron bars, and pulled on them, and tugged on them and shoved on them, and I swear them bars bent a little, but maybe it was just my imagination. For the moment, King Bragg's pa was there, across from his doomed boy, and maybe the boy would teach him a few manners.

TWENTY-EIGHT

Mr. Bragg, he sure was noisy back there. He wanted to post bail. He wanted his lawyer, Stokes. He even wanted Judge Nippers, even though a few days earlier he'd tried to make the judge a hostage. I told him I'd let him out at eleven the next day. He had something to watch about then.

"What are you holding me for?" he asked.

"I'll think of something."

"It's illegal, keeping me in here without charges."

"Maybe so. I'll read a law book sometime and find out."

"Watch your back," he said.

That's how he thought. If he couldn't get what he wanted, try a threat. But I would watch my back, all right.

I left him in Rusty's care, but Rusty didn't like it none, and said he was tired of being persecuted and maybe I should give him a day off or some hardship pay. I told him he could have a day off soon as we cleaned out the cells, which would be tomorrow, unless we had to throw a few more cowboys in between now and the big event.

"I guess I have to put up with it," he said. "What do you want me to feed him?"

That reminded me of something. "King Bragg gets whatever he wants for a last meal. Ask him what he wants, and we'll do what we can for him. It's owed him, a good last chow down."

"Ask him yourself," Rusty said. He was being ornery, now that I'd put two Braggs in his care. Next thing, he'd ask for a raise or a month-long leave.

"I'm going out," I said.

"And leaving me here."

"Watch the place, and keep them scatter-guns handy."

Rusty sighed, poured some week-old java from the speckled blue pot on the stove, and settled into my chair.

I was glad to get outa there, and into some fresh morning air. The sun was out, but it wasn't a nice day. The whole town of Doubtful was brooding, waiting for the next day, or maybe waiting to get past the next day. I saw Mayor Waller putting up some broadsides on his store, advertising "Courthouse Specials" at twenty percent off. I guess

Courthouse Specials were really hanging specials, which he would offer to the mob that would assemble on that patch of grass the next morning. But just now, there wasn't a soul on the streets.

I made my way to Saloon Row, hoping to find Mrs. Gladstone open for business. I pushed through the batwing doors into the Sampling Room, which was empty except for one drunk asleep on the billiard table. Mrs. Gladstone saw me and froze into an iceberg. I didn't blame her any; she'd tried and lost, and I was halfway embarrassed myself. She stood behind her bar, rigid and frosty, waiting.

"You sure are a beautiful woman," I said.

That didn't melt one particle of ice, but maybe a little more heat would.

"I guess you're just about the finest gal in the territory," I said.

She stood unmoving.

"You had something about King Bragg that you was thinkin' of sharing with me the other evening."

She studied me, a sudden gentleness in her face. Then she nodded slowly.

"Something you thought might help the boy."

"It wasn't anything," she said. "Not something that would stop this — this legalized murder."

"But you thought it was something."

She was plain embarrassed. But then she started in a little. "You know, they were waiting for King. They waited a long time for King to come here. That foreman, Plug Parsons, came over here from the Last Chance every few minutes, looked around here, and left."

"He'd come in with several T-Bar men. Their horses were tied out front."

"Crayfish with them?"

"Why, yes. He was there."

"How do you know that?"

"I saw them ride up to the hitch rail."

"Who else?"

"I don't know all those T-Bar people. But the ones that got killed, they came too."

"The Jonas brothers and Rocco?"

"Rocco I know. Every woman in Doubtful knows Rocco."

"And Parsons came looking for King Bragg?"

"Like clockwork. Every few minutes, he just poked his head in here, looked around, and left."

"What did he say?"

"His boss wanted to talk to King."

"After the shooting, what happened?"

"I saw Crayfish in the alley. He had come

out to, you know, relieve himself."

"And did he go back in to the Last Chance?"

"I don't know, Sheriff. I was wondering about the shots next door."

"Is that it? What you wanted to tell me about?"

"It isn't very much, Mr. Pickens."

"Would you come tell this to Judge Nippers?"

"But I would have to close up."

"Maybe it's worth closing up."

Well, she did. She pulled off her apron, fluffed up her hair some, and closed her saloon.

"Do you think it will help that boy?" she asked.

I couldn't say. "The judge wants a witness, someone who saw Crayfish pull the trigger on those three."

We walked up empty streets, but I saw some of them riders lurking in the shadows, seeing what kind of trouble they could stir up. There was T-Bar men on the left, and Anchor Ranch men on the right, staring at each other across the wide clay street. Every last one of them was armed.

Me, I walked Mrs. Gladstone straight up the middle.

Judge Nippers wasn't in yet, but I set Mrs.

Gladstone down and went hunting for him. He was over in the beanery polishing off some pig knuckle stew, and I told him Mrs. Gladstone had a thing or two to say.

He belched some, and looked unhappy, like he hadn't started his daily sipping yet, and it was keeping him out of sorts. But he paid up, started along with me on his gouty feet, past the gallows with that noose dangling there for all the world to see, and finally we got up the stairs to his chambers, where Mrs. Gladstone sat primly. She looked him over as she would a potential lover, while he pushed a skeleton key into the door and let us all into his office.

"What now?" he asked.

I nodded to Mrs. Gladstone, and she sort of started in.

But she didn't get halfway through before he interrupted.

"You see those three get shot?"

"No, Your Honor," she said.

"So you don't have a shred of evidence," he said.

"It's worth a stay of the execution until we find out more. There's a real question here," I said. "I'm no lawyer, but I know there's doubts, real doubts."

He looked at me impatiently. "Sheriff, you come up with evidence. Evidence. And don't bother me again unless you've got a witness."

I guess that was how all this would end.

"Until then, that boy's guilty as sin," he said.

I helped Mrs. Gladstone to her feet. She was fighting back tears, but Nippers pretended not to notice.

We walked all the way back. It seemed like the longest walk I ever took, like we were walking back into sadness.

I went into the Sampling Room with her, and next I knew, she was crying her heart out. She left the CLOSED sign in the window. She just sat there on a chair, too broken to move, the tears leaking down those soft cheeks. I ached to help her, but there wasn't a thing I could do. I couldn't help her and I couldn't help the boy and I couldn't help this town of Doubtful.

The door opened and Queen come in. I'd never seen her in there, and I was sure her pa never let her come close to the place, even if it was the saloon that Anchor Ranch riders always come to and called their own.

She looked at me, and at Mrs. Gladstone, whose tears flowed steadily, and she sat beside the older woman and held her hand. I thought maybe Queen was going to cry too, but she didn't. They sat there in their helplessness. There was nothing they could do, nothing I could do, nothing anyone on earth could do.

Unless I could rattle a confession out of someone, or some testimony out of someone.

It was up to me. It was always up to me. There wasn't no one to help me.

I left them two women in the closed saloon, stepped into the bright sun, not knowing where to start. But the court testimony depended on two witnesses, Plug Parsons, and Carter Bell, so I supposed that was where to start.

I didn't know where they might be, or what I'd do if I found them, but the Last Chance was right next door, and that was where they'd likely be, and where the murder of three men had happened not long before, and where I'd open the case if it was to be opened. So I sucked in some fresh June air and stared at the snow-tipped peaks off to the west. Eternity was up there somewhere, nature so big it didn't matter what a few poor folks called trouble. That reminded me I'd have to round up a preacher for the boy. He had a right to a preacher and a last prayer if he wanted it. He had a right to all of that. Most of the churches in Doubtful were served by circuit riders, since no one could afford a full-time preacher, but there'd be someone, somewhere, to pray over King Bragg, and I'd find one.

I pushed into the Last Chance, and was hit by a wall of foul air. It was sweat. Everyone in there had been sweating, and stinking the air. The smell clawed at my belly. I waited until my eyes got used to the darkness. There were plenty of T-Bar men in there, and they'd turned silent when I walked in. But I didn't see the big body of Plug Parsons, or the short and rat-faced one of Carter Bell. What I did see was a lot of riders who were wearing one or two side-arms, and whose shirts had big black sweat stains under the armpits. It wasn't real hot out, but this place was as sweated up as a racehorse after a run.

Sammy was behind the bar, eyeing me like he didn't want me in there, but I was in no mood to leave.

"Gimme a sarsparilla," I said.

Sammy looked annoyed, but he uncorked the jug of it and poured a tumbler full. He snapped the glass down so hard in front of me that it didn't take any smarts to figure how he felt just then.

I laid a dime on the bar, and he swept it away.

The sarsaparilla was warm and cheesy.

"You find what you were missing?" I asked, knowing he hadn't because them knockout drops was in my office safe.

"I'm not missing anything," he said. "False alarm. I thought I was, but I wasn't. I've got what I was looking for."

"So you never told me what you thought was missing," I said.

He shrugged. "I thought someone nipped a bottle of gin."

"But it was here?"

"Drunk up now. Crayfish, he sure likes good London gin, and has me order it in."

"Well, tomorrow it'll be over," I said. "You must be glad to see justice done. Them three that King Bragg killed, were they friends of yours?"

"Rustlers and a pimp is what they were. King Bragg did the world a favor."

"Did he shoot them in self-defense?"

Sammy eyed me cynically, like I was being dumber than usual, and then laughed smartly. "You're a card, Sheriff."

"King must've been fast, pumping six rounds into them three before they knew what hit 'em."

"They sure weren't expecting it. They were just sipping suds when they began taking on lead pills."

"Too bad you was back there and didn't see it," I said.

"That kid was wild, and when someone like him pulls an iron I don't want to be around. I'm alive to tell about it."

"Well, it'll all be over tomorrow," I said. "Justice done, and everyone in Puma County'll forget it ever happened."

"That's what we're counting on," Sammy said.

"One thing, Sammy, and I want you to spread it. No sidearms, no weapons in the courthouse square or anywhere in town tomorrow. Not one. Anyone shows up armed in any way, my deputies will toss him into the tank, and he won't see his sidearm for thirty days. And he'll be charged with disturbing the peace."

"How many men you think that's gonna stop?" Sammy asked.

"As many as we can arrest and haul away," I said. "I've told Crayfish. He's got the word. I've told Admiral. He's got the word. Now I'm telling these here men, so they got the word. And next I'm gonna tell the Anchor Ranchmen, so they get the word. There's not going to be one person on the courthouse square tomorrow who hasn't got the word. We're going to have a peaceful and proper hanging, and there's not going to be any trouble."

I knew every man in that place was listening real hard.

TWENTY-NINE

The sun was getting low, and so was I, when Caboose, the little breed boy that Big Lulu hired, came trotting up.

"Miss Lulu, she wants to see you. Someone in there worrying her," he said.

"Caboose, you tell Lulu I'll get on over real quick."

Caboose trotted toward Red Light Row, and I started in behind, wondering what was troubling such a pleasant and religious old madam.

When I did get there, Big Lulu was doing her afternoon concert at the piano in the parlor. This time it was "Faith of Our Fathers," which got a little mangled because some of them keys were out of tune. Doubtful must have been five hundred miles from the nearest piano tuner, which didn't help the town anytime it came to music.

I peered around, and didn't see much of any trouble brewing, except that over in a corner was Carter Bell. And none too sober either. I'd been looking for Carter Bell. He was one of them witnesses I wanted to rattle a little. He sure was different from the other riders. He liked to fancy himself up some, but he still looked like a rat. He scraped his cheeks most every day, and scrubbed his britches most every Sunday, and got himself clipped and combed so often he must've spent a lot of the wage that Crayfish Ruble laid on him once a month in the tonsorial parlor. He knew he had a little polish, and used it on women. The girls in the houses all liked him because he smelled good, or at least didn't stink, like the rest of them cowboys. He was skinny and the girls didn't mind that he looked like a rodent. He carried a revolver like the rest, but it was all for show. I don't think he could hit an elephant at ten feet. That gun of his, it was a show gun, with pearly grips and some inlaid gold. It sure shone, but I wondered if he ever scrubbed the black powder out of the barrel.

I was glad to see him; I'd been looking for him and for Plug Parsons, seeing as how they were the only witnesses to the killing of them three T-Bar men. But I didn't approach him just then. Big Lulu wanted me, so I just hovered around the upright piano and waited for her to wind up. She was singing away, reading the sheet music. "Modern Hymns," it said. Her girls were serving the town fathers, as usual. There was the mayor, George Waller, being uplifted as usual. After closing the store, he would go to Big Lulu's for the happy hymn time, and a half-price girl sometimes.

There was two, three girls in gauzy gowns serving whatever there was to serve around there, and I spent my time sort of peering through that gauze and being uplifted by them hymns. But all good things come to an end, or maybe all ends come to good things, but finally Big Lulu finished her matinee and turned to me real quiet.

"Carter Bell's scaring us. He's over there pouring red-eye down, and getting angry, and even pulling his gun out and waving it around."

"Any reason?"

She sighed. "He says he's the next Rocco."

"Next Rocco?"

"Crayfish told him he would replace Rocco. Get women for Crayfish. Take care of all that, for a five-a-month pay raise."

"And Carter didn't refuse?"

"You don't refuse Crayfish. You know that. And Crayfish told him if there was trouble, he'd get what Rocco got."

Suddenly, I was real interested. "Which was?"

Big Lulu smiled. "A bullet through the heart, dearie."

"It don't make sense to me," I said. "It being King Bragg's bullet."

She played a gloomy chord on the piano, striking a few of them notes that was out of tune. "You've always been a little slow, Pickens."

She started in on "Amazing Grace," and sang it in a wobbly warble. "Amazing Grace, how sweet the sound . . ."

Pretty soon Mayor Waller and half them businessmen in Doubtful was singing right along with her. It sure made the place seem holy, and put just the right mood on them when they took advantage of the half-price happy hour girls. I'd heard tell Mayor Waller sometimes performed temporary weddings, because sometimes a feller came in there that just wanted to be married for half an hour or so, so the mayor would do the ceremony and Big Lulu would play the wedding music, and off the feller would go with the gal, and everyone would be happy.

I got a couple of tumblers of red-eye and headed over to Carter Bell, who was sitting in that dark corner looking real blue.

"Maybe this'll cheer you up, Carter," I

said. "I saw you sitting here looking like things ain't so good, so I come along with a little liquid comfort."

He eyed me with a faint smile. "I could use it," he said, and swiftly drank the whole tumbler. That must have been a red-hot volcano going down, because the red-eye hadn't been aged for more than a few weeks. But he just belched and patted his mouth. He was real genteel that way, not like the usual cowboy. I heard tell once he even used talcum powder on his cheeks after he shaved. I sure don't know what a feller like that was doing around Doubtful, but there's all sorts of strange types floating around.

"I'm pretty blue myself," I said, "having to hang a feller in the morning."

"Well, he earned it," Bell said.

"Guess he did. Either that or he deserved a medal for bumping off some miserable specimens — like Rocco."

"Rocco . . . yeah, he deserved it all right, trying to double-cross Mr. Ruble."

"That's what I heard," I said. "Sure was fortunate for Crayfish that the Bragg boy come along and kilt off Rocco."

"Just between you and me . . . ," he said, and then quit. He wasn't gonna spill any beans if he could help it.

"Big Lulu says you've got Rocco's job," I said, fishing a little.

"Five-dollar raise and bring him women whenever he wants one. Yeah, I got the job even if I didn't want it. That's how he is. You do what he says."

"You could always pack up and vamoose," I said.

He stared hard at me. "Maybe I should. Sooner or later Crayfish . . ."

His voice trailed off again, and I felt like I was so near to something important that I could hardly stand it. But it just didn't happen. Carter Bell, drunk or not, wasn't going to spill his guts to the sheriff. He wasn't going to say what happened that afternoon when they lured the Bragg boy in, knocked him flat, and someone, probably Crayfish himself, made use of the boy's gun and then stuck it in the boy's hand.

"You know what, Carter? My friend the judge, Nippers himself, really enjoyed that trial, and keeps askin' about all the witnesses and how they're doing. You want to share some real good bourbon with him? It ain't red-eye. It's good Kentucky. He's a real good drinker, and likes company."

"What are you talking about, Sheriff?"

"Old Nippers, he sure enjoyed that trial. He'd sure enjoy a little palaver with you."

"I'm not inclined to drink with a judge, Sheriff. I'm not in that class of people."

"No, not drink. Swap a few stories, tell a few yarns. I bet you could tell him some dandies."

"Well, I could," he said. He eyed me. "Lead the way. I don't know if I'll stay there. I've got a few stories to tell him, and I'll just see what he thinks of some cowboy."

I steered him out of the parlor, and got me a grateful nod from Big Lulu, who was plenty happy to see Bell out of her place, with no damage done.

She started in on "Onward, Christian Soldiers" as we slid outside. The shadows were growing long, and that kid was lighting her red lamp that hung on a bracket at the door.

"Is there something here I'm not figuring out?" Bell asked.

"If there is, I wish someone would tell it to me," I said. "Nippers is the stubbornest mule in Doubtful, and when he believes something, there's no way to shake him loose of it. He always said your testimony and Plug Parsons' testimony was what put the noose on King Bragg."

Bell wasn't talking anymore, but neither did he quit me, so we hiked up Wyoming Street, toward the courthouse square. Nippers would be in; in fact, he'd be there all night, hoping as much as I was hoping that someone would give him a reason to call off the necktie party. Maybe Carter Bell would give him a reason. But it wouldn't happen if the Sheriff of Puma County was hanging around listening to the pair of them drink and talk.

I steered Bell up the stairs and down a dark hallway to a lamplit open door. Just as I figured, there was old Axel Nippers in his swivel chair, about half asleep. He wouldn't sleep this night any more than I would, and he wouldn't budge from his office through the endless night.

"Ah!" He came awake. "You, is it? What you got for me, eh?"

"This here's Carter Bell, Judge."

"Of course it is. How could it be anyone else? Pickens, there are times when I wonder about you."

I sure didn't know what to say to that. "I wonder about me too, Your Honor."

He motioned to Bell. "Pull up that stool and have a nip with me."

Bell, he sort of eyed me, but he did it.

"The judge has the best Kentucky in the Territory," I said.

Nippers handed Bell his slender bottle, and Bell took a nip.

"I thought you fellers might have a fine time," I said. "Bell here's replacing Rocco as Crayfish's fetch-it man."

"You don't say? What do you fetch, eh?"

I kind of figured I'd best get out of there and let that there conversation go wherever it would go.

"Bell got a five-dollar raise for it," I said. "Five dollars or get out of Puma County."

Nippers' eyebrows raised like a pair of caterpillars, and lowered again.

"Have a nip and tell me," he said.

I left the judge and Carter Bell in there, and hurried away. I doubted that Bell would spill any beans, but that sure was what I hoped. Even pie-eyed, Bell wouldn't say anything that would contradict his testimony in court. Unless he slipped up.

It sure was lonely in that dark hallway, where my boots echoed on the floor. I slid down in the dark and out the front door, where it was twilight and the last light caught the noose dangling from the gallows, ready for use at eleven.

I didn't much care to stand there in the chill. Some cold air was lowering off the mountains, and it sent a shiver up my spine. I was about to get back to the sheriff office when I seen a ghost. That's what she seemed at first, but it turned out to be Queen,

331

dressed in white, with a white shawl around her neck. She come on over and stood near me, and we both were lost in our thoughts, or maybe we didn't have a thing to say. I was going to be her brother's hangman, and that kept us quiet.

"How's my father?" she asked finally.

"Don't know. I've been trying to come up with something, but I ain't got anywhere."

"I'm glad you hauled him away."

"He's just the same as anyone else. Assaulting a peace officer, and he gets himself in trouble."

"He's never spent an hour in a jail."

"It's been most of a day now," I said. "I'll let him go when the time comes."

I heard the catch in her breath. "I told the ranch people not to come armed. I think they'll heed me."

"You've done a good thing."

"No, I haven't done anything good. There's no good in the world. There's only grief and tears. And death."

I kept quiet. A breeze was twirling the noose. She saw it too.

"I have to decide what to do with King after — after it's over," she said. "My father thought it never would be — over. He was ready to shoot his way out. But it's going to be over, and we need a grave, and since he can't think of it, I have to. I want it to be a good place for my brother. I want it to be a place where I can go, and sit on the grass, and think of him and look at my memories, one after another, and not let go of him."

"If I could change it, Miss Bragg, I surely would."

"You don't have to tell me."

"I'll look after your father," I said.

"He needs looking after. No one ever looked after him before, because we were all too busy obeying."

I took her hand and held it a moment, and let go. She continued her vigil at the gallows, while I pushed through the darkness.

THIRTY

I found Rusty and Burtell holding the fort.

"Any trouble out there?" Rusty asked.

"It's quiet. You fellers go on home. I'm staying here tonight, and can't sleep anyway."

"But what if they rush you, try to spring the kid?"

"You'll hear it, and I'll have help."

"Doesn't seem right," Rusty said.

"Here's what you do. Rusty, you patrol Saloon Row and then call it quits. Burtell, you check the rest of the town and call it quits. And I'll see you both in the morning. You'll need your sleep because tomorrow we got to be sharp."

Rusty stared at me. "It's you that's carrying a lot on your back."

"Yes, I am," I said.

They slid into the night, and I barred the door behind them. There was only one kerosene lamp lit, and the whole office was thick with shadow, which is how I wanted it. I unlocked the jail door, and sure enough, Admiral Bragg started bellowing at me.

"You let me out or you'll pay for it," he said.

"You're staying put."

"Clean my pisspot."

"I'll do that in a little bit."

He clasped the bars and rattled them. It seemed almost like he could bend them apart and step through and come at me. But the bars held.

Then he picked up the bucket and threw the contents at me. The bucket clanged hard against the bars. There wasn't much in it, and it missed me and puddled in the aisle.

"Kind of a stink to live with, ain't it?" I said.

I stepped over the puddle and headed for King Bragg's cell, down one and across.

He lay on his iron bunk, staring upward. He seemed lost to the world already, as if he had somehow passed away, but he was alive still.

"They treated you all right?" I asked.

He didn't reply.

"You get the meal you wanted?"

"I don't want any food. What good is a last meal? A fancy last meal does nothing for a man about to die; it's offered so the hangman can feel better."

I guessed that was true.

"You want to come out and stretch in my office?"

He stared, absorbing that, and nodded.

I unlocked, and stepped aside, wary and ready for anything. But the kid just stepped through, and walked ahead of me down the aisle past his pa.

"If you can let him out, you can let me out," Admiral said.

"I'd be a foolish sheriff if I did that," I said.

"You already are," he said. "And you won't be sheriff for long. You'll be out of office — one way or other — in hours."

"Thanks for the warning," I said. "Your daughter's told your men to put their guns away tomorrow."

Bragg loosed an animal yowl that scraped my nerves, but I ignored him. I let the kid out in the office, ready for trouble, but he just stood there in that lamplight.

"Have a seat," I said.

King Bragg sat, staring at the walls, at the gun rack, at the stuff on my desk, and then sort of sagged into the chair.

"Anything you want to talk about?" I asked.

"No. There's nothing. There's no tomorrow, so there's nothing."

"Anything you want me to do? To tell people? Anything you want to write?"

He stared into the lamp so long, I thought he wouldn't say anything. "I have a question you won't like," he said. "How can you sit there talking to the man you're going to hang in a few hours?"

He was right. I sure enough didn't like that one. I guessed that most hangmen don't want to meet or know the ones they slip the noose over.

"Just dumb, I guess," I said. "You want to know how I feel? I feel like opening that door and telling you to fly into the night and don't never come back to Puma County. But I can't. I got a duty and I got to do it, and what I feel don't count."

"I hoped for it," he said. "Maybe it would be good. But mostly I'd be a fugitive, my life no good."

His pa was back there bellowing some. "Let me out, you son of a bitch," he was saying.

"My ma would take offense," I said.

"My mother wasn't like my father. He controlled her, just like he controlled Queen and me and his men, and tried to control his neighbors, and the politicians, and you, and tried to control the rain and the snow and the land and the water and the stock and the game. She simply died, because that's all she could think to do when she got tired of being his woman. He taught us to be like himself. He gave me a gun four years ago and told me to make the whole world afraid of me, and then I'd be a real king." He stared at me. "Look what it got me."

"You and Queen, you've both busted loose of him."

"Too late," he said. "She set herself free?"

"She did."

"That's why she'll live a good life. I was too late."

We sank into one of them silences, and I watched a moth flit around the lamp. It'd likely get itself burnt pretty quick.

"Do you think there's an afterlife?" he asked.

"I'm inclined against it, but I haven't got it figured out yet," I said.

"I guess I'm slated for hell," he said. "If I killed three men, that's it. So God says, get down there and suffer, and get burned up, and know there's no hope from now until the end of time. Maybe that's it. Maybe this is just the beginning. Maybe this is the easy part, getting my neck snapped in one bad moment. It's the slow stuff, the roasting in the flames. A thousand years from now, ten thousand years from now, I'll still be roasting away down there, and there's no getting loose."

"Sounds almost as bad as heaven," I said. "I sure get myself in a snit when I think of getting stuck there. I don't know how to play any harp. I wish there was some sort of in-between place where I could have a rip-roaring time now and then, and then get a good beefsteak and a shot of red-eye, and find me the prettiest gal anywheres."

"Do you believe it? Really, really believe it?" he asked.

"Heaven and hell? No, not like that. Not eternal damnation, not eternal wandering around on streets paved with gold. No way."

"Maybe just a little time in heaven or hell, and then — you know, nothing?"

"Makes more sense to me," I said. "But my ma always told me I'm a little slow, so don't take my word for it."

"Do you think I'd get to see my mother?"

"That would be the good part of it, if you get the chance."

"Do you think I'd have time enough to tell her that I got into trouble?"

"Maybe you could tell her you stood up to your pa, and made yourself a man."

I saw him start to crumble, and I was

afraid to say anything more. He didn't quite. He just struggled to hold it all in, and pretty soon he did.

"I guess you can take me back there now," he said. "I want some time alone."

"You want a preacher tomorrow?"

"It doesn't matter," he said. "I don't know what I believe, and he'll just pray for mercy, and that's about the last I'll ever hear."

"I'll rustle up a preacher; it can't do no harm," I said.

"Maybe it will do harm," he replied.

He stood, making himself stand real tall and straight. I could see that in him.

I unlocked the jailhouse door, and took him back to his cell. We stepped around that puddle of slop. He walked in, and I locked him up, and he settled down on his bunk, staring at the ceiling. He had a few long hours left, and was probably wishing they'd go fast. He wasn't fighting or pacing or yelling or weeping or even hoping. He was already gone, at least in his head, and probably that numbness was keeping him quiet. It was hard even for me to look at him there.

I started up the aisle, knowing I'd not get past Admiral, and I didn't.

"Put us out of here, both of us right now, and you can retire for life," he said.

"I'll tell Judge Nippers of your kind offer," I said. "I'd be a lucky feller, getting to retire at my age."

"You can have Queen if you want her."

I stared at him, not quite believing my ears. But he'd said it. It didn't seem worth an answer, so I headed out of there, glad to escape the stink. I locked the jailhouse door, got me the mop and poured some water into the bucket, and then went back there and mopped up his slop. I wasn't gonna let any man stink up my jail more than necessary. So I mopped it up until it was halfway decent in there, and then locked up the jail again. I decided not to empty the mop bucket. I'd have to go outside for that, and I wouldn't do that, not this night.

There sure was a lot of quiet in there by then. It wasn't late. I had a long night ahead, and a longer day tomorrow. I checked the shutters, checked the barred door, checked the gun rack, and all seemed to be as tight and ready as I could make the place. So there was nothing to do but wrap a blanket around me and sit in the swivel chair until dawn.

We had a seven-day clock in there, one you wound up on Saturdays, and it was clicking away. I was glad that the kid wasn't hearing that clock tick like that, because he would be counting the ticks, adding them up into minutes and hours. So it just ticked away, and I sat in the chair with a scatter-gun on the desk beside me, and waited for the seconds to come and go.

I got itchy every little while, and hiked around the office and tried to settle back in my chair. The kerosene lamp burned away, and the reservoir went down some. I wanted real bad to see the sky, see the stars that would be up there long after I left the world, but I didn't want to open them shutters. I didn't know what was out there. But the itch became so big in me that finally I decided to try it. I turned the lamp wick down until the flame blued out, and it was dark as hell in there. I felt my way over to the window up front, and opened the shutter a little, half expecting a pole or something to crash through the glass. But there was no one out there, and no one could see me looking out in that darkness. The stars were up there, cold chips of light that comforted me some.

It was real quiet back in the jail. I closed and barred the shutter again, and settled in my swivel chair, and left the lamp unlit so it was pure dark in there, and all I knew was the ticking of that clock. I got to hating the clock because pretty soon it would be telling me of the things I had to do, and so the clock was my enemy, ticking away, ticking me toward the time I took that kid up onto the scaffold with his hands tied behind him and fitted the noose around him and turned it a little to the left and tightened it just right.

That's when I heard a sharp knock on the barred front door.

"Just a minute, just a minute," I said, tossing aside my blanket. I made my way through pitch dark to the door, and felt around some for the bar.

"Who's there?" I asked.

"You know perfectly well who it is. Who else, eh?"

"I sure don't," I said.

"You're slow, all right, Sheriff. I keep telling you, smarten up."

I knew who it was then. "You alone?"

"I wanted to bring that idiot with me, but he sobered up first and got out while I was still soaking the sauce."

I eased the door slightly, knowing that in pitch darkness I wouldn't be much of a target.

"Dammit, Sheriff, open that door," Judge Nippers said.

I did, and he slipped in. I closed it behind him and dropped the bar once again.

"What are you trying to do, save the

county a nickel of lamp oil?"

"You just stand right there, and I'll light up," I said.

I felt my way back to my desk, found a lucifer, and thought to hold it far from me, just in case I was a target. I scratched it to life with my thumb. The flare was blinding. And there was Judge Nippers, looking the worse for wear, holding his flask of Kentucky, glaring at me.

"That punk Carter Bell perjured himself," the judge said. "You got some paper and nib and ink?"

"I do," I said.

"That's good, because I've got some court orders to write," he said.

THIRTY-ONE

I rustled up some paper and a nib pen and inkpot and blotter, and set them before the judge, who had settled his bulk in my swivel chair.

"Should have made it sooner," he said, uncorking the ink and dipping his nib into the ink. "Trouble is, I soaked my gizzard more than usual, and catnapped. The rascal decamped, though I'd intended to collar him. He was swizzled, and I didn't discourage it. He's a blabbermouth, and after a dozen little sips, which I'll charge the county for, he began to undo his perjury."

He studied the naked paper, his pen poised and ready.

"What are you writing?" I asked.

"I'll show you in a minute."

"Print her out," I said. "Then I'll get them letters right."

"No, I'm going to scribble, and then I'll read it to you."

"What you got going there, Your Honor?"

"Hush now, this taxes me. You can't stay up all night and write a bulletproof court order now, can you?"

I figured I'd just have to wait. I slid a shutter open a little, and saw that the new day was quickening, and soon there'd be full light to shine upon the day's slaughter. I sort of wished the light would never come, and this here day wouldn't begin. But I didn't have any skill at stopping clocks. And the seven-day clock on the case there was showing almost seven. It sure was quiet. Not a peep from back in the jail either.

Judge Nippers scribbled a little and then paused. "That soak you sent my way was entertaining. After we'd shared a few shots, I asked him what happened over there at the Last Chance, and at first he just smiled some and allowed it was just like his testimony in court. I eyed him and said, 'Horsepucky.' He laughed and said that was rich. Horsepucky was it, all right."

"What was horsepucky?"

"The whole story. It took another dozen sips before the wretch began to spill any beans, but when they spilled, they scattered all over my floor."

"There's another story?" I asked.

He glared at me. "You sure are slow, Pickens. I don't know what to do about you."

He paused, pen poised over the paper. "I don't quite know what to do yet. But I'll do something," he said. He reached for his flask and took a long, deep suck on her, and then hiccuped and belched real fine. That judge could belch his way right through an hour if he wanted.

"I sure had to pump the little turd to get it out, but I got it out," he said.

"You mean Carter Bell?"

"He's the only little turd in town, Pickens."

I peered out the window, looking for signs of life, but it still was real quiet out there on Doomsday.

"After we soaked his brain a little, he told me how it happened. Crayfish had it in for the three crooks he employed, he being a bigger crook and now having smaller ones nibbling at his ankles. There were the Jonas boys, dumb as stumps but smart enough to slide out and turn the T-Bar brand into the Double Plus, by extending the T into a cross, and turning the bar into a cross. Now you'd think some crooks would be a little cautious about claiming a brand like a Double Cross, but these dopes thought it was clever. It didn't fool Crayfish for an instant.

"Rocco, the remaining deceased, was another sort of cat. Crayfish had some appetites that would have made Paul Bunyon look like a midget, and Rocco was hired to keep him supplied. But Rocco came out of Hell's Kitchen, and saw ways to make money. So Crayfish thought it was time to ventilate Rocco, along with the Jonas lads.

"Now here's the fun of it. Crayfish amused himself with the idea of pinning the whole thing on King Bragg, son of his rival Admiral, who had a nasty habit of strutting down Wyoming Street with a custom-made revolver, looking for someone to kill. Well, my friend, it was easy to set up. Carter Bell had no notion he'd be a witness. He was simply told to wait in the Last Chance. That crappy bartender Sammy Upward was recruited to dose some red-eye he would serve the kid. After that, Plug Parsons wandered next door now and then looking for King Bragg to come in, as he usually did, and simply invited him over. It was easy. Bragg showed up, landed on his face, Crayfish pulled the kid's Colt, executed the three on his list, and stuffed the gun back in the kid's possession, where it remained until the kid awakened. That was the afternoon's entertainment."

"The boy's innocent?"

"Now I'm not saying that, Pickens. I'm saying that we've got to have another trial and Bell's going to cough up."

"He's not going to say one word in court against his boss," I said.

"Then I suppose the kid'll hang," the judge said. "Won't be the first time an innocent man got hung."

I sure was having a bad time of it. "What are you going to do?"

"Stay the hanging until there can be a new trial."

"Why not just let him go?"

"And deprive Doubtful of a good hanging? Not on your life, Pickens." He yawned, and set the pen down. "That's what I get for burning the midnight oil," he said.

His head slumped forward, and his body relaxed.

"Your Honor! Get that thing writ up!"

He muttered something, and sunk deeper into my chair.

"Wake up! Write it up!"

"Oh, I will, give me a minute," he said, and settled into another snooze.

"Your Honor, you have to do it right now. Now."

Nippers just smiled, eyes closed, and wobbled in his chair.

"I'll help you up. We'll walk some," I said.

I headed for the chair, tried to lift his massive bulk, but he sort of swatted me away. "Five minutes, boy. Five minutes," he muttered.

"Just finish it up, write it up," I said.

But he pitched forward, splaying himself over my desk.

I guess I never did get myself into such a pickle. That seven-day clock was ticking and tocking and there wasn't four hours until I had to take the Bragg boy out there to courthouse square and do what had to be done.

Five minutes, then. The minute hand had crept past the hour, and onto the ten. It was three hours and fifty minutes until the hour of tears.

I wrestled the half-done paper out from under him. It was dated, all right, and it said, far as I could tell from that curvy script, that the execution of King Bragg would be stayed for one week, until — And that's where it quit, and wasn't signed, and wasn't worth beans without him signing it.

I eyed that flask, and slid it away from him just in case he woke up and got a new thirst to put himself back to snorin' again. I paced around, and discovered the blue speckled coffeepot. It hadn't been washed in a while, maybe two weeks, but I set to work on her, and scraped all that brown coating off. I'd have to built a little fire in the stove to heat it up, and it was going to be a warm day. Maybe I could just go over to the diner and get me a cup and bring it over for the judge. I'd hold it up and pour it down his gullet.

I ached to go back there to that cell and tell the boy that he'd live to see another sunrise, but I couldn't do that. I couldn't say stuff to that, and then break his heart if the judge decided to let the hanging go ahead.

It sure was quiet back there. I wondered if them Braggs heard any of it. They might have. But I didn't have anything good to tell them. I peered out the door, and wondered where Burtell and DeGraff and Rusty were. They should have been in by now. I didn't see a soul out there, even with the sun up and the day stirring. If one of them would show up, I'd send him over for some coffee, and get the judge honked up a little so he could finish up that paper.

I watched that clock tick away. Every once in a while, it would have a convulsion and tick twice and tock once, but it kept time pretty good, and got past those five minutes. So I went and shook the judge on the shoulder, and he just wobbled like a dead dog, and flopped like a twice-caught fish, and muttered. So I thought I'd give him another five, and then it would be all right, and he would finish up that document, and I would halt everything, and maybe I could free the boy. I wasn't inclined to let his pa get out, not until eleven, just like I said, but the boy, he could vamoose.

So another five rolled around, and I tried to wake up Judge Nippers, but he just said "Eh!" and started snoring. This here was getting a little chancy, so I figured I'd just have to quit the sheriff office long enough to get some coffee and pour it down his throat. That'd do it. I'd get some java and hold his head up and pry his flaky lips apart, and aim it between his yeller teeth, what was left of them, and pat him on the back some, and pretty soon he'd pop right up and whip that paper into shape, and I'd spring the kid.

That clock was clattering away, and the minute hand was spasming along, like it should, and the hour hand was crawling slower, like it should. It was getting bright out there, with the sun up and the early light slanting across Wyoming Street, so some buildings were lit, and the others were casting shadows.

I was getting real ornery about my deputies. Where was Rusty? Where was DeGraff and Burtell? Maybe they wasn't men enough to face this day. I began going from window to window, opening the shutter for a look, and finding nothing but a real empty street and alley out there, and the clock was ticking away.

I tried rattling the judge again, but he just said something blasphemous and waved a hand at me, and then it was eight in the morning, and pretty quick it was eight-thirty. And still them lazy no-good deputies of mine hadn't showed their faces.

The bunch collecting down the street a way looked to be armed to the gills, in spite of my ban on weapons this day. I could only wait and see which outfit was defying me, and it didn't take long. That bunch was T-Bar, and they was strolling straight toward the county sheriff office and jail, and they was staying apart some, not bunched up, like a battle line, and I knew straight off there would be more trouble than I ever faced in my life.

Sure enough, there was Crayfish, back a little, and in front of the usual bunch of rannies and gunslicks and riders. Plug Parsons was leading that parade, looking like a bull, and sure enough, there was Carter Bell in there, wearing his fancy artillery. And I sure wasn't seeing no deputy of mine, and it was dawning on me that I wouldn't, because this outfit had collected them and held them somewheres. That was bad news too. It meant they was going to do what they were itching to do all the time they camped in Doubtful.

I had to make some decisions real fast.

I shook the judge until he finally rattled awake and sat staring at me silently.

"Write that thing."

He collected himself a moment, and nodded. His hands shivered and shook like one of them belly dancers, but he set to work, and made them wobbly letters and words, while I watched real sharp. Then he eyed me, dipped the nib into the well, and signed the thing. He eyed the clock and added the time to it, and handed it to me.

"They're coming," I said.

"Who?"

"Crayfish and his bunch. They're armed. They got my deputies off somewhere, so I'm holding the fort."

He sighed. "I'll talk to them. In your hands is a legal stay of execution, pending a review."

"The boy ain't free to go?"

"He might be. But I'm going to see whether Carter Bell sober says the same thing as Carter Bell lit up. Maybe later today. *In vino veritas* isn't a legal doctrine."

I sure didn't know what the old goat was talking about, but it didn't matter. In a moment, King Bragg's life would change.

I tucked the stay of execution into my pocket. It felt light as air. It made me feel real light, like a ton of hemp rope was lifted off my shoulders. I'd tell the boy that he was off the hook. It'd all work out. Nippers sure wasn't gonna let the kid hang now.

I heard the bunch collecting outside the door, and then someone yelled. I knew that voice. It was Plug Parsons, who was probably leading this bunch, while Crayfish hung back a little.

"Open up, Sheriff. Open up, and you won't get hurt," Parsons said. "We've got some business to do."

THIRTY-TWO

I turned to the judge. "You stand back, over there," I said. "I'm going to open that door, and there might be some lead flyin' through."

"You'd open up to them?"

"I don't know what they want. They're armed and violating my order. No guns in Doubtful this day. And if they're up to no good, I've got to put a stop to it."

"It's dangerous," Nippers said.

I nodded. A man wearing the badge has to put himself in harm's way now and then. I waited until he shuffled off to one side, over near the jail door, and then I lifted the bar and opened up.

They didn't have any weapons pointed at me, at least for the moment. But there was plenty of fingers hovering over holsters, and itchy eyes.

There must have been fifteen, twenty of them, all T-Bar men. And Plug Parsons was leading the pack, and standing in front. Crayfish was there, but at the rear, like he wanted to be as safe as he could get. I saw Carter Bell back there some, but most of those fellers were simply T-Bar riders and gunslicks. I thought maybe I knew what they had in mind, which was an early hanging just to make sure it got done, before crowds around the gallows might change things.

I looked the lot over, but it was Plug Parsons who caught my eye. He was standing there, solid as a bull, wide as a beer barrel, and smug as a bridegroom.

"Where is he?" Parsons asked. "We're going to push this necktie party ahead, just so nothing much goes wrong today. The law won't mind."

"There'll be no hanging today," I said. "I got a stay of execution right here, signed by Judge Nippers. You fellers go on out to your ranch and call it a day."

That sure rocked them back on their heels.

"A stay? What are you talking about?" Crayfish yelled.

"There'll be no execution. There's new evidence the boy didn't do it. And that's what the judge is going to be looking at. Now go home. You're all violating my order. No guns in Doubtful today. So get out, before I get a little pissed off."

They sure were taking their time absorbing that, but I wasn't seeing anyone turn around and walk away, neither.

"What evidence?" Crayfish yelled.

"That's for the judge to look over. But there's a witness sprung up."

Carter Bell looked pretty solemn, but he wasn't shaking in his boots neither. Still, Crayfish had three lying witnesses: Bell, Parsons, and my friend Sammy Upward, the sneakin' bastard that slid them knockout drops into the boy's booze. I looked for him in that mob, but he wasn't there. This was all T-Bar men.

Things seemed to teeter like that for a moment, and I thought maybe they'd pull out, but then Axel Nippers himself showed up beside me, huffing and puffing and trying to control the shakes from a hard night of sipping.

"Here now," he bellowed. "You quit this place. There'll be no hanging on this day. I've heard new evidence and I've issued a court order. I'm holding a hearing in my chambers in one hour, and I want every witness who testified at the trial there. That includes Parsons there, and Bell there, and you fetch Upward too. I'll expect you there, and I'm going to be asking some questions and you'd better be giving me the right answers, or you'll be facing the music."

"What questions?" Crayfish asked, real quiet.

"You won't be there. You'll just wait and see. You're going to deliver Mr. Parsons, Mr. Bell, and Mr. Upward, and then you can wait for the verdict."

"I asked what questions."

"And I told you."

"It seems that justice won't be done this day, unless we do it," Crayfish said softly.

Nippers pushed pugnaciously into that crowd. "You'll have your justice. You'll have it every which way. And those who are guilty will hang. And those who lied will spend a long time thinking about their crimes. And this mob is going to disperse right now. You heard the sheriff. No guns. I'll throw every last skinny-assed cowboy into the slammer until you're all feeling sorry if you don't get yourself out of town right now."

"You won't hang King Bragg?" Crayfish asked.

"I'll hang the man who murdered those three men, and you can count on it, Mr. Ruble."

"And who would that be?"

"You'll know when the time comes," the judge snapped.

"I guess we'll have a couple of hangings today," Crayfish said.

He nodded at Plug, who manhandled the judge.

"You varmint, take your fat paws off me or face the music," Nippers roared.

I got my revolver in hand real quick and aimed it at Parsons.

"Let him go," I yelled.

"You piece of pig manure, get your hands off me," Nippers snapped.

Parsons and the judge was wrestling some, but the beefy foreman sure had the upper hand. He swung the judge around between my Colt and himself, and putting a bullet in him and not in the judge would have been like shooting two dogs in heat. So I hunted out Crayfish, but he was already racing toward the gallows, and out of range.

I fired in the air, but that didn't slow anyone down.

I waded in, but there was a mess of T-Bar riders blocking the way, and I sure enough got into a brawl with three or four, and they were piling on me from all sides, and them fat fists were landing on me. One knocked my revolver into the clay. I slugged back, and kneed one of them boys in his basket, and he whoofed and doubled up, but every time I got ahead, two more came at me. I could feel my blood up, pounding in my head, and I gave more than I took, because I use all of me in a fight, including my thick skull, but I was plain outnumbered, and in a bit they had me down and was kicking my ribs real hard.

I heard a shout and they all quit pounding me and was running toward the gallows on the courthouse square. I tried to get up, but there was something tore up in there. They'd quit me and was hell-bent to get to the gallows. I crawled to my feet, hunted around for my revolver, but it wasn't there. Someone had took it. I got to standing, and stared at the open door of the sheriff office, wondering how many of them T-Bar men was in there, and what they were doing to my prisoners.

I could hardly stand. I made myself stand. I raced back to the office, and up the steps, and entered. There wasn't a soul in there, and the jail door was locked tight. So I grabbed a double-barrel scattergun and limped out, closing that office door behind me, wishing a few deputies would show up, now that a shot or two had been fired. But I knew they wouldn't because they were prisoners somewhere.

Up ahead a block, that mob was propelling the judge straight toward the gallows.

There was a few town people running for cover, and a few more who had come to see the show. I could hear Judge Nippers bellowing up there, but couldn't make out what he said. I knew it was ferocious, whatever it might be. But words don't cut into a man the way a bullet does, and they were paying him no heed.

I trotted along, feeling pain in my ribs and a lot of other places. I had two loads and that was it. But they were double-ought buckshot, and that always gets some respect. They seen me coming and one tried a potshot, but he was most of a block away. This was shaping up into a real bad mess. I followed along, but now Crayfish himself was turning some of them boys my way and they was popping their six-guns at me, and they was going to hit me pretty quick.

The rest, led by Plug Parsons, was manhandling that judge forward, dragging him when he quit walking. They sure was going to hang the judge, unless I could stop them. And Crayfish was urging them on. Kill the judge before the judge got any more curious about what happened that afternoon in the Last Chance Saloon.

I could see I was losing out. They'd reached the gallows, and were hoisting Nippers up them steps. Now there was two or three of them cowboys who just plain halted to shoot at me, and one bullet sizzled through my sleeve. I veered toward the doorway of Maxwell Funeral Parlor, and got into the entryway, where I was safe for a moment, but a couple of bullets splintered wood right where I'd been a moment before.

I was trapped. They had me penned. I crouched low, and sneaked a peek or two around that corner, only to see what I sure didn't want to see, and could hardly stand seeing. They was shoving the judge up, and pushing him toward the trap, while some ranny was tying the judge's hands behind him with a borrowed belt. The judge, he wasn't taking it lying down, and once in a while I could hear him yelling.

Down below, Crayfish was quietly pointing a few of his rannies into a perimeter, their six-guns pointed at the spectators. He didn't want no town folk messing up the death of the judge. Up on that gallows, Plug Parsons was calm as could be, lowering the noose over Axel Nippers' old neck and tightening it some. Down below, a couple of them cowboys was keeping an eye on the doorway where I was crouched. I wished old Maxwell would open up. I might get a shot at them hangmen from a window. But Maxwell always waited politely for death before he ventured out, and he wouldn't show up until there was a body and someone wanted to pay him to do something about it.

I heard Nippers bellow out his last words: "You baboons," he said.

That was his final observation on life in Doubtful, Wyoming. Plug Parsons swung that lever. The trap dropped. The judge dropped hard and fast, with a loud crack. He shuddered once and then went limp.

The thing was, the whole place went quiet. Even the wind quit. After all that ruckus, there was no noise, no movement except for the swinging body up there, and no talk. Them T-Bar men just stared at the judge. Even Crayfish just stared. I wondered what was going through their heads. Every last one of them was engaged in murdering a district judge of the Territory. A judge who knew something, and who had stopped an execution, only to trigger his own. He just swayed up there, limp and twisting slowly. The spectators didn't move neither. It was too much to absorb, so they just stared. There was no law in Doubtful. There was no justice, no decency, no safety.

I was mad at myself because I couldn't get in there and make it quit. But I didn't, and now it was too late, and I was still pinned in that entryway.

And the sheriff office and jailhouse stood unguarded.

I edged out, heading toward my office. I had other lives in my care. I heard a shout behind me, and a couple of pistol shots sailed by, but nothing came close, so I just kept on going, my hurt ribs pretty near torturing me, along with a mess of bruises. But I was going to get back there and defend that boy, defend that boy with my life if it came to that.

I made it back all right. The T-Bar men didn't try to catch up. They probably thought they could tear the place apart any time they chose.

There wasn't a soul in my office, and the jail door was still locked. I closed and barred the front door, laid out some scatterguns on my desk, and a box of shells, and drank a tumbler of water since I was parched. There was blood on my shirt and arms, but I didn't know whether it was mine or someone else's.

I thought maybe I had a few moments, so I unlocked the jail door and headed in there.

It was real quiet. Old Man Bragg stared at me. The boy was simply lying on his iron cot and waiting for the end. The sadness was so thick I could feel it chill my heart.

I unlocked the cell door and swung it wide. The kid glanced at me and lay quiet. I didn't know what time it was; it might seem like eleven to him.

"King," I said. "It's not gonna happen. You're free to go."

He stared at me.

"You're free, boy. No noose."

The young man closed his eyes. "Don't try to make it easy for me," he said.

He didn't get the message. I dug around in my shirt. The stay was folded in there, so I pulled it out. It was bent some from all that fighting.

"Read," I said.

He eyed it, and the paper dropped to the floor. I picked it up and stuffed it at him. He took it and read.

"It's just some legal stuff," he said.

"Get up, get washed. I need you. We're in trouble. You'll need to defend yourself, maybe."

He stared at me like I was nuts.

Now his father, Admiral Bragg, was up and rattling the cage. "What's this? What's this?"

I thought about letting him out, but he would do some damn fool thing, like trying to shoot me.

"I'll tell you later," I said.

"Let me out, damn you."

The kid was dazed. I pretty near shoved him out of the jail and locked up behind him.

"You're free. Judge Nippers heard some evidence of what really happened. You were knocked out with some stuff, and Crayfish borrowed your gun. There's a lot more, but we got trouble. You can vamoose if you want, and if them T-Bar men don't kill you. They're coming. You're free, but I need you."

He stared at me.

"Take this scattergun, boy. You may need it," I said.

He hesitantly lifted the shotgun, wondering whether I'd shoot him, I guess, and stood there in the middle of the office, freed but not knowing it, and neither of us knew what would come through that door.

THIRTY-THREE

I sure get itchy behind walls, forted up. Sooner or later someone's gonna bust in or starve me out. And this was going to be soon, since it was me against fifteen, twenty T-Bar men ready to tear the place apart and drag the kid to the gallows. I had only moments before that bunch quit staring at Judge Nippers dangling out there on the courthouse square, and started coming for the next ones, namely the Bragg kid and me.

"King, we're going to get out of here. You hear? I'll unlock your pa. I'm going out with my scattergun and I'm turning left and heading straight for the courthouse. After a moment, you and your pa slip out and turn right and get out of sight fast. You're on your own. Try to hook up with your sister and your Anchor Ranch men. That's all I can do."

King, he still was trying to get all this

straight. Minutes before, he was waiting to be hanged. But he nodded.

I plunged into the jail and unlocked his pa.

"Get out of here. King will tell you where to go," I said.

"Are you giving me orders?" Admiral Bragg snapped. "You haven't even fed me. I'll hang you from the nearest street lamp."

"Move. If you want to live, move."

"What's all this?"

"Judge Nippers is dead. He stayed the execution and got hanged for it. Now move."

"Dead? Well, he deserved it, sentencing my boy to be hanged."

That did it. I pushed him back into the cell. He tumbled onto his bunk while I slammed the door shut and locked it. That lock snapped like a rifle bolt.

"You're leaving me to that mob?" he howled.

"Not if I can help it," I said.

I locked the jail door, thinking maybe that would slow down the T-Bar mob, and I picked up a few buckshot cartridges. Enough to fire until my trigger finger went dead.

"You ready, boy?"

"What about my father?"

369

"He wants his breakfast."

"But —"

I ignored him. "Do what I say. I'm going to slow that mob. You go the other way. Find your sister, and get out of town."

King stared at me, and nodded. "Thank you," he said.

"Thank Judge Nippers."

"If there's any way we can help you —" he said.

We were out of time. I raced to the front door, opened it a bit, and saw the T-Bar men staring at that limp, twirling body up on the gallows. I nodded to the kid and stepped out, leaving the door wide. It would shield the boy if he was smart enough to jump off the steps and skirt the building.

I moved slowly down them steps, and turned left just as I said I would, and started straight toward that mob on the courthouse square, my shotgun cradled under my arm. I thought I heard the boy slide out, a soft drop to the grass, and then he was crawling back along the wall. Good. He figured it out. Now that bunch out there on the square saw me, walking slow, in no hurry because I wanted the kid to move his butt far away.

I was going to do what I had to do, which don't mean I wasn't scared. I'd end up a

370

piece of Swiss cheese, or maybe they'd pull the noose free of Judge Nippers and fit it to my scrawny neck. But I didn't have time to worry about that. The square was empty except for all them T-Bar men, who were mostly watching Nippers dangle and twirl. Everyone had fled. It felt sort of funny, walking right into that bunch, but I kept on, one foot at a time, that side-by-side shotgun ready.

They saw me coming. Crayfish was staring, and so was Plug Parsons, and so was Carter Bell. They stayed bunched up, not spreading out in a skirmish line, just staying tight around those gallows, with that body dangling there real quiet. I just kept on walking, one boot at a time, and they just kept on staring, first at me, then at Crayfish, and then at Judge Nippers, slowly swaying there, looking testy.

It was odd. I was all alone in the world, but there were people everywhere, watching from every window and doorway, ready to duck when lead started to fly. I wished my deputies would show up, but they'd been taken hostage or they'd be here at my side. I glanced at the hotel, and thought I saw Queen in a shadow there. Then she moved swiftly, and there was some commotion over there. But I was still walking, and getting close to revolver range now, but still too far for a short-barreled shotgun.

Me, I just kept walkin'. There wasn't anything else to do but to walk. Now they was all staring at me, and a few had their paws sort of hovering over their six-guns. I was real interested in Crayfish, who simply stared, not moving a muscle. He didn't give me a clue. He stood like a statue on the outer edge of that bunch, his hands at his sides. I thought maybe the T-Bar would wait for him to make the call. So I slid my barrels a little his way. You don't have to aim a shotgun full of buckshot. All you got to do is point.

I just kept on walkin' and nothing much happened. I was getting into range. Any one of them riders could pop one at me if he was real careful about where he aimed. But it wasn't happening. They'd just hanged the judge, and now the law was coming at them one step at a time, and the law wasn't slowing down.

The other feller who was real important to me was Plug Parsons, standing there like a snorty bull, his hand still on that lever he used to spring the trap and send Judge Nippers to eternity. But Parsons wasn't edgy like the rest. He was the calmest in the lot, just watching peaceful, like this was a

372

Sunday morning and the church bells had rung. He was armed, like all the rest, but he didn't bother to lower his paws so he could grab iron if he needed to. He just watched, and waited, and was ready to back up Crayfish's play.

It got real quiet. But I just kept on walkin'. It all happened so fast I couldn't sort it out. A bunch quit the pack and began trotting down Wyoming Street, not quite running like some yellow dogs, but just pulling out of the contest. Then a few more followed, looking back over their shoulders at me.

I just kept on walkin'. Then the rest quit the gallows, this time in a trot because I could spray a lot of buckshot into them now. And then Crayfish himself, after a frozen moment, took off hard, almost loping out of range, and wanting some distance between my buckshot and his flesh.

It was odd. I can't explain it. The bunch was fleeing. Like they all knew what they had just done, hanging the judge. Fleeing because the law was coming and the law wouldn't quit, and the law was still walkin' straight toward the gallows. I watched the whole bunch flee. Except for Plug Parsons, him who slid the noose around Judge Nippers and then pulled the lever. He just stood there, sort of smiling, half protected by the gallows, but some of him showing.

I just kept on walkin'.

"You want to come with me to the jail, Plug?" I asked.

It was funny how he smiled, and said nothing, and just stood there.

"I guess I gotta collar you, Plug. Hanging a judge."

Parsons had shaded a little behind the gallows to give himself some protection, so I just worked sideways myself, and when Plug saw how it would go, he simply pulled at his revolver, and I shot him. He took about half of them buckshot in the chest and head and toppled like a big old tree. There was a little powder smoke drifting in the breeze, and it was real quiet. Plug shivered a bit and then quit living. He was all red.

I reloaded, and watched them T-Bar men head for the Last Chance. I feared for my deputies. I didn't know where they'd been hid or who was guarding them, but I was having a bad moment.

There wasn't nothing to do but climb that stair to the gallows platform. I tried to pull the noose loose, but them things are designed to go one way, tighter, and I couldn't. I dug around in my britches and found my jackknife and pretty soon sawed through the rope, and stretched the judge out on the platform, and then I cut the noose loose. He stared up at me, like he was expecting something.

"I got one and I'll get the rest," I told him. "That's a promise."

I saw Maxwell, hovering at his door, looking for business, so I waved at him. He leapt into action, and began hauling an ebony two-wheel cart out to the gallows to fetch the judge. He had a small sign screwed onto the side, that said SEE MAXWELL'S FOR A DIVINE PASSAGE. I waited, and pretty quick Maxwell pulled up. I lifted the judge, who weighed a lot, and carried him down the steps and laid him in the cart.

"You treat him good. You treat him better than you ever treated anyone in your life," I said.

"Certainly, certainly, that's my business," he said. "I always treat everyone best."

I got to thinking about that, but it still didn't make any sense.

He took off with the judge, and I recovered my shotgun and watched him wheel that cart across the courthouse square and into his alley door. I peered around, wondering why I'd let myself stand around, but if there was someone on the square, I sure didn't see him. It was like I was the only one on earth left alive.

I stared at Plug Parsons, or what was left of him. One of the buckshot had hit him in the mouth, shattering what was left of his teeth. Another had passed through his bull neck. Two more had hit his chest, another his arm, and one had almost severed his left hand. I didn't much care whether Maxwell hauled him off or not.

There wasn't nobody in that square. My ma used to tell me if there was no one that came close to me, it was time for a Saturday night bath. It wasn't Saturday night yet, so people would have to put up with me for a while. Them T-Bar men had vanished. My pa used to quote the Good Book: The guilty flee when no man pursueth, or something like that. I could never figure out why they didn't use plain English, like pursues, instead of that pursueth. They was fleeing, all right, and I was pursuing, and I was going to keep on pursuing.

I didn't see a soul, but I thought a few hundred eyes was watching. I headed back to the office, thinking I owed Old Man Bragg a breakfast, even if I didn't care whether he ate for the next week or two. I got to worrying about all them deputies of mine, and wondered whether I'd see them again, or how I could find and free them.

They might not even be alive. They might also be hostages. Well, I'd find out soon enough.

When I got back to the office, there was King and Queen in there, both armed to the teeth.

Queen rushed up to me, and danged if she didn't wrap her arms around me. I don't mind being hugged, but not by a woman with a six-gun at her hip.

She started crying again, and pretty quick her tears were dampening my shirt, and she clung to me like I had done something real fine.

"I got things to do," I said.

She let go, and brushed back her tears.

"I guess you two need to hear the story," I said. "But first I got to feed you pa. He's in there hollering for his breakfast."

"Let him holler," she said. "Just tell us what happened."

There hadn't been time to tell King Bragg when I let him out. Just that the judge had signed a stay of execution. So I told them the whole shebang, about the judge and his drinking buddy Carter Bell, who got himself swizzled enough to spill a few beans. How Crayfish had set it up. He wanted to execute them T-Bar men that was on his hit list, and thought it would be entertaining to pin the whole thing on King, and watch the kid hang for something he didn't do.

They listened quietly.

"I got a few things to do," I said. "I got to find my deputies. I got to arrest Crayfish for murder. I got to arrest Sammy Upward for putting them knockout drops into your redeye and being part of it, and lying about it. I got to nab Carter Bell for lying on the witness stand and being a part of it. I've got to open up them graves you showed me, Queen, and maybe charge Crayfish with some more murders. I got to shut down Crayfish for good, before he starts worse trouble."

"Carter Bell went to see Judge Nippers?" King asked.

"I took him over there," I said. "I told him the judge was a good man to drink with."

"You took him there?"

"Yep. He was acting sort of squirrelly, like he wanted to brag some, only he didn't want to brag to the sheriff."

"And that's why the judge stopped the hanging?"

"Temporarily. He said he needed a sober confession before he'd call it off for good."

"Am I still in trouble?"

"I got to let them lawyers figure it out," I said.

They absorbed that bleakly.

THIRTY-FOUR

I didn't want that skunk Admiral Bragg stinking up my jail, so I let him out. I hardly got the cell door open, but he lunged at me in a rage.

"I'll have you strung up in a week," he said. "Abusing prisoners."

I pushed him aside. He stomped into the office, where King and Queen were waiting for him.

"How come he's out?" Bragg asked. "How come he's not hanging?"

"Because one of the lying witnesses squealed. Crayfish did the shooting and tried to pin it on King."

"What took you so long? How come you haven't shot the whole lot?"

I was tired of this. "Get your ass out of here," I said.

"You're in trouble with me, Pickens. You'll be out of the county in a week."

"Father, shut up," Queen said.

"Where are my weapons? I want my derringer," Admiral said.

"Come back in a month and I'll give it to you," I said.

"You expect me to go out there unarmed?"

"Our men are waiting behind the hotel," Queen said. "They're ready to ride. There are horses for you and King and me. Come along, Father."

"You telling me what to do, girl?"

"Yes," she said.

"Come on," King said. "Let's get out of here."

"You telling me what to do, boy?"

"Don't come then," King said. "Stay here."

"Get out right now or I'll lock you up," I said.

He paused, his face purpling with rage. "I strung you up once, Pickens, and next time it'll be for real."

I didn't have nothing more to say to the turkey, so I just stood there.

The Bragg girl and boy finally hustled Admiral out the door. I wondered whether he'd soon be bossing those two children of his around again, but it didn't look like it. They'd growed up overnight. They headed straight for the hotel, which was wise. I was glad to see King outside the jailhouse, alive and free. There sure would be some explaining to do when the mayor and all them people caught up with me, but I had Judge Nippers' document in my pocket, and that's all that mattered.

I slid out the door after locking up. I had missing deputies to hunt for and some people to invite to a hanging.

It sure was quiet. Over on the square, a rope hung from the gallows, with no noose on it. I could see Plug Parsons lying near there. A few puffball clouds were steering across a blue sky. I hardly knew where to go first, but the Last Chance Saloon seemed likely. It was funny how empty Doubtful was. The hardware was closed. So was the mercantile. So was the milliner. So was the blacksmith. The whole place looked like a ghost town. There were people peering from windows. I could see that. But there wasn't even a dog sniffing along the street. I carried my shotgun cradled on my arm, but I didn't see any sign of trouble. It looked like everyone in Doubtful was scared and hiding.

I got to Saloon Row, and came to the Sampling Room first, but Mrs. Gladstone had locked the door. There wasn't any Anchor Ranch men in there. I wanted to tell them to get out, and go back to the ranch.

So I headed for the Last Chance. The double doors were shut tight. I wondered what might be on the other side. Maybe the whole T-Bar outfit, ready to blow away anyone come through there. But I didn't see no horses at the hitch rails. When an outfit's in town, you see the horses. I knew half of them and had ridden a few and I knew the brand, but there wasn't no horses around Wyoming Street on this hangman's morning. I rattled the doors, but nothing happened. I booted the door a couple of times, but no one opened. I trotted down a piss-soaked space between the two saloons and tried the alley door, but it was shut tight. So I reared back and cut loose, and smacked it open with my shoulder, and ducked to the right, expecting some flying lead. But none came at me, and I raced into that dark, stinking place where men had died and swung my muzzles around, but there wasn't anyone to shoot.

I could have sworn someone was in there, but I didn't see no one. I shoved the back room door open. There wasn't any light back there, but enough come through the door so I could see bodies on the floor. One of them was twisting around some, so I dragged him by the feet into the light, and it was Rusty. I pulled the gag off his mouth and cut him loose of all that cord they'd wrapped around him.

"Knocked us cold," he said.

"Knockout drops?"

He nodded. "You hang the boy yet?"

"I let him go. Judge Nippers —"

"Let him go? I'll be damned."

Rusty looked like he couldn't make any sense of it.

I cut the rest loose, but them three were still mostly knocked out still, and Rusty didn't look exactly useful.

"Rusty, the Bragg boy's innocent and the judge turned him loose. Crayfish is the guilty party, just like we figured. So they hanged the judge."

"Say that again," he said.

That stuff was still wearing off, and he was slower than I am. I thought I wouldn't have me any working deputies for a few more hours, and maybe not until the next day. But I sure was glad to find them alive, even if they couldn't add two and two.

"Look, you help these fellers get themselves awake and then get out of here. Go on down to the jail and fort up. I've got a job to do."

"I don't get it," said Rusty.

"You'll get the whole story soon enough. I've got some business to do. But first tell me how you got here."

"T-Bar men pulled us out of bed, hauled us over here, every gun pointing our way. Upward pushed some tumblers of whiskey in front of us and told us to drink up. That's the last I knew."

"It's that stuff Upward's been using," I said. "You get back to the jail and be real careful."

Rusty was still pretty dazed-looking, but he nodded. I hated to leave them in there unarmed, so I poked around and found Sammy's shotgun under his bar. I didn't see any blue bottles this time, but Sammy had a stash of that stuff somewhere. I took the shotgun back to Rusty and gave it to him. He was pretty groggy, and maybe it wasn't the smartest move.

"This here's some protection. It's Sammy's."

Rusty nodded. "It'll serve," he said. "I couldn't hit a barn with a revolver."

"I've got work to do," I said, and left them there.

Out in the alley, there wasn't no one stirring. I wanted three men: Sammy Upward, Carter Bell, and Crayfish Ruble. Him most of all. They might still be in Doubtful. There wasn't any reason for them to git out, what with all the deputies knocked flat and me alone. I tried to figure what Crayfish knew. He knew that Judge Nippers had stopped the execution, but he didn't know why. Or maybe he did. If he knew someone had sung a song or two, it would have to be one of three people: Sammy, Plug Parsons, or Carter Bell, them that testified in the trial that King Bragg had shot and killed them T-Bar men. Plug was lying in the dirt at the gallows, and wouldn't be singing any songs.

I was pretty slow to come to it, but when I did it hit me hard. If them other two witnesses got kilt, Crayfish would be home free. There'd be no one around to point the finger at him. There'd be no reason to worry about anything. I had to find them two, Sammy or Carter, and get them out of harm's way.

I started toward Red Light Row, and sure enough, there was all them T-Bar horses tied to the hitch rails, slapping flies with their tails, yawning, and dropping green piles on the clay. At first I thought to storm into Rosie's place, but that might not be so bright. Especially if they was all in there waiting for me to walk through the door. I thought maybe to see what I could find at Big Lulu's house first. I eyed the windows at Rosie's, and saw a few faces duck away, so I knew I was being watched real hard. There wasn't going to be any surprises, and I wasn't going to collar Crayfish unannounced. I sure wished I had some deputies handy, but that bunch was so hung over it'd be a week before they'd be back on their feet.

Lulu's then. I eyed the windows. It was midday, not a time for much business in that trade, and most of the ladies were snoring away in there. But I pushed the door open and slid to one side. No shots met me. I got in there and took a hard look at the parlor, and all the horsehair furniture with the doilies pinned on it. It sure was quiet.

I was about to ring that bell they keep when a customer wants service, when Lulu herself showed up in her gray wrapper with the purple petunias on it.

"You got any T-Bar men in here?"

"Why, Sheriff, I wouldn't think of violating the privacy of my patrons."

"You got T-Bar men? You tell me right now or I'll shut you down real quick."

She eyed me like I had just broken all the china. "We might have one or two," she said.

"Where are they?"

"They are pleasuring their temporary wives, Sheriff."

"Who are they?"

"I couldn't possibly — well, you must be discreet."

"If you don't tell me real quick, I'm gonna start opening doors here and having a look-see."

"Oh, sir, don't do that. We don't want to violate the sacrament."

"Sacrament?"

"Why, their sacramental union. It's sacred. It is a private matter between a man and a woman."

"Well, if you don't tell me who, and where, I'm gonna start looking in on a lot of them sacraments."

"Surely, Mr. Pickens, you wouldn't do anything so, so, so . . . distasteful?"

"I sure would. You can distaste me all you want, but I'm about to go hunting if you don't steer me fast."

She sighed, and I thought she would tell me she had a headache or something. She wiped her eyes with her soft hand and sighed again.

"Mr. Upward is in room seven with Mrs. Cardwell. And Mr. Bell is in room five with Mrs. Boyd."

"Mrs. who? How come they're married?"

"We offer experience, Sheriff. What can an inexperienced temporary wife offer? A perfect sacrament requires deep experience, and then the result is sacred. So all my ladies have been married, or may say they have."

"All right, I'm gonna bust in on them. I want both of them fellers, and if I can catch them with their pants off, all the better."

I headed down the hallway while she stared at me and plucked at her purple petunias.

Room seven was silent. I pressed my ear to the door and heard nothing at all. I tried the door knob, and it opened the door, and no lead blew past me. So I looked in there. There was no girl in sight. Sammy Upward lay on his back, staring open-eyed at the ceiling. He was wearin' all his clothes, including his boots. I slapped him once or twice, but he wasn't moving, and his lungs weren't working, and I figured out that Sammy was history, and he'd been dosed to death with that knockout juice. Just to make sure, I looked for any bullet holes and blood, but there were none. There wasn't a mark on him. Poor old Sammy had bought the farm this time.

"So long, Sammy," I said. "You can pour me one in hell."

I was pretty sure Carter Bell would be in the same boat, but first I went back to the parlor and got aholt of Big Lulu.

"He's croaked. How'd he get put in there? You tell me fast and true."

She looked frightened out of her wits. "Oh, sir, Mr. Ruble brought them in, Mr. Upward and Mr. Bell, and said he wanted two private rooms for them to sleep off a drunk, and they shouldn't be disturbed, and for me to say they were enjoying the company of my temporary wives."

"How long ago?"

"Just a little while ago, sir."

"Were Upward and Bell on their feet?"

"Oh, yes, sir. They were joking with Mr. Ruble. It was all very jolly. He told them it was time to celebrate, and he'd foot the bill."

"Where's Ruble?"

"I wouldn't know, sir. He left here a little later, in a very good mood."

"Did he say anything?"

"Yes. He said, 'Let them sleep. They need rest.' And he said if they wanted one of my wives after they woke up, I should provide one."

"Did he pay you?"

"I always expect a gratuity, Sheriff. I'm in the temporary marriage business."

I headed down the hall to room five, found the knob, and pushed in real quick. There was Carter Bell, faceup, eyes closed, fully clad, and dead as a mackerel. I shook him a few times. I slapped his rat-face a few times. I found a hand mirror on the dresser and held it to his nostrils and found no moisture on it. I felt his hand, which was still warm but not like he was alive. There was a half-filled tumbler of booze on the dresser. I knew what was in that booze and I knew who poured it into Bell and Upward. Just to make sure, I checked him for bullet wounds. There were none, no blood, no cuts or bruises, nothing busted.

He sure looked natty, clean shaven, dressed real nice. "Look what you bought when you got to telling the judge a few things, Carter," I said. "A dose of that stuff. Chloral hydrate, that's what Crayfish served up for you. Guess you'll be visiting the devil."

I closed the door and got out of there. I'd collect the bodies later.

I knew that Crayfish Ruble was scot-free. All them witnesses that testified that King Bragg shot them T-Bar men were dead. There wasn't nobody left to take back the court testimony, and not only was Ruble free, but King Bragg was still in trouble, and once they got some new judge in here, the boy might still be hanged for a crime he didn't do.

391

THIRTY-FIVE

It wasn't any trouble finding Crayfish. He was in Rosie's parlor, running his paws over all them smiley girls, and having himself a fine time. There wasn't anything to run from, so he was back with the ladies once again, while Rosie was watching over the parlor so things didn't get too rowdy.

I simply wandered in there, ready to swing my shotgun into action, but no one seemed to care any. The girls were more interesting to Crayfish than any lawman. He patted one on the behind, and she winked at him, and Rosie smiled because she might get a cut of the business.

"You came just in time for the party, Sheriff," Crayfish said, running a feral hand over another behind.

"I got to take you in for questioning, Mr. Ruble."

He looked annoyed. "For what?"

"We're gonna talk about a lot of stuff," I said.

"Oh, the hanging. I tried to stop it. Judge Nippers was a friend, you know. But my boys didn't much like it when he stopped the hanging, and they got a little frisky."

"Well, we're gonna talk about that some."

"I'm not inclined to go. You can see I'm busy with important things. Try me tomorrow morning — early. We're heading back to the T-Bar around noon." He smiled. "Any earlier and the boys would be fighting hangovers."

He slid an arm around a real pretty little thing, who chirped cheerfully.

"I'll send him over when he's done here," Rosie said. "Now don't you go cheating me out of a sale."

"Your sale's gonna wait, ma'am," I said. I turned to Crayfish. "You coming or do I get serious?"

I moved the shotgun muzzle a notch or two, and it didn't escape him.

He sighed, smiled, and surrendered. "I'll be back in a few minutes," he said to Rosie.

The pretty little thing pouted and rubbed his belly.

"Evangelina, he's gonna stay in his pants," Rosie said.

"I'll take a rain check, honey," he said.

I followed him out the door and into a fine June day. Doubtful was stirring a little. Them merchants was finally opening up. People had figured out there wasn't going to be no hanging this day, at least not of the Bragg boy.

Ruble tried to walk beside me, but I motioned him to stay in front of me.

"It's a pity, losing that judge," he said. "Now that kid's loose and who knows who he'll kill next."

"We're gonna have some real serious talk about that," I said. Truth was, I didn't have much to go on. All three witnesses dead. And I had no real good proof he killed the other two. No real proof of anything. But we were gonna have us a long talk anyway, him on one side of the bars, me on the other.

A few merchants were at their doors, shouting questions.

"Is the judge dead?" George Waller asked.

"Yes," I said, but didn't want to spill any more beans. "You'll get the story soon as I'm ready."

We reached the courthouse square and something was sure different. Then I knew. There was a new noose on that gallows. I'd cut off the rope to get Judge Nippers down, and now there was a big noose dangling there.

And a mess of Anchor Ranch men swarming toward me from all sides, including behind. I spotted Big Nose George, and Alvin Ream, and Spitting Sam. Sure enough, there was Admiral Bragg hovering back a way, but I didn't see King or Queen around. And behind me was Smiley Thistlethwaite. I didn't see any of my deputies, and doubted I would. They was all too far gone to do much.

"Crayfish, you keep on walkin' straight to my office. Don't slow down, not even if they say stop. I'll be right behind you. We're walking to the jail, and that's the safest thing I can do."

"I should have shot you," he said.

But he walked steadily now, even as all them Anchor Ranch men tightened their noose around us. I could shoot a few in front of me, but them behind would make quick work of me and my prisoner. My ma used to say I could talk my way out of a whippin', and that's what I'd have to do.

Big Nose George was bossing this parade.

"Stop right there, Sheriff."

"You're not going to interfere with the law."

Then Admiral Bragg was moving in from

the side. "Matter of fact, we are. You turn him loose and we'll turn you loose."

That's when Crayfish took matters into his own hands. "Admiral! Good to see you, my friend. Our slightly retarded sheriff seems to think he can hold me on general principles." He laughed, and veered straight toward Bragg. I could hardly swing the shotgun around before there was a mess of barrels pointing my way.

Bragg, he smiled and shook hands with Crayfish Ruble, like they was a couple of old buddies. I'd lost my prisoner.

"Sheriff, you'll want to set down that shotgun real slow," Big Nose said.

I sure hated to do it, and thought maybe to check out by spraying the neighborhood with buckshot, but I saw how it was. So I settled that shotgun on the clay and stood up.

"You'll be a witness, Sheriff," Bragg said. "A little justice, long overdue."

I was sort of getting the drift of this, and so was Crayfish, who smiled cheerfully.

A few citizens were collecting, braving the chance of some stray lead flying their way. I was sure feelin' like a fool, disarmed and standing there. But I'd be even dumber trying to shoot my way out of that one.

Bragg, he had an arm around the neck of

his new friend Ruble, smiling away like it was some party. And Ruble, he was chuckling and snorting and enjoying the get-together. Bragg, he was steering Ruble into the courthouse square, and all the rest of them Anchor riders were making sort of an escort for them, like a pathway straight toward that gallows. I followed along, though there were men with drawn revolvers right behind me, keeping me goin' toward that gallows. That noose looked real big there, a good clean knot with the coils just right. I wondered who had tied it. Maybe the same Anchor Ranch feller who'd tied the noose for me when they were tryin' to scare me into springing the kid.

I wondered where the boy and girl were. They sure weren't a part of this bunch. I wondered whether their old man had gotten real tough on them.

We kept right on walkin' straight to the gallows, and then Bragg was manhandling Ruble around toward them steps up to the platform, and Ruble, he wasn't smiling anymore. But Ruble was no match for Bragg. Ruble had spent years tomcatting, while Bragg was running his ranch, and now it showed. It was like Ruble was being dragged by some giant force to them steps and up them steps, walkin' where he didn't want to go, not at all.

And then Big Nose George was up there with a cord, binding Crayfish Ruble's hands behind him real tight, wrapping that cord around his wrists so tight it made Ruble wince, and then they sort of pushed him onto the trap, and Crayfish wasn't smiling at all. He was just staring at the sky. Bragg, he lowered that noose over Ruble's head and tightened it a little and turned the knot to the left, and made sure everyone saw he was doin' it and no one else. This was Admiral Bragg's show, from start to finish.

It got real quiet, and some puffball clouds skidded across the sky, shadowing the gallows and Crayfish and Bragg, even though the rest of Doubtful was blotting up sunlight. It sure was quiet. I'd never heard it so quiet. There was a mess of people watching now. Every shopkeeper in town was out, and so were all the women and children.

Admiral Bragg pulled the lever. The trap dropped, and so did Crayfish. There was a loud crack, like maybe a neck bone was busted, and then Crayfish swung and twitched and turned real slow. And he was smiling to beat the band.

There was that feeling you get right after you see someone die like that. You're mostly thinking it could be you. And for a moment,

I wondered if Bragg had me on his list, just as he threatened a few times. But no one was paying me any attention. I could have walked to my office and no one would have known it.

You know, it was a funny thing. The law said this was wrong. Ruble hadn't been tried. He'd been lynched. And I sure would have trouble coming up with real good evidence. He had killed the Jonas boys and Rocco, but proving it was something else. There was a bunch of stuff needed looking into, including them graves out on his place.

Still, I had something to do. I pushed through them people until I got to Admiral.

"Got to take you in, Bragg."

"Of course you do. But I might not go."

"You come along now."

"I tell you what. You come along with me," he said. "To the courthouse."

He plunged through the gathering crowd, like a horse with no bit, and I raced along making sure I didn't lose him. He swung open the door, and headed up them wide stairs toward Judge Nippers' chambers, and stopped at the big desk there.

He handed me a paper lying on the desk. It was in Nippers' hand, all right, but I sure couldn't make out all them curly letters. Bragg stared at me, annoyed.

"It's Bell's confession. Nippers wrote it all down. How my boy was framed. And that's Bell's X for a signature."

"That don't make it right, what you did," I said. "You got to come in and get yourself tried for that hangin'."

"Come get me," he said, "whenever you're ready."

I collected that confession, before someone else took it off.

Bragg knew he'd never spend a day in my jail, at least not for that. Them good folks in Doubtful would cut him loose, especially when they saw the confession Nippers had gotten out of Bell. I knew it too. They'd figure everything was even and justice got done. At the moment he held the cards, and the biggest one was the revolver hangin' from his hip.

I followed him out, into the silent square, where Crayfish Ruble was twisting and turning in the June breeze.

"One thing more, Bragg. Where's King and Queen?"

"Locked in the hotel liquor closet," he said. "They've betrayed me. They'll never set foot on Anchor Ranch again."

"Might be a good deal for them," I said.

He laughed. "Cotton, you're a card," he said.

I'd get over there in a moment and spring them and make sure they was both all right. They weren't the same two Braggs as they once were, and I was sort of sneakin' proud of them defying that holy terror of a father of theirs.

Next I knew, all them Anchor Ranch riders were collecting their horses and riding out. I saw some T-Bar men riding out too. They'd have no payday there. I wondered who'd get the place and all them cattle out there. Them T-bar men would likely alter a few brands and take some beef with them. I thought that the whole ranch would vanish in about a week, and there'd be a few riding the owlhoot trail. There was nothing permanent about that place. Crayfish hadn't built anything for the future. And the future ended on that gallows a little while before.

I had some business to do out there. Four graves to open up. Four women to identify. I thought Lulu and Rosie would shed a few tears.

There was plenty of folks standing around the square, gawking.

"Get on away from here," I said. "Go home."

But no one did.

My landlady, Belle, as wide as she was tall, come steamin' up. "It's a good thing," she said. "That Crayfish. There's not a virtuous woman left in town, except me."

She looked like she wished she weren't.

I spotted Rusty wobbling along with Burtell and DeGraff, so all the lawmen were present at last. They paused in front of Crayfish, who was sort of smiling down at them.

"Serves him right," Rusty said. "You do the honors?"

"Nope, it was Bragg done it."

"You arrest him?"

"I tried to."

"Glad you didn't," Rusty said. "That Bragg. He's a son of a bitch, but my kind of son of a bitch."

"He's not my kind," I said.

ABOUT THE AUTHOR

William W. Johnstone is the *USA Today* bestselling author of over 130 books, including the popular *Ashes, Mountain Man,* and *Last Gunfighter* series. Visit his website at www.williamjohnstone.net or by email at dogcia2006@aol.com.

J. A. Johnstone is a Tennessee-based novelist and the author of the exciting new series *The Loner.*

The employees of Thorndike Press hope you have enjoyed this Large Print book. All our Thorndike, Wheeler, and Kennebec Large Print titles are designed for easy reading, and all our books are made to last. Other Thorndike Press Large Print books are available at your library, through selected bookstores, or directly from us.

For information about titles, please call:
(800) 223-1244

or visit our Web site at:
http://gale.cengage.com/thorndike

To share your comments, please write:

Publisher
Thorndike Press
295 Kennedy Memorial Drive
Waterville, ME 04901